Ronald Hugh Morrieson was bor [barcode] where he lived until his death at th small Taranaki town and lived all born. He never married and he earned his living as a music teacher. He published four novels: *The Scarecrow, Came a Hot Friday, Predicament* and *Pallet on the Floor*, and wrote several short stories.

PREdicAMENt

RONALD HUGH MORRIESON

dUNMORE
PUBLISHING

All the characters and events described in this book are fictitious, and
any resemblence to actual persons, living or dead, is purely coincidental.

First published by Dunmore Press 1974
Published in Penguin Books, Auckland 1986

Reprinted in 2009 by
Dunmore Publishing Ltd
P.O. Box 25080, Wellington
books@dunmore.co.nz

© the Estate of Ronald Hugh Morrieson

National Library of New Zealand Cataloguing-in-Publication Data

Morrieson, Ronald Hugh, 1922-1972.
Predicament / Ronald Hugh Morrieson.
Previous ed.: 1974.
ISBN 978-1-877399-38-1
l. Title.
NZ823.2—dc 22

Cover design by Vasanti Unka
Printed by Astra Print, Wellington

Introduction to the first edition

Ronald Hugh Morrieson was born in Hawera, South Taranaki, in 1922. He died in Hawera in 1972. He never left the house where he was born; he never spent more than a few days outside the only town he knew. In life, as in literature, he was an utter original: a prisoner of place in a land where most are footloose, an author innocent of literature. All he had – and it was more than enough – was the imagination to see his home territory as a wild wonderland, with the cruel and comic at every corner, and a talent for telling a tale. ('The same week our fowls were stolen, Daphne Moran had her throat cut,' begins *The Scarecrow*.) Travel had nothing to teach him. Nor had other writers. Let them get on with telling their yarns; he had his own.

One searches for comparisons when trying to define Morrieson, and always returns empty-handed. There is, and has been, no one quite like him. I must have given away at least half a dozen copies of *The Scarecrow* – having found myself inarticulate about the writer and finally, in despair and passion, pressing the book itself upon friends. I remember first reading it in 1965 at the suggestion of an equally passionate friend, and being quite stunned by its bawdy verve.

I then discovered his second novel, *Came a Hot Friday*, which confirmed that the first was no accident. The latter still seems by far the funniest book ever written by a New Zealander – a ribald riot of a book, rich with incident; its rollicking prose seems a repository of New Zealand folklore.

A folk writer, then? Yes, but that is hardly adequate: just too convenient a critical pigeonhole, and unjustly patronising.

A primitive? Again too dismissive a description: there's nothing primitive about his craft, about the way he makes his narrative spark and crackle. Nor is there anything insubstantial about his vision. There are genuine' thunderclaps among the fireworks: his comedies seem to bring the cosmos down; his colliding images, as extravagant as his language, have a cumulative effect so that one enters a feverish and hallucinated reality. Reminiscent, yes, of Dickens, and in fact one Australian reviewer in the distinguished literary journal *Meanjin* did suggest that if Dickens had been born in backblock New Zealand in the twentieth century, he might well have written *The Scarecrow* – or, for that matter, *Came a Hot Friday*, *Predicament* and *Pallet on the Floor*.

You will search in vain for such reviews of his work in New Zealand literary periodicals. Nor did he have in his own country the commercial success he had in Australia. In his lifetime he published two novels which should by rights have been New Zealand's best-ever sellers: all the popular ingredients were there. I doubt if either sold more than three or four hundred in New Zealand, and then mostly in his home town of Hawera. The fault was in his stars, perhaps, but also in his Australian publisher: the books were poorly publicised and indifferently distributed, and moreover appeared at a time (in the early 1960s) when New Zealand publishers appeared determined to kill the growing market for New Zealand fiction with a flood of ephemeral rubbish. That-tide soon ebbed, but Morrieson was still lost to sight. Perhaps he would have been anyway: such is often the fate of original writers. And Morrieson offered little to the sociologists who pose so bleakly as literary critics in New Zealand; he had none of the more conventional New Zealand literary preoccupations, or rather was entirely innocent of their existence; he wrote for the hell and joy of telling a tale. And in the, process, perhaps, fell between two stools – between the clichés of popular fiction and the novel of social or moral purpose, the familiar terrain of critics. (It would certainly be asking too much of New Zealand critics to suggest that Morrieson's work be considered as metaphysical comedy.) In 1968 H. Winston Rhodes published a 'critical survey' called *New Zealand Fiction Since 1945*: Morrieson didn't even rate a casual mention.[1]

Since there has been little about Morrieson written for the record, I should convey my own limited experience of the man here, and confess my own weakness for his work. I once knew Morrieson's South Taranaki territory of Hawera, Patea and Opunake for almost a year of my life; I was familiar with the booze-and-betting ethos from which his stories sprang. I even thought, when I first read him, that I could recognise some of his characters, and later it turned out that we did have mutual friends. I wrote to Morrieson in the year I read his novels, expressing

---

1 To be fair, essayist M. H. Holcroft had observed Morrieson's strength in a piece called *Isles of Innocence* three or four years earlier. This, though, only makes the myopia of Rhodes and other unadventurous (and critically inter-changeable) commentators on New Zealand writing all the more amazing.

both pleasure in his work and my distress that it had been so little noticed by his fellowcountrymen. We began to correspond fitfully.

At the beginning of 1966 I stopped briefly with Ron in Hawera. It was the first time he'd met another novelist. He was a bulky, likeable man of large enthusiasms, a heavy drinker and big eater. Ron Morrieson was, in truth, a Morrieson character. That was the first shock. He was not only inseparable from the environment he wrote about, he was also indistinguishable within it. After a long and confusing tour of Hawera pubs, all swarming with other Morrieson characters and bristling with Morrieson dialogues, we drifted home with four flagons of beer and a bottle of whisky to see us through the night. Somewhere along the line we shared a couple of pounds of steak and a dozen eggs. For breakfast next morning we had another dozen eggs and a pound of bacon. He lived in a large gloomy old house on the south corner of Hawera's Regent Street with his indulgent and loving mother – he was an only child, his father long dead – and an elderly aunt. Ron and his mother were music teachers. Ron also played in a dance band around South Taranaki halls. He began writing experimentally in his late thirties: *The Scarecrow* and *Came a Hot Friday* were the first things he ever finished and were immediately accepted by a publisher. Without the beginner's usual run of rejection slips, then, he was poorly conditioned to sustain the inevitable disappointments and frustrations of the literary life which came later. But in 1966 he was still ebullient, if mildly dismayed by native neglect – his dazzling Australian reviews were more than adequate consolation.

At some point that evening he asked me confidentially: 'Hey, tell me about this Southern Gothic business, can you?' I was baffled briefly. 'Southern Gothic?' 'Yes. You see, this professor bloke interviewed me for Australian Broadcasting. He asked me how much I was influenced by the Southern Gothic novel. I wondered what the hell he was on about, but I pretended I knew. Perhaps you can tell me.

The penny dropped. The professor's question was not altogether unreasonable. After all, Ron Morrieson clearly saw Hawera, South Taranaki, as intensely in imagination as William Faulkner had seen Oxford, Mississippi. So I mentioned Faulkner and other southern U.S. writers: Truman Capote, Carson McCullers, Calder Willingham …

'Tell me,' Ron broke in, after the point had been sufficiently elucidated, 'do you crack a smile when you read these people?'

'Why?'

'I can't stand reading books where you never crack a smile.'

So much for literature, so much for influences. Ron was always on his own. He explained, 'I have these majestic themes in my mind, you see, big things, shapes like music, but the trouble is getting the characters to fit. I mean, they're not up to the themes; they just turn out funny. So what do I have to do? I just have to make the best of it.'

Whatever else he was, then, he was also a storyteller in deadly earnest, always restless within his flamboyant narratives; it was never just a matter of throwing words down on paper. He made a kind of madcap poetry out of the only world he knew.

What might have happened if Ron had left Hawera? My guess, not especially informed, is nothing; he might never have written. He did try Auckland University once, but after a couple of days, on hearing a piano played while walking past a stranger's house, went back homesick to his mother in Hawera; he was never really to be prised away again. Even the trip forty miles north to New Plymouth was a rare and wild adventure. Near the end of his life he was persuaded to attend a writers' conference at Palmerston North: again a couple of days were enough. He got drunk, had a fall, and left before the conference ended. After my visit in 1966 I often tried to persuade him to come up to Auckland to stay for a break. He was always coming, but never arrived. Perhaps he sensed that his fictional world might fracture; that Hawera might seem something less than a riotous fantasyland if he went too far away.

In 1968 his mother died. He never really recovered. I spoke to him on the telephone, and sent him letters urging him to keep writing as a way of easing grief. He insisted that he had no wish to live. Literary disappointments were, besides, beginning to pile up. A new novel became the subject of dispute with his original Australian publisher, and was then turned down by a couple of uncertain New Zealand publishers, by then cautious about any native fiction at all and especially about such an outsize oddity as a Morrieson manuscript. (I did, as it happened, have the chance to make an enthusiastic reader's report for one publisher, but it didn't seem to help.) Ron, meantime, spent much time in hospital. About 1970 we began to correspond again. He had started another novel, he said, and was revising the rejected one; he wasn't giving up. He telephoned me often – almost invariably drunk, but excited about writing again, new ideas bubbling; these toll calls would go on for half an hour or more. Around this time too he wrote two fine short stories

Cut My Throat and Hope to Die and *The Chimney*. Both were published posthumously. In 1971 I tried to interest one or another publisher in his work. In one instance the New Zealand office of an English publisher was enthusiastic, but was finally overruled by a perplexed London editor. In that year too I learned that Frank Sargeson and C. K. Stead had given Morrieson long and warm critical treatment in *Landfall*. I sent Ron a telegram of congratulation: recognition seemed on its way at last, and perhaps he would find another publisher now.

The expectations aroused then only made his last year more cruel. I visited Ron in January 1972. He was a shaky shadow of the man I saw in 1966. It was the day after his fiftieth birthday. He had been up drinking, solitary, until two in the morning – 'until the half century clocked over' – and was putting away a couple of bottles of sherry before lunch.

He had just suffered another rejection, but I did my best to kindle hope again. By the end of the visit he was reeling off racy anecdotes in fine Morrieson style. He allowed himself only one flash of bitterness: 'I hope I'm not another one of these poor buggers who get discovered when they're dead.' We never met again. He died in late December that year. A number of other notable New Zealand writers – James K. Baxter, John Pascoe, Eileen Duggan, Charles Brasch – died around that time too, and were substantially mourned. Ron's death was barely noticed, but a brief and rather confused Press Association message out of Hawera did call him a well-known philosopher. Perhaps it was Ron's own Hawera at ghostly work.

Now that town's curious solitary of literature has gone. What went wrong? Nothing was stock about Ron Morrieson, as a man or a writer, and that may have been his downfall. With any justice he should have been New Zealand's most popular writer ever. On the reasonable working assumption that there is no justice, then, we must ask ourselves another, more pertinent, question: What went right? For the miracle of this hermit of Hawera is that he wrote so wonderfully well, and indeed wrote what he did at all. How he composed such colourful and uninhibited fictions in a small town as inhibited and colourless as most will always remain a mystery to me. How that robust, eccentric and comic vision sprang to life so fully-armed, from that rambling gloomy house on the corner of Regent Street, will never cease to surprise me. For me, at least, he places a vivid question mark at the centre of literature, at the heart of all creation: his magic is that of the first storytellers, and our delight is that of the first listeners to their wondrous tales. Morrieson may not safely be called New Zealand's best writer – so long as the ghost of Mansfield lingers, and such as Sargeson and Frame remain substantially in the flesh – but he certainly takes first place in our eccentric tradition: he is by far our most original writer. And thus by far, perhaps, our most precious.

Maurice Shadbolt
9 August 1974

1

IN THOSE days motorists could fill up with Big Tree gasolene at the blue pump and the only guys with anything like a Beatie haircut were Hitler and one of the Three Stooges.

One day in the mid-thirties, just before the end of the year, a boy of fifteen and two young men became involved in a bizarre, macabre and altogether despicable adventure.

Their paths had not crossed until then although they lived in the same small town. But, although unaware of each other's existence, two of them – Cedric Williamson, age fifteen, and Ernest Fox, age twenty-two, who was the attendant at the new gas station and lubritorium which had gone up only three hundred yards from the front gate of the Williamson property – entertained notions concerning the attractions of a young girl, Maybelle Zimmerman, and both hated a certain Blair Bramwell.

The main fuel stoking this burning hatred was envy – envy of Blair Bramwell's world of easy money, open cars and beautiful women. Unlike young Cedric, Ernie Fox was not envious of Blair Bramwell's looks: he thought he was better looking himself. Blair Bramwell was tall but Ernie Fox was an inch taller, broader in the shoulder, and, whereas Blair's glossy hair was as slick as a skullcap, his own was an unruly mop of dark curls.

However, better looking or not, he still had to blow up the tyres and wipe the wind-shield of Blair Bramwell's maroon Auburn roadster – quite a car, with glistening exhaust-hoses sweeping out of the long bonnet on each side – while Blair sat behind the green steering wheel and smirked superciliously.

The Auburn revved and ripped away without the driver uttering a word of thanks.

Back in the office, Ernie Fox, after wiping his hands on a piece of cotton waste, entered, on the Bramwell card, the gas and oil the Auburn had taken. He had a shrewd idea that the business was owned, or part owned anyway, by Blair's father, Vernon Bramwell, and that went for all the other property that was being built at this end of town. There was virtually a new suburb springing up. Man, he reflected, how he could live it up with that sort of money! At the thought of the smug and arrogant Blair, he made as if to spit.

But thoughts of Maybelle Zimmerman soon crowded Blair Bramwell out.

Ernie Fox put his hands in the pockets of his white overalls and stared out the office window. From here was visible the extraordinary tower which was being constructed in front of the Williamson mansion, but Ernie Fox had been employed in this job for over a month by now and the spectacle barely registered on his brain. He desired dalliance with Maybelle Zimmerman badly but he knew she was under the age of consent and that was playing with fire. He should never have started flirting with the kid, he knew, but, brother! she was a sexy little piece. Well, he'd got to within hitting distance: he was on a promise. As soon as school had broken up she had gone for a holiday, but, over the phone, they had arranged to meet the night she arrived back – the night before New Year's Eve.

"If I had the brains of a woodpecker," Ernie Fox muttered, "that's one date I wouldn't keep. I'd stand her up. But what a mug I'd be to dip out on a dish like her! Maybelle can keep her mouth shut. She'd better, by God!"

Blair Bramwell had a woman on his mind too and he didn't really see the Williamson tower either as he went past. That is, he saw it – not to see it was impossible – but it didn't filter through his preoccupation. He also was playing with fire, but he was getting a great kick out of it. He was so besotted with his particular amour that he couldn't think straight any more. What a set up! He grinned. His blood raced like his car and so did his thoughts. Fancy the old man bringing home a smasher like Margot! Fancy an old shrewdie like him getting taken for a ride like that! He must be going into his second childhood. Well, boy, I'd be a mug to have any scruples. Bring a hot pants little fraud like Margot into the house and he deserved all he got.

Cedric, from an upstairs window of the Williamson mansion, saw the Auburn whip past, going up through the gears, with the grinning Blair at the wheel. Naturally, Cedric thought it was the sight of his father's tower which so tickled Blair Bramwell. Behind his spectacles, spleen hooded his eyes.

2

BECAUSE HE was fifteen years old many years before the ill-fated James Dean starred in *Rebel Without a Cause*, Cedric Williamson was an adolescent – as distinct from the genus 'teenager': his two pairs of long trousers had twenty-two-inch bottoms; he let the barber decide how to cut his hair; included the words 'fabulous' and 'fantastic' in some corner of his generous vocabulary but rarely used them; exclaimed, 'hot-diggity' not 'like crazy, man'; addressed his contemporaries as 'boy', not 'father' or 'chief'; referred to girls as 'sheilas' or 'dames', not 'birds' or 'darlings'; put an apple in his pocket and not a transistor radio; had no ambition to become a millionaire by learning five chords on the guitar and waggling his bottom as he strummed them; no interest at all in pop songs and no money to be gulled out of by big recording concerns if he had had. In fact, Cedric had little money to spend on anything at all. But being broke didn't precipitate his descent into the maelstrom of crime although it may have given him a push on the way.

Boredom was partially to blame – a boredom as grey and monotonous as the Sunday afternoon pavements of his home town. Perhaps sport would have helped to alleviate this boredom, but if there was one thing Cedric definitely was not it was a sportsman. Organized games appalled him. And this led to loneliness. Gaining a nickname is supposed to be a sign that a big step has been taken towards popularity, but with two nicknames Cedric was still a lonely boy with no real friends. To add to his introspective depression he was a living lie. His slight stoop, his spectacles and bookwormish habits had won him the nickname 'Professor', but for all his scholarly appearance he was near bottom of his class in every subject except English. True, he had always managed to scrape through end-of-year examinations and, at fifteen, was in the lower fifth form of the local Technical High School, which entitled him to have a tilt at the University Entrance examination known generally and erroneously in those days as 'Matric'. His chances of passing were estimated by his teachers as nil. This was a gloomy view shared by himself, but perplexed and despondent he brooded studiously over his textbooks far into the night.

So, in what appears to be emerging as a brief for the defence of Cedric Williamson, we find boredom; unpopularity; a deep interior dissatisfaction with his lot; a brain that sought refuge in the world of fiction he so loved but was now denied by the exigencies of a grim, steep, hopeless academic haul, and, on top of these things, all the turmoil of old-fashioned adolescence evil passions; pimples; dandruff; shaving; brand-new Adam's apple; a voice with a hairtrigger range; unrequited love for a second cousin called Jasmine who might as well have been dead, having gone to live in far-away Cape Town (Maybelle Zimmerman did not loom in his dreams like Jasmine: she was merely a complication) and a sad, smouldering, savage envy of boys better built and better looking than himself, which, Cedric had come to feel, meant the jolly lot. To top off Cedric's psychological predicament, as if being called 'the Professor' wasn't bad enough, he was also known as 'Pisa' Williamson – after the celebrated Leaning Tower.

Cedric's papa was a screwball. Martin Williamson had been known to appear dressed in a shiny double-breasted navy-blue suit and a bowler hat, but, on all other occasions he was to be seen in tight saddle-tweed trousers tucked into socks at the ankles, clodhopper boots, a heavy jersey, a working shirt of some coarse material, but buttoned nevertheless at the neck to sport a crumpled tie. He was a thick-necked, paunchy, big-bottomed, florid-faced man, a little over average height, who looked out through cherubic blue eyes that had all the vague serenity of one from whose brain some embittered concept of reality had departed and, in striking camp, had left nothing behind. He was oblivious of the giggles and temple tapping that took place as he ambled by with his wheelbarrow in front of him. Martin Williamson was not seen around the streets on foot very often but, when he was, he was never without that trundling wheelbarrow.

Somewhere in his middle forties, Martin Williamson had retired from the rat race, up-stumped his end of the unequal struggle, and begun to build a tower. They didn't have an atom bomb in those days but if they had, this whacky tower would have been Martin Williamson's answer.

Martin Williamson's father, who was dead long before Cedric was born, was a General of Her Majesty Queen Victoria and subsequent monarchs. When his family, who owned a big block of land about ten miles out, died off and the land was sold, the pensioned-off General built a big house at the end of the main street right where people coming in couldn't miss it. But by the mid-thirties no one looked at the two-storeyed mansion; they stared at the tower on the front lawn. They used to stop and back up their cars and laugh until water ran down their cheeks and, on some not entirely authenticated occasions, down their legs.

Cedric, from the age of thirteen, had watched in horror the tower grow taller and taller and with every heavenwards thrust more cockeyed. Cockeyed as the tower was to behold, it was as solid as the Rock of Gibraltar because its off-plumb appearance was deliberate and stemmed from its builder's unique conception of the finished edifice.

The tower was a series of single rooms, each new addition diminished in area by a few square feet, but, instead of being centralized on the top of the bigger room beneath, it was placed flush with the left hand side so that the first five storeys gave the impression of being some fairy-tale staircase for a giant. At this stage Martin Williamson had played his trump card. The next flight of rooms (two had been completed and the third was under construction about the time the drama now to be related began) was built flush with the right side of the storey below. A fascinated town had now some glimmering of the awesome sight the tower would present by the time it tapered into nothingness, if that were indeed Martin's ultimate goal. Because Martin only had money to buy timber every so often, the curious had a long time ahead of them to wait.

The tower was also remarkable for its windows: doublehung windows, casement windows, fanlights, louvre-type ventilators from water-closets, port-hole windows, even a stained-glass window with some bearded men and Mary and the Infant Jesus depicted on it. Never a building was pulled down around these parts but Martin Williamson arrived to negotiate with the demolisher for the purchase of some windows.

However, for all its weird and crazy appearance, the tower was structurally sound. Its safety had baffled the local building inspector, who could only advise the Borough Council that, short of making retroactive changes in the by-laws, they were powerless to condemn. With great cunning Martin Williamson had even had the foresight to trick them into granting a building permit. The authorities had no reason to suspect when they gave it, that the applicant was losing his grip. The Williamson name was well respected. The councillors decided to shrug their shoulders and, for the time being, see the funny side. So the tower continued to rise in spite of the jeers of the curious, the scowls of the inspector and the complaints of neighbours. The General's son just turned a deaf ear and was never rude to visitors, no matter how thinly veiled their derision or hostility. He appeared pathetically proud to show them 'up and over' as he put it. He waved in a pleasant, modest way to hysterical sightseers out on the road. Cedric, peering through the curtains, was never able to bear his mounting shame and mortification for long and would skulk off to his bedroom or the meadow. "This is the end, the bloody, bloody end," he would groan.

3

CEDRIC NEVER remonstrated with his father, because his grand-mother, hugging him, had asked him not to and he loved his old granny, the General's widow. He also loved his loopy father in a warped sort of way and managed sickly smiles while he endured proud prattle about the tower and showing people 'up and over'. But next to his granny in his affection ranked Gus, the aged half-draught horse that inhabited the meadow behind the mansion. The blue gums and pines which fringed the meadow had watched Cedric grow from an insignificant child into a puny youth; watched happiness turn sour; watched the mighty Gus grow pensively old; and soon the friendship between the human brooding weakling and the lumbering inarticulate creature deepen into love. Beneath these trees, in sunshine and shadow, Cedric had sprawled in the yellow grass among fragrant blue-gum leaves, cones and pine-needles and read everything he could lay his hands on, from comics and sixpenny novelettes to classics and even, in certain moods, poetry, although his true penchant in literature was the sensational – crime, adventure, mystery.

To list the stuff that over the years Cedric's spectacles glistened over in his bedroom, at the table, under his desk and in the meadow would make an amazing catalogue, but now, although his self-discipline was nearly at breaking point, he took with him into the meadow a textbook of Latin prose composition, a pad and a pencil. For Mr North M.A. and the Rev. Dr Hillard D.D., the compilers of this book, he developed a bottomless loathing. The book was second-hand, and he was not blazing a trail in harbouring these emotions as he deduced from a scribbled inscription on the flyleaf:

Stay for me, I shall not fail
To meet you in that hollow vale,
But what a rumpty there will be
If thou shouldst bring this book with thee!

Some afternoons, Granny Williamson, feeble and stooping but indefatigable, would cross over to the meadow and 'hear' Cedric's most recently learned exercise in Latin vocabulary. These were peaceful scenes, far from gay but very memory saturating: the quiet voices, the birds, the munching and champing of Gus. They ignored the distant sounds of sawing and hammering where work continued on the tower.

The whole town knew Gus as well as they knew Martin Williamson and his mother. Once a month Gus plodded right through the centre of the town, harnessed to the old cart, with Martin holding the reins and his mother, a shawl over her shoulders, sitting silently beside him. They were on their way to the timber mill and the whole town knew as soon as they went by that the old lady had received the pension due to her as a General's widow. To some it was funny, to some it was sad, but everybody wrung their hands at the thought of all that money being gobbled up by such a lunatic project as the tower. Nobody really knew why the old lady always accompanied Martin on this monthly expedition to the mill. Maybe she had it figured that at least her pension owed her a ride across the town and back.

Cedric suffered. 'Pisa' Williamson. He tried to bluff it out by pretending not to hear or care, but one day he cracked up and flew at a persecutor – which got him a thrashing and broken spectacles.

Some said it was the early demise of Martin's wife which sent him around the bend and on to this tower-building kick. Some said he had fallen from a scaffold and knocked his head. He had been educated to be an engineer but his father had financed his start as a master builder, and it was true that once on a construction job he had lost his footing and fallen some distance. But most people said it was because he was naturally simple and unworldly and when the legal firm of Bramwell and Thorne, in cahoots with Vic Prout, the Mayor, swindled Granny Williamson out of the land, some one hundred acres right alongside the mansion – land into which she had sunk all her money – he just slipped away into a world of make-believe. This could well be so, particularly as the fraud came hot on the heels of some financially disastrous building contracts. To make matters worse the Williamsons were not only given a dirty deal – they had their noses rubbed in it.

4

It was Granny Williamson's plan or dream to have the hundred acres surveyed and carved up into streets and building sites on which her son Martin would build modest but pleasant homes. Even the deep gully at the back of the block was to be graded and landscaped. This residential development was to be the Williamson's little empire. It wasn't a gamble because the town, and for that matter the world, was in a bad state right then, but she was convinced a boom would come and, of course, she was right. The trouble that Martin had struck, a spell of inactivity owing to an illness during which time he was badly cheated, had strained his mother's resources so that she was obliged to approach Bramwell and Thorne to see what she could raise to launch her big building project. There were signs everywhere that prosperity was staging a comeback and she wanted to move quickly and head off rising costs. Vernon Bramwell asked for a day or so to look into it. At their next consultation he shook his head sadly. The scheme was not only unsound, but impossible. It was too bad, but all the land in that part of the town had been declared a commercial zone in the new, undisclosed, town plan. This meant that the building of residences in the area was prohibited. It was very unfortunate, but unless she could interest the owners of shops or factories in purchasing her land (and he, Vernon Bramwell, personally couldn't see much hope of that for many years yet), she might as well realize the holding was 'a – ah – *white elephant*'.

The Williamson mansion with its neat hedges just high enough to shelter the charming lawns and gardens was a showplace in those days and it broke the old lady's heart to think that one day it would be hemmed in with factories and workshops and noise. She protested at the unfairness of it all and Vernon Bramwell was very sympathetic and arranged a meeting between her and the Mayor who was also very sorry about it all but adamant. The town plan stood. The area was zoned commercial and there was nothing anybody could do.

One night, after dark, Vernon Bramwell called at the Williamson house. Martin had retired early. Cedric was in the kitchen tormenting the maid every time she turned her back by tugging at her apron strings so that the bow-knot slipped.

Vernon Bramwell was taken into the big blue-carpeted bay-windowed drawing-room in the front of the house.

"My dear Mrs Williamson," portly Vernon Bramwell, hands behind his back, said, "I have accomplished what is little short of a – ah – *miracle*. I trust you will be very discreet about this. There is nothing underhand involved you will realize, only that we feel some leniency should be extended to such a respected member of the community as yourself. While not underhand, it is very – ah – *hush – hush*, the big thing to bear in mind being the undesirability of establishing a – ah – precedent. There are many people in the same boat as yourself and a wholesale relaxing of the town plan is to be avoided at all costs, as our mutual friend the worthy Mayor trusts you will – ah – *appreciate*."

Whenever Vernon Bramwell paused and wedged in an 'ah', the next word was always doubly emphasized by sudden leaning forward of his person and a downward jerk of his fuzzy dome tilted to the left. The word was synchronized with the faintest of arch smiles followed by a momentary pious lowering of the heavy eyelids.

The fruity voice resumed. "In a nutshell, my dear Mrs Williamson, we, the worthy Mayor and myself, have managed to hit on a scheme which should prove to be the – ah – *solution*. While there is, unfortunately, no great financial reimbursement to yourself in what I am about to divulge, there are, however, various aspects which should appeal to you. Briefly, the town needs a second park, a pleasant domain to be planted with trees, provided with a fountain, garden, shady walks, some facilities for weekend recreation." Vernon Bramwell spread his hands. "Can you imagine a more pleasant vista from the windows of your lovely home, the value of which will, of course, be greatly – ah – *augmented*. Thus, in one fell swoop as it were, hah hah!" He smiled his arch smile. "You benefit in a worldly way and the menace of having either idle land or a sprawling eyesore of commercial ventures at your doorstep has been removed. Believe me, my dear Madam, a great deal of astute arguing on my part has been called for to achieve this compromise with the inexorable march of progress. It has distressed me more than I can tell you to dwell on the monstrously unfair position in which you found yourself placed. I strongly advise you to avail yourself of this opportunity. Your previous plan may have been a more ambitious project financially, but, even allowing for its validity, which unfortunately is not the case, it was fraught with commercial pitfalls, whereas this move will result in a nice safe nest-egg to sustain you in your – ah, um, – ..."

"Declining years," said Granny Beatrice Williamson. "Precisely. The transaction would of course be done through Bramwell and Thorne. This stipulation is not prompted by avarice but – ah – *diplomacy*."

He named a figure. Granny sold out.

Granny was trusting and the papers she signed further defrauded her. Surveyor's fees and legal expenses nearly halved the payment for the land.

Martin entered the building arena again and met fresh disaster both financially and physically, to wit his fall from the scaffolding.

For a year or so the ground remained in status quo except for flourishing weeds and then, as the boom got into its stride, a service station went up with a semi-circular drive-in, a row of gas pumps, a lubritorium and a big neon sign with glittering ribbons of blue light advertising Big Tree gas. Then roads were driven through and the first of the neat small bungalows appeared. Men and machines assaulted the gully. They called the first street Dale Lane after the wealthy Dale family who had produced no sons but whose daughters had married influential and prosperous men. The other streets, one after the other as they appeared, were named after these men: Bramwell Avenue; Dean Crescent; Hoskin Place; and running right through the development to rejoin the curving main road, Prout Parade. Vic Prout was not married to a Dale but politically he played ball and they liked him in the team. Vernon Bramwell raised his hat to a frail, trembling Granny Williamson in the street but she cut him dead. So it came to pass that the Williamsons looked out over a little empire after all but the paint peeled off the walls of the big house and the General's widow scrubbed her own floors.

The convalescing Martin sank his pride and took a job with one of the contractors building the new houses. He spent a morning on a concrete mixer and then went home, saying nothing to his mother. A week later he began the tower.

The tower was now seven-and-a-half storeys high and Cedric was fifteen years old.

5

IN NOVEMBER Cedric sat the examination referred to as "Matric", and turned in a series of smudged, slip-shod and incomplete papers. The results were not out until late January at the end of the summer vacation, but Cedric knew he had failed and that he should return to his swot, thus getting a start on the term ahead. However, the days ticked past without his opening any books other than fiction, but as he read, guilt built a wall between his brain and the words, making him irritable and depressed. One afternoon he got out his old bicycle and pedalled into the town. He would make a start on his studies after Christmas Eve, he decided.

"Hi, Professor!"

"Hi," Cedric called back hopefully. "It's old Pisa, Pisa-Pisa ..."

Cedric, who had intended to spend his only sixpence on a milk-shake, propelled himself away from a main street bestrung with sad foolish bunting and finally found himself sitting on a bank in a dead-end part of the town close to the timber mill which his father patronized so consistently. He had been in such a miserable state of mind that he could barely recollect bouncing over the four sets of railway tracks across which he now stared at the dingy station. A goat tied to a stake regarded him importantly. The mill timber, stacked like tall wigwams, resinated the air. Cedric lay back on the bank and put his hands behind his neck. A few little white clouds floated like paper boats. The long grass stirred and sighed in its summer dream.

Soon the bells began clanging at the level crossing and Cedric propped himself up to watch a train with one passenger coach at the end of a long line of freight wagons grind to a halt at the platform. A girl waved to him from the carriage.

Scarcely crediting such an adventure could be happening to him, Cedric waved back. There was at least a hundred yard between them, but Cedric knew that she was beautiful. She held up a comic, open, outside her window. Cedric spread out his hands. Then he put his hands together, edge to edge, as if they were an open book and pretended to read furiously. (Afterwards, in love-lorn retrospect, he would blush suddenly as he reflected what an ass he must have looked.) The girl leaned out her window to make it plain that she was eating an orange. Cedric, inspired, plucked out a long piece of grass and began chewing it.

They began a long-range pantomime. When the train pulled out the girl blew him a kiss. Then a lorry rumbled along the dirt side road behind the mill and shut off Cedric's view. In the distance, the steam locomotive bellowed. It was a still afternoon and Cedric could hear the pounding of the wheels for a long time after the train was out of sight. Once, from far off the uh-whoo-ee-duh-who-ee of the whistle drifted back to him again.

He thought his heart would burst.

So it came to pass that every afternoon for the rest of the week Cedric returned to this enchanted spot to watch for trains and induce in himself a pleasant melancholy by murmuring such lines as, 'Ships that pass in the night' and 'Quoth the raven, "nevermore"'. His cousin Jasmine who had gone to Cape Town and the girl on the train had blended into the one misty dreamlike being. Maybelle Zimmerman, who got top billing in more carnal moods, was not honoured by his meditations.

On the Sunday afternoon, Mervyn Toebeck gate-crashed his life.

Cedric had been sitting on the bank mooning away for about three quarters of an hour and was on the point of stirring himself to go for an aimless cycle ride when he saw a fat young chap of twenty or so wearing tennis shoes, crumpled grey slacks and checked shirt crossing the railway lines towards him. The stranger jumped across a ditch without removing his hands from his trouser pockets and landed only the width of the narrow street from where Cedric sat. He paused, produced a handkerchief, and wiped his forehead.

"Hot day," he said. His voice was high-pitched.

"Yeah," agreed Cedric.

"'That your grid?"

"Yeah."

The plump fellow mopped his pale blubbery face again and put the handkerchief away. "Didn't I see you around here the other day?"

"You, could've," Cedric admitted. "I go out for a few rides. It's the holidays, y'know. Nothin' to do."

"And a long time to do it in. I know, I know, I'm one of the great unemployed. If anyone knows it's me."

Cedric, the great reader, liked the phrase 'the great unemployed'. He grinned. "Out of work?"

"Superannuated," said the newcomer with a dignity that Cedric realized could only be facetious. Cedric had automatically classified him as 'common' and he also felt instinctively that the fellow was just as aware himself of being common, and when he used grandiloquent phrases he did so in a deliberate way to upset people. Cedric was pleased by the diversion. He wanted someone to talk to.

"Sunday makes it worse," he volunteered.

The fat chap sauntered across the road. "A fugginsight worse."

Downright common, Cedric thought. However, he was not displeased when the chap sat down a yard or so away from him on a bank. Anything was better than boredom.

"Everything shut up," the chap said. "Town like a morgue. Snip's shut up. Can't play snooker. Just ridiculous. And on the seventh day thou shalt rest. But I notice the cows still have to be milked. An oversight on the Almighty's part, doubtless."

This sort of talk put Cedric in mind of one Tomblinson, a freethinking schoolmate who had now left town. He decided to say nothing, but hating to be rude, compromised by sniggering.

After a few minutes silence Cedric's new companion said, "I see by your socks you're an inmate of our local high school."

"That's right."

"Went there myself. Briefly. My name's Mervyn Toebeck. You can call me Tubby if you like. Some do. I don't care. I've been insulted by experts."

"I'm Cedric Williamson."

They reached to shake hands and some sparrows which had come daringly close flew away.

Cedric regarded his dusty shoes. Mervyn Toebeck plucked at a piece of grass and chewed it. He said, "It's enough to drive a guy nuts."

"What is?"

"Doing nothing. Sunday. Everything."

"Certainly is," said Cedric.

"The trouble with me is I haven't any mates," Mervyn Toebeck confided.

"Me neither." Cedric had decided there was no harm in swapping confidences. It seemed the time and place. They had the world to themselves.

"You haven't?" Mervyn Toebeck looked astonished. "Well now, I just can't understand that at all. With me it's different. No one wants to pal with a guy whose old man's a metho king."

"How do you mean?" asked Cedric. "Is he religious?" Mervyn thought this was a high old joke. He laughed for some time. Then he said, "Religious! If my old man went into a church, it'd be to burgle the poor-box. No, Cedric, he isn't a Bible-banger. He drinks methylated spirits."

"That's bad," said Cedric, shaking his head.

"It'll kill the old reprobate, that's all. And the quicker the better."

"That's an awful thing to say," Cedric said, not really thinking because his mind was digesting the word 'reprobate'.

"You sit there and tell me it's an awful thing to say! What the hell do you know about it?"

The anger in his companion's voice frightened Cedric. "I'm sorry," he said meekly. "I didn't mean that."

"Well what *did* you mean then?"

"Oh well," Cedric stammered. "Well, y'know, my pater, my old man, he's a bit dippy but I don't wish he was dead, sorta."

"Is he a metho king?" asked Mervyn Toebeck. He sounded quite genial again. "When you say dippy you wouldn't have the word dipsomaniac in mind by any remote chance?"

Cedric frowned. "No, it isn't that. He's sorta odd. He's building a tower. And so I'm like you. It's made me a kinda laughing stock. That's why I haven't got any friends."

"Well now, what d'you know!" exclaimed Mervyn Toebeck. "If that isn't the darndest coincidence I ever heard of in my whole life. Not long ago someone asked me if I'd seen some tower a nut's building right on the main street – is that it?"

"That's it all right," Cedric said:

"Well, I never get past Snip's billiard-room so I haven't see it. Just what's the strength of this tower business?"

"Oh it's hard sorta to explain," Cedric said, feeling very ashamed and disloyal to his family, but nevertheless glad in a way to unburden himself. "He just lives in a world of his own and builds this tower. It's as high as anything and all sorta lopsided. It's right on the street and everyone laughs themselves sick when they go past."

"Look here, old son," said Mervyn Toebeck. "Can I see it? For some reason this appeals to me."

"I suppose so" said Cedric, unhappy again.

Mervyn Toebeck stood up immediately. Cedric decided just as suddenly he wasn't going to be pushed around like this.

"Look here," he said. "I just don't want to go and look at that tower right away. Tell you the truth, Mervyn, I came out on the old grid this afternoon to get away from things like the tower. Some other time, huh?"

Mervyn Toebeck said, "Well, all right then, but I'm beginning to get mighty curious. First I get told about it, and then blow me down if I don't run into you here like this. Now I feel I must see this darned tower for myself. It really is your father's tower?"

"Of course it is," said Cedric, raising his voice to try and sound convincing, it being a weakness of his that whenever he was accused of duplicity he immediately turned shifty eyed no matter how unfounded the charge. "Gee, Mervyn, why should I make up a crazy story like that? I didn't think there was anyone living in this town who hadn't seen my father's tower."

Mervyn shook his head. "It's just about the darndest thing I ever heard of. What would possess a man to start him off building a tower? I'll have to see it for myself just to prove people aren't out to pull my leg."

"I'll show it to you all right, but I don't want to go home so early, Mervyn. Haven't you got a grid or something and we can go for a bit of a spin somewhere first?"

As soon as he had spoken Cedric wondered if perhaps the idea of going for a spin on a bicycle would sound a bit childish to one who had obviously reached – even if he hadn't crossed – the threshold of man's estate. He estimated Mervyn's age at about nineteen or twenty. At any rate the suggestion was brushed aside.

"It strikes me you're ashamed of the tower," Mervyn Toebeck said.

"Well, of course I am. Wouldn't you be? All the kids throw muck at me about it."

Toebeck didn't speak for a few moments. He rubbed his close-cropped brownish hair with the palm of his hand. Studying the plump countenance Cedric thought it revealed a great unease about something or other. When Mervyn did speak, it was as if it were the outcome of deep deliberation.

"Well now, look here, Cedric old son, I'll tell you what. We'll make a deal. You're ashamed of this tower and I'm ashamed of my old man. Now what say I take you round and you can have a peak at my old man first? Once you've seen the conditions I live under, boy, you'll never be ashamed again, I'll bet. You never know, but seeing my old man might cheer you up just like hearing about your father's tower interested me."

Cedric found himself frowning. It was just about the oddest invitation that had ever been extended to him. In the end he said, "I don't care. As long as we don't go near home for a little while yet."

"Just leave your mangle where it is," said Mervyn Toebeck, nodding at the bicycle. "It's only a hop, skip and jump to our shanty. We can take a short cut through the mill. They only have a watchman on."

6

"WHAT D'YOU work at, Mervyn?" Cedric asked when they had climbed over a high gate and were following a narrow-gauge set of tracks which wound through the tall stacks of timber. "I mean, did work at?"

"For a while I worked here, right here," Mervyn replied, pointing briefly to the ground. "But the management and me didn't see eye to eye on some trivial matters."

Every so often as they walked along Mervyn would espy a short length of timber lying on the ground beside one of the stacks, cross quickly and drop it down his shirt front.

"Terrible short-sighted a lotta people are," he explained.

"Just because it's fine weather nowadays, they forget the long winter nights ahead. A little foresight can prevent a lotta hardship. Here, my shirt's full, drop this hunk in yours."

Although Martin's eccentricity had stigmatized the Williamsons' name socially, Cedric had been raised in accordance with a strict moral code and he accepted the block of wood apprehensively and reluctantly. He would have liked to throw it away but he was a little frightened of Mervyn Toebeck.

Struck by a sudden thought Mervyn Toebeck stopped dead.

He snapped his fingers. "Throw it away!" he said. "What must you think of me!" He peered at an alarmed Cedric. "You must think I'm just a common thief. And I am, I am. Poverty has driven me to it. But it's never too late to mend."

He took the block of wood from Cedric's hands and threw it away.

He moved to one of the timber stacks and emptied out his own shirt. He looked solemnly at Cedric. "My strength is as the strength of ten because my heart is pure."

After scrambling over another gate they crossed the street and turned down a short, blind lane which ran between neglected boxthorn hedges. Facing them up the lane was an old house with a high hip roof and blank staring windows. The boxthorn hedge in front of the house was the only one in the street which had been slashed low.

Cedric stopped. He said, "Look Mervyn, there's no need for us to go and see your old man, I'll show you the tower."

Mervyn Toebeck looked at Cedric curiously. "No, you might as well see him. It'll show you what a cross I've got to bear. You and your old tower! It'll be an object lesson to you what bad booze can do to a man. Not that the old man would ever drink blue meths. He's fussy about things like that. Always gets the clear white stuff. God knows where he gets it. Must belong to a club or something."

Cedric looked down at the house. It looked sinister.

"Oh for God's sake," said Mervyn irritably. "C'mon, c'mon."

He walked on down the land and Cedric followed reluctantly. He had a feeling there was something screwy going on. Mervyn waited at the gate for him. Cedric recognized the gate as being the end of a single bedstead, looped with fencing wire to a post. Mervyn lifted the gate to open it and Cedric noticed that his hands were shaking.

"Hey, is your mother alive?" Cedric asked. He wouldn't have been able to explain why he felt so alarmed.

Mervyn shook his head.

"Maybe your old man won't like visitors," Cedric said, but Mervyn was already walking along the clay path that led round the side of the house to the back. Uneasily Cedric trailed along. The back of the house was an unsightly lean-to that ended in the tumble-down porch. The piles had sunk and the floor was nearly at ground level. Cedric sniffed. He didn't like to ask Mervyn what was causing the smell.

Mervyn opened the back door and stepped inside. "Step into my squalor, old son."

Cedric made to follow but the smell was overpowering.

And Cedric knew what it was. It was gas.

Mervyn plunged forward through the small scullery just inside the door. He shouted, wrenching at the handle of a further door which

Cedric, despite his mounting terror, observed was totally riddled with borer holes. The door flew open and Mervyn charged into the dark room beyond, only to come immediately reeling out again. He grabbed up a wet, stained dish-cloth off the sink-bench in the scullery, clapped it over his nose and mouth, and entered the inner room again. Choking, Cedric retreated out on to the dirt path. Mervyn's bulky stooping figure emerged into the porch backwards. He had the ankles of a prone man under his armpits. He dragged the man right out on to the path and turned him on his back. Cedric, retreating in horror, tripped and sat down. He scrambled up regardless of his jarred spine to see the puffed purple face of the man. He turned away and staggered out to the grass where he began to retch violently.

He heaved for a time, hands on knees. He knew Mervyn was standing close to him and he looked up at Mervyn's fat chalk-white face. He had his hands up to his mouth and seemed to be gnawing at his finger-tips.

"He's done himself in," he said. "God awmighty! I'll have to stay here, Cedric. Make a bolt for that grid of yours, will you? and head for the cop shop. Tell 'em to get a doctor. Get an ambulance. Go like blazes."

Cedric began to run stiffly, crazily, like a robot. He fell as he lowered himself over the gate that led out of the mill to the street where his bicycle was leaning against the bank. He didn't feel the pain in his grazed knees as he picked himself up and ran for the bicycle.

7

IT HAD been mid-afternoon when Mervyn Toebeck and Cedric Williamson made their grim discovery, but it was nearly seven o'clock in the evening before they came down the steps of the police station together. The street lamps had just come on and there were a few tiny stars and a pale moon hanging in a remnant of daylight.

Now that all the excitement of being questioned by the police and making a statement was over, Cedric was anxious to get home. Once he had recovered from his first shock he had felt very important but, as the time passed and still Mervyn failed to emerge from the side room where a typewriter inexpertly tapped out his statement, and there were long spells during which a deep voice was just audible but not Mervyn's high-pitched voice in reply, he had become fidgety. His grandmother would be very worried about his whereabouts by this hour. The afternoon had simply melted away. First the report from the hospital had been long in coming. Then the police had made heavy weather of gleaning the facts. Not that Cedric had minded. He didn't even want to admit it to himself but he couldn't remember a more enjoyable and exciting afternoon. As it grew later, however, and he was left alone, he began to tap his foot and bite his nails. The Williamson house was not equipped with a telephone. He could have gone without Mervyn, he supposed, but to do so didn't seem right somehow. He paced up and down the room across the passage from where Mervyn was being interrogated.

"I'm sorry, Mervyn," he said awkwardly as they now walked away from the police station, Cedric wheeling his bicycle, towards the main street. "I guess meeting me doesn't seem to have brought you much luck."

"It's not your fault, old son. It's just one of those things."

Mervyn sighed heavily. "The old devil was in the ding-bats half the time. I guess he had it coming. Poor bastard. What sort of questions did the demons ask you?"

"The demons?"

"The police," said Mervyn. "The bulls. Did they ask you where you met me and all that? Did they ask you what time you met me and put you through the hoop generally?"

"Yeah, they asked me how we met and all that. I just said I met you back of the railway station and we got yarning and you invited me down to your place. I didn't mention us going to look at my Dad's tower or anything like that. "Did you?"

"No," said Mervyn. He stopped and said, "Look here, did they think it was funny me inviting you down home when we'd just met each other. Did they keep on harping on that?"

"Well," said Cedric, thoughtfully. Mervyn was holding on to one handle-bar of the bicycle, which was between them, and Cedric saw his grip tighten. "I suppose they did a bit. They asked me if I always went home with strangers and I said, no, but we both had nothing to do and it just sorta happened."

"That's more or less what I said, too. Cops have got an absolute flair for making a mountain out of a molehill. As if a man wasn't grief-stricken enough without being put through a bloody third degree. As for the blasted hospital, words fail me. Don't they know a dead man when they see one? I could've screamed sitting around the copshop like a half-sucked blackball."

When they reached the main street they stopped again. "What a mess I'm in now," Mervyn said, looking most dejected. "God. I couldn't face spending the night in that house. I'll never go back. Never. And I haven't even got the price of a feed in my pocket. I'm starving and I'll have to sleep under a hedge."

Some inner voice warned Cedric he was on the verge of making a mistake, but he was a kind-hearted boy and he could feel Mervyn's eyes fixed on him. He couldn't just climb on his bike and ride away.

Mervyn put his hand on Cedric's arm. "You've been a real pal to stick with me this afternoon, old son. But now I'm alone in a hard old world. Alone, hungry, broke and nowhere to put my head tonight. God help me."

"I suppose ..." began Cedric. He wasn't looking at Mervyn, but he could feel the touch on his arm and he heard Mervyn snuffle as if on the verge of tears. "I suppose I could put you up for the night. I don't think Granny would mind under the circumstances. You could have some tea, anyhow."

8

CEDRIC WASN'T sure whether he felt relieved or disappointed at not being mentioned by name in the Monday evening edition of the local paper, but only obliquely referred to in the sentence, "discovered by the deceased's son, Mervyn Toebeck, who, with an acquaintance, had returned to the dwelling ..." The report went on to add that an inquest for the purpose of identification had been adjourned *sine die* and concluded by quoting the police as stating that there were no suspicious circumstances. Mervyn read this phrase out aloud and gave a curious chuckle. Cedric looked at him questioningly and Mervyn said abruptly, "I wonder what drunk they roped in to identify the poor old devil? A man's own son isn't capable, I suppose."

The paper was on the streets at about four o'clock in the afternoon. A boy on a bicycle tossed the copy perused by Mervyn and Cedric on the Williamson front lawn at four-fifteen.

A few minutes later a copy landed with a slap at the feet of Ernie Fox standing in the doorway of the office at the gas-station. Business was slack and Ernie had plenty of time to spread the paper open on the office desk and glance through it. Because his thoughts were elsewhere he only skimmed over the headlines and he missed completely the two paragraphs which the late Stanley Toebeck had earned when he put his head in the gas oven. Had be seen it, he would have been interested, because he lived in the same part of the town although three blocks away from the lane behind the mill.

Bored with the rantings of the comic German dictator Adolf Hitler, Ernie picked up a pencil and in the margin of a page beside an advertisement for Three Castles Cigarettes began to sketch some curved lines representing his impression of Maybelle Zimmerman, undraped, supine, her legs abandonedly bifurcated. Blood bubbling like a pot of porridge, he began to fill in the centre of the spread-eagled figure with various black lines, wriggles, ovals and circles and then, carried away, he even tackled the problem of dimension by attempting to portray the presence of another figure – this time revoltingly and incredibly male – astride the first, until his handiwork reached (to his own informed eyes) such a pinnacle of obscenity he felt obliged to score it out heavily.

9

A CAR pulled in by the row of gasolene pumps and Ernie Fox slouched awkwardly out to attend to it, his hands deep in the pockets of his white overalls. When he saw the silver-grey two-seater Alvis with its hood down and the petite, provocatively pretty Margot Bramwell behind the wheel, his hands came out of his pockets as if he were reaching for his guns. He tossed a dark lock of hair back from his forehead and his slouch became a self-conscious swashbuckling swagger.

Margot, Vernon Bramwell's second wife, was fully aware of Ernie Fox's masculine appeal and had several times given him an approving *coup d' oeil*, but she had been careful that her appraisals should be unobserved. When Margot had left her home town as the bride of Vernon Bramwell she slammed a door on her torrid past, her slum home, her fat mother with her red rough hands and varicose veins, her jack-of-all-trades father with his duodenal ulcer, and if she ever spared a thought to all this it was that it all belonged to some prior existence. Sometimes a feeling of unreality actually did possess her as if, by some miracle, she had become a different person. From the day she had gone to the races and backed a winner and then, by a sheer fluke, a sort of ricochet from the bet itself, met the successful owner Vernon Bramwell and been escorted by him up into the stewards' stand to drink champagne, Margot had decided to be her own fairy-godmother. The Ernie Foxes of this world were now strictly on the outside looking in. Sitting in the Alvis she favoured the smirking young man with the coolest of gracious smiles.

Margot had not been behind the door when senses of humour were handed out, and although hers was the deluxe malicious model, it helped her to weather the patches of boredom that were the only drawbacks in her wealth and leisure. Out driving on her own, purring along a country road in the open Alvis, Margot had sung, "I'm only a bir-r-rd in a gilded cage," rolling the r's in a comic parody of music-hall presentation and grinning her elfish grin as she reflected that her particular gilded cage ran to a luxury bedroom with its own dressing room and shower; a forty-by-thirty lounge equipped with a grand piano and a semi-circular bar; a maid, a cook and a gardener to call her 'Madam'; a cheque-book to use within reason and no questions asked; an open-sesame to the Pioneer Club, the best homes in the town and the most exclusive circles of the racing world (which she revelled in most of all); her own glittering sportscar and, to top everything, a built-in lover in the shape of a handsome stepson who followed her around aflame with desire to console her for her sugar-daddy's near impotence.

Young Blair attracted Margot a great deal but he frightened her a little. He was too ardent to be able to conceal his infatuation as carefully as Margot would have liked. Old Vernon might have lost his dash as a bed partner but he was nobody's mug. It had happened once and Margot frequently closed her eyes for an instant and drew a sharp breath as she realized what a risk she had taken. Right on the lounge sofa – and two minutes later Celia had come in with a tray of sandwiches! Blair had darted in behind the bar and grabbed a cocktail shaker so that the maid wouldn't see that his buttons were undone and his shirt untucked. It had been one great thrill and her heart had pounded deliciously for ages, but the price could have been outrageously high for both of them. Silly Blair didn't seem to care, but of course he was half-primed all the time and an arrogant young rake-hell to start with. Well, it wasn't going to happen again, not like that anyway. And those dozens of stolen kisses every time they were alone for a minute! They were out too. If he couldn't put his thinking cap on and make some careful plans he could whistle for it.

Margot turned the Alvis out of Bramwell Avenue – I've even got a street named after me, she thought not for the first time – drove slowly across the nearly completed culvert, ignoring the labourers (one or two of whom touched their foreheads), stepped on the gas to soar up the rise of the gully, and spun in through the open wrought-iron gates of the imposing new Bramwell residence, set into the rising terrain so that its full basement garage gave the impression of being a ground floor. The house seemed taller than its two storeys. The Alvis curved its way around the drive and came smoothly to a stop beside Blair's Auburn in the garage. Reminded of Blair, Margot muttered to herself, in the jargon of her buried past, a phraseology which had the advantage of being more colourful than the refined mode of speech her new status demanded, "No bugger's going to put my weights up just to have a blow-through."

Blair himself opened the door for her and bowed.

"Blair," said Margot, "I declare you're intoxicated. You know your father is against this daytime guzzling. Why are you home so early anyway?"

"I will hearken to my father," said Blair, "when he practises what he preaches. I came home early to dream and scheme. Alcohol seemed essential for inspiration. I am developing into a drinking thinker, I mean a thinking drinker. My word, do you realize that's impossible to spoonerize?" He put an arm around Margot but she ducked under it and went down the hall.

"Fool," she whispered, but couldn't resist an over-shoulder smile.

In the lounge, turning to him as he followed her in and closed the door, she said, "The thrinking dinker. There you are. Nothing's impossible."

Blair took both her hands and looked down into her pert and sly, but

33

unquestionably bewitching features. "It's you that's impossible. Margot kid, I'm going slowly crackers with desire."

"Shut up," said Margot. She looked quickly around the big lounge.

"There's no one around," said Blair impatiently. "The skivvies are both in the kitchen juggling the flesh-pots. Christ, Margot, we could slip upstairs now and no one would be any the wiser."

"You *must* be drunk," Margot said, pulling her hands free and wheeling from him. She dawdled across the floor. In the oval mirror above the mantel she saw Blair spread out his hands and shrug his shoulders. He looked almost comically forlorn. Blair was such a clown Margot was never quite sure if he was in earnest or not. She met his eyes in the mirror and she closed an eye at him. He put his head ruefully on one side and smiled his charming smile. He's good looking enough to be a film star, she thought. Despite her resolves she began to feel excited. Damn it, she thought, the old boy trying to hose it into me for hours every night is only making things worse: he's just priming me up. She sank down on the sofa, crossing her legs with a calculated carelessness that gave Blair a fleeting and tantalizing glimpse of embroidered scanties and long black suspenders clinging sinfully to the softly swelling thighs.

Blair put an ivory tipped De Reszke between his lips and approached Margot holding out his gold cigarette case. She accepted one and he flicked his lighter. "Margot ..."

"Fix me a gin sling, would you, Blair? You know my formula. There's a dear boy."

Blair laughed. "Dear boy. That's rich."

"What's so funny?" Margot said, blowing out a thin stream of blue smoke.

"Nothing." He went over to the bar. When he came back with two drinks he sat down on the sofa very close to her. "This couch has very tender memories for me."

Margot took the glass from him, sighed, and with a series playfully exaggerated bounces moved along the sofa away from him. Primly she said, "We must learn to behave ourselves."

"Look," Blair began, then stopped and looked thoughtful.

He stared down into his glass and pursed his lips.

"And how was the world of high finance today?" Margot asked.

"Fairly depressing. My trouble is lack of concentration. Now I wonder what could possibly be distracting me?"

"I wonder."

Blair took a pull at his drink. "I think: it's most unfair of you to frustrate me like this, Marg. You wouldn't like to see me getting deep-seated inhibitions or something neurotic like that, would you?"

"Inhibitions," Margot scoffed. "You're the most hibited person I ever knew."

"And possibly the most amorous."

"Certainly. Also the thirstiest and by miles the most reckless."

"There's an element of risk in everything," Blair said smugly. "Everything worthwhile, anyway."

"Some of the things you've got in mind aren't just risky they're downright crazy. Blair, let's be sensible shall we? You know, well ..."

"Go on."

"Well," said Margot. "I love, I respect your – well, Vernon – very much." Margot realized how phony she sounded.

"How interesting. Proceed."

"Aw hell!" she said. She put her glass down on a small coffee table, then turned and stared at the faintly smiling Blair almost fiercely. "All right then, I'm only human. I do like you, Blair – you do things to me, boy. But I'm not absolutely rotten. I do care for Vernon. When I agreed to get married the difference in our ages didn't seem to matter." She studied the tip of her cigarette and sighed. She stubbed it out carefully in an ash-tray on the coffee table. "I hadn't counted on you being around like this all the time to bring home to me just how big the difference is."

"Would you like me to go away?" Blair spoke softly. It was as if he just mouthed the words and she were expected to lip read them. More loudly he demanded, "Is that it?"

"No, no," said Margot. "Please!" She pressed the knuckles of both small fists against her chin. What a little actress you are, Blair thought. After a long moment's silence he touched one of her silk-sheathed calves lightly with his toe.

"Go on, darling."

"There's nothing to say." She looked at him with despairing big eyes. Blair got up and took a turn around the room studying his glass and rattling the ice in it. He said, not looking at her, "Margot, I'm not rotten either. I've always respected the old man but well, dammit, this is too much."

"Ssh," said Margot.

"There's no one around."

"So you say. What about, you know, Celia the other day?"

Margot hung her head as if in shame.

"It was wonderful though, wasn't it?" said Blair.

When Margot looked up and smiled a wicked ashamed smile Blair knew the day was won. He resumed, speaking with less urgency, "Marg, you're beautiful. You say you didn't count on having me around. Well, how about me? I didn't count on a package of dynamite like you either. Marg, how can I possibly think of a lovely girl two years younger than me as my mother? It's ridiculous. I refuse to entertain the idea. I should ignore you or just be polite, but I'm a man, Margot."

"You can say that again," said Margot.

"Well, where does that leave us? If I thought for just a minute that you didn't like me, even despised me for feeling this way, I swear to you I'd never make another pass at you. I wouldn't hate you for it, I'll always care for you, but I wouldn't ever be a nuisance again. But after what's happened what am I to think?"

Margot sighed. "I know I was a fool. God, what a tramp I am!"

"Do you wish it hadn't happened?" Blair asked softly.

"I don't know what to think."

"I'm glad it happened," said Blair. "Glad! At least I'm being honest, honey. I feel a heel in some ways and then I think how marvellous it was, how marvellous it can be, so what the hell! Marg, we're not to blame for this trap. If my father hadn't let his tool run away with his brain ..."

"Blair!"

"Well, it's true," said Blair. "A sensible man of his age would have introduced a girl like you to his son and tried to play Cupid. But the old goat leg-ropes you for himself. Kid, you can't buy love. You can't buy your youth back. You can't turn an Indian summer into spring."

Margot chuckled. "That's not bad. You say some clever things, Blair."

"Oh, I'm clever all right. So clever I'm in love with my stepmother."

"Blair!" Margot looked angry. "It's no good talking like that. Anyway you're not in love with me. Not the teeniest bit. You may think you are but you're not. You're far too selfish. You just want me, that's all."

"And you want me," Blair said in a soft way, putting his head on one side and lowering his eyelids as if to hear his own voice.

Margot looked up at him. She lowered her eyes again. "You could put it like that, I suppose."

"Darling," Blair crossed over to her and put his empty glass down on the table.

"Please!" said Margot, raising a hand to stop him. "Now that's what we've got to get straight. I don't understand you, Blair. You're clever, you're an accountant, and yet in some ways you're plain silly. Anybody could walk in that door. Celia, the nosey little hussy, your father, he's due here. All right, we've agreed to be naughty ..."

"Attagirl!"

"But that doesn't mean in this house. Not at any time. Ever. That's out. And back seats of cars are out too."

"Those days are over, eh?" grinned Blair.

"Oh, shut up. Yes, if you must know they're over. And some damn bench in the park is out too. All that back street, kid stuff is out. I'm not sticking my chin out like that. People are getting to know me around here and I want them to respect me. I want them to keep on respecting Vernon too and, as his son, so should you. It's up to you, if you're so keen, to think of a set-up that's safe."

"Okay, okay," said Blair. "That makes sense to me. Here, let's have another drink."

"Mix three," said Margot. "That was Vernon's car door slamming. See what I mean?"

10

VERNON BRAMWELL was carrying the evening paper under his arm. He put it down on the coffee table and gave Margot a light peck on the brow. Blair appeared at his elbow with a tray and three tall drinks.

"Thank you, thank you," said Vernon Bramwell. "You got away early, Blair."

"Headache," said Blair. "Felt the need of something long and cool."

"You look a little flushed" his father commented. "I think we'll have to pay a bit more attention to our policy of letting the sun get further down in the west before we imbibe."

"If that's the case," said Blair coolly, "you'd better leave your own drink to settle for half-an-hour or so. It looks pretty bright outdoors to me."

"Aha, hoist with my own petard. Well, with your headache and a little item I noticed in the paper, I think perhaps we can make this an – ah – *exception*."

"Something interesting?" asked Margot.

"Hardly to you, my dear," said Vernon. "But for Blair and myself the item has a certain significance, certainly a reason for mild celebration. Briefly, my dear, an unmitigated scoundrel and inebriate who once–ah pitted his wits, or what was left of them, against the Bramwell clan has–ah–shuffled off this mortal coil." He beamed down at Margot and she smiled her elfish smile in return.

"What a cute expression," she said.

"The rogue put his head in the gas oven," said Vernon Bramwell. "A fitting end." He picked up the paper, found the item and handed it over to Blair.

"Hum," said Blair. "Stanley Toebeck. I'd almost forgotten that old drunk. So perish all blackmailers."

Margot piped up, "What's it all about, Blair? Do tell." "It's nothing really," said Blair.

"No, of course it isn't," his father agreed. "Nevertheless it gives me satisfaction to know the fellow died in abject misery. Blair once had a slight collision in his car, Margot. This fellow, Toebeck, an absolute dead-beat, saw the opportunity of making some money. He did get away with a, certain amount too, unfortunately. He threatened to give evidence against Blair. An absolute – ah – *fabrication* from start to finish but nevertheless awkward to disprove. However, we outwitted him. The Bramwells have a certain – ah – *flair* for strategy, my dear."

Blair held the paper up so that he was hidden behind it from his father. He winked at Margot. "We certainly have."

Margot looked away and reached for her glass.

"Well, Pop," said Blair. "There should be time before dinner for me to slip down to the village. I want to see Monty Harrop about a little matter."

WHEN BLAIR had gone Vernon Bramwell sat down by his young wife
and patted her knee. "How wonderful, when the weary day is over, to
come home to you."

Margot looked at him in a dazed sort of way and then, snapping out
of her trance, smiled and said, "Darling." She patted his hand. "Just wait
a moment. I'll catch Blair. He can pick up some cigarettes for me."

She caught up with Blair when he was halfway down the steps to the
basement garage.

"Blair," she said. "If you've got in mind what I think you have, you
can forget it. I don't trust Monty Harrop. He hasn't a brain in his pin
head. I know he's got a flat of his own. That's the general idea, isn't it?"

"Not really. You're on the right lines though."

"Well, I don't like it," snapped Margot.

"Look, no one's going to know. Not a living soul. I'll tell Monty I've
got a popsy, of course, say she's married. He's no saint, old Monty, but
he'll never know who it is. He'll never dream of you.'"

"And us using his own flat," sneered Margot.

"No," said Blair patiently. "Not this flat. There's a bloke called
Gerard Hemingway has a flat on the same floor with its own entrance
and everything. Absolutely ideal. Now this is the big deal. This chap
Hemingway is a bit of a mystery man. He's wealthy. He's a globe trotter
and a big game hunter. He's got land around here somewhere and he
uses this flat of his for a base every so often. He's going overseas for a
trip, this rooster, any day now, and Monty could get the keys, I'm sure.
I've an idea he leaves the keys in Monty's care. Anyway it's worth a try."

"I'm not sure I like it," said Margot.

"Well, hell! I tell you it's perfect. You couldn't ask for anything
sweeter. The flats are right across from the parking lot. You could be at
the movies or anything; paddy playing poker at the Pioneer Club …"

"While you're poking me," said Margot.

"Jesus, I like you when you're nice and crude," said Blair. "It suits you,
kid." He came up the steps towards her with animal passion blazing in
his eyes. Giggling, she backed away then turned and skipped up to the
top.

"Bring me home some Du Maurier Filter," she said with an imperious
wave. "That's what I came to tell you."

"You think of everything," said Blair.

"I have a certain-ah-*flair* for strategy," Margot retorted.

12

BENEATH THE blue sky of Christmas Eve, at eleven o'clock in the morning, the body of Mervyn Toebeck's father was lowered into a pauper's grave – a drab little ceremony witnessed only by the undertaker, the sexton, a Salvation Army preacher (whose Adam's apple stole the show during the recital of the 23rd Psalm), a tall, skinny, toothless hag who gave the impression of having parked her broomstick behind a tombstone, Mervyn Toebeck, Cedric Williamson and the inscrutable eyes of destiny.

Cedric had deceived his grandmother for probably the first time in his life. She had expressly asked him not to attend what she had referred to as 'this sad business'.

"We are doing all we can for poor Mervyn," she said. "We've let him stay here until the funeral's over. There's no need for you to get all upset. There is nothing you can do. I've given Mervyn money for a wreath."

In the sleeping porch, Mervyn, who had slept in this room for the last two nights, said to Cedric, "I won't feel so bad if you're with me, old son."

He donned a black suit coat which belonged to Cedric's father. Granny had suggested he wear it over his check shirt.

"Look?" Cedric told him. "You walk on up to town ahead and wait for me by the post office. I've got to go and get meat and things and I'll follow you as quick as I can."

From the post office, Mervyn who was heavier by a good ninety or more pounds, had doubled Cedric on the bar of Cedric's bicycle to the cemetery where they had waited for the hearse to arrive from the morgue. The Salvation Army preacher had turned up first in an Essex Super Six. He had shaken hands with Mervyn and Cedric. Cedric felt a little ashamed, immediately after, of the alacrity with which he had disclaimed being Mervyn's brother.

"This is a sad business," the preacher said, which reminded Cedric of his grandmother and made him feel uncomfortable. "That your father had his failings we know only too well, but this morning I was deeply touched by hearing an old, er, friend of his refer to him as a white man, a real white man."

"Yeah," said Mervyn, "that's right. He never touched the blue."

The preacher looked puzzled and Cedric had a coughing attack.

"Who was that woman?" Cedric asked Mervyn as they walked back to where the bicycle was propped against a hedge. "Boy, didn't she look like a witch."

"I didn't see any woman," Mervyn said in a flat voice.

Cedric knew this couldn't possibly be true, but after a glance up at Mervyn's expressionless profile he decided not to pursue the subject. A passing reflection that she might be a relative, even Mervyn's mother, gave Cedric a nasty feeling deep down inside. He also decided against making any mention of what had become of the wreath.

As if reading Cedric's thoughts, Mervyn said, "In my grief-stricken state I forgot to buy that wreath. I shall buy Granny's Christmas present with it instead."

The familiar way Mervyn used the term 'Granny', even addressing her in that fashion to her face, irritated Cedric, but he knew he only had himself to blame, for it was in this wise he had introduced them. Granny herself had not seemed to mind. All in all she seemed, quite taken with Mervyn who, Cedric had to admit, had put on a very smooth act and behaved himself almost obsequiously. He had been politeness itself to Cedric's father and been shown 'up and over' the tower with great ceremony. That he had made a big hit with Martin Williamson was obvious. On the Monday morning Mervyn had even spent an hour or two passing timber up through the trapdoors of the tower. While this was going on Cedric had retired to the meadow in a state not far removed from the sulks. He had an uneasy feeling that Mervyn was going to prove difficult to get rid of. Cedric had longed for companionship but now found himself standing jealous guard over his solitude. He had been a lone wolf for so long he wanted friendship to be on tap as it were, to be turned on and off.

"Oh well," Cedric communicated to Gus, who nodded sagely, "we'll see what happens after Christmas."

AFTER LUNCH on the day of the funeral, as soon as Martin had left the table and gone back to his labours, Mervyn said, "You people have been so kind to me I could cry, I really could."

The dining-room of the big house hadn't been used for years: Granny, Cedric and Mervyn were sitting around the table in the kitchen.

"I really don't know what to say," Mervyn went on. "If it hadn't been for your kindness to me in my grief it's hard to say what would have happened to a man. As I told Cedric, the idea of going back to that house was just too much. Not only that, I'd've starved for sure."

"Oh shucks," said Cedric.

"It's all right for you to say 'oh shucks', Cedric, but you and our Granny and Mr Williamson have saved my, bacon and I'm not one to forget it. I'm going to reward you people handsomely for all you've done."

"Oh nonsense, Mervyn," Granny interrupted. "You've had a terrible experience and Cedric was quite right to offer you some hospitality. Life can be very hard at times and the least anyone can do is give a helping hand to a fellow pilgrim. To fail a fellow pilgrim in an hour of need is not the act of a Christian."

"That's all very well, Granny, but I've made up my mind to prove to you people that I'll be grateful all my life for the kindness you've shown me in my hour of grief. I've got my pride and I don't want to take charity. As soon as Christmas is over – Christmas, oh God! – I'll get a job. I can work hard, Granny, really I can, and as so as I've got some money in my pocket I'll try to prove how grateful I am."

"Oh nonsense," Granny said again.

"To think ..." Mervyn sniffled. "My ... father, ... father, was buh-burried in a puh-puh-pauper's grave at Kuh-Christmas tau-tuh-time. Tuh-tuh think ..."

"Oh dear, oh dear," cried Granny, springing up and going around the end of the table to put her hands on Mervyn's quivering shoulders. "Now then, Mervyn, you must be a brave boy. None of this nonsense. You've had a big strain but everything will soon be all right. Cedric, pour him out another cup of tea, there's a good boy. He'll feel better if he has a nice cup of tea."

"I'm all right now, Granny," Mervyn said, taking his hands away from his eyes and pulling himself together. He put a plump paw on top of the thin, blue-veined hand resting on his shoulder and patted it. He shook his head quickly. "Can't imagine what got into me all of a sudden. I s'pose I've been bottling up my grief, that's what it is."

"Here, Mervyn," said Cedric, pushing across a cup of tea.

"You drink your tea," Granny said. "Take it with you and go and lie down for a while if you like. Perhaps if you had a little …"

"No, no," said Mervyn, "I'm perfectly all right now. Just lost control of myself, that's all. Heavens, I've been a big enough nuisance now without making an exhibition of myself."

"You drink your tea," said Granny.

"Well, I just want to say this: I want you to know I'm going to show my appreciation of your kindness if it's the last thing I do."

Cedric and Mervyn helped Granny with the dishes and then Mervyn, drying his hands on the towel behind the door, said, "I don't like to ask this but I wonder if you good folks could stand my company for about two or three weeks? I promise I won't be in the road and as soon as I've got a job I'll make you take some money even if I have to send it through the post. I hate throwing myself on your mercy like this but I just want to get sorta organized. It's been an awful blow my father dying like this and, frankly, I'm all at sea. If I just had a week or two, or even maybe a few days, to get organized and recover from my grief."

"Of course," said Granny.

"I'll have to do some swot," said Cedric. "As long as you don't mind my being, y'know, getting away on my own in a corner with my books some of the time."

"I should say not!" exclaimed Mervyn. "The very last thing I want to do is interrupt a fellow pilgrim from trying to get ahead in this cruel world. Look, Cedric, you won't know I'm around the place. I'm dying to have a browse through some of those books you've got in that wonderful big library room. I'll be like a little mouse unless you want me for something. Anything you want done, I'm your man. I don't know how to thank you people. I'd be at my wit's ends if it wasn't for your kindness."

That afternoon Mervyn borrowed Cedric's bicycle and made two trips to his old home to pack his belongings. Cedric never saw that sinister house again. Sometime in the following year it was pulled down.

Apart from a change of underclothing, Mervyn, it seemed, owned only the clothes he stood up in. He had a handkerchief, a comb, a razor and a hot-water bottle, but the rest of his gear consisted of dog-eared dilapidated books – two sugar-bags full. Many of them were new to Cedric and looked interesting. That Mervyn was an avid reader promoted him in Cedric's estimation. While they looked the books over in the sleeping-porch, discussing them, Cedric and Mervyn's friendship strengthened.

14

THAT EVENING, Christmas Eve, Mervyn and Cedric set off for town together on foot. Mervyn still wore the black suit-coat he had been lent for the funeral. Cedric was wearing his long trousers, in one pocket of which was twenty-five shillings – more money than he had had in his possession since probably the same occasion the preceding year.

Cedric was glad to have Mervyn's company. Now that Mervyn had made it plain he realized he was an intruder and had no intention of foisting himself on the Williamsons indefinitely, Cedric was prepared to make the most of having a friend. It was a relief to have noticed on previous excursions together that nobody seemed to know Mervyn or suspect his lowly background. Cedric told himself that he was not a snob, but still, what with the tower and being poor and everything, one did not wish to play into the hands of the enemy. After all he *was* a General's grandson and, whatever his father's peculiarities, drinking methylated spirits, even white methylated spirits, was not one of them.

Cedric was rather touched at the way Mervyn entered into the spirit of buying Christmas presents for Granny and Cedric's father. Cedric told Mervyn he intended to buy his grandmother a pair of warm slippers but confessed that choosing anything for his father presented a problem.

"He's not a man that seems to *require* anything," Cedric said. "About the only thing that he'd really appreciate would be timber."

"Does he smoke?"

"Well, you know, it's funny but I can't tell you. I remember he always used to have a pipe, but, blow me if I've seen him with it lately."

"Well, look here, old son," Mervyn said. "You run along and get Granny her slippers and I'll poke around and see what I can see. I'm an amazingly versatile shopper. You'd be surprised. I'll meet you here in half an hour or so."

"Okey-dokey."

Mervyn was a long time keeping the rendezvous and Cedric stood at the edge of the footpath with Granny's slippers wrapped up in a box under his arm and got more and more miserable.

Each end of the main street had been roped off to stop vehicular traffic and allow people to wander on the road as well as on the sidewalks. The entire shopping area was like a fair-ground, everyone jostling and shouting and the kids blowing whistles and twirling rattles. Cedric began to wish someone would squirt him with a water pistol or throw rice over him in the same way they were treating everyone else or even yell out the hated 'Pisa', but even his classmates went by in excited groups without apparently seeing him.' Some of the prettiest girls at the school seemed to have been picked up by the meanest, lousiest so-and-sos that ever made Cedric's life miserable. No one spoke to him. He felt invisible.

"Riff-raff," Cedric muttered and then, spleen finding obscenity a better vehicle than disdain, said out aloud, "Dirty lotta shits."

A woman stepping over the gutter with an armful of parcels gave him a horrified look. Hot faced, he moved down a few yards.

Cedric's emotions when he beheld the approach of Mervyn Toebeck were mingled. He was glad to see him, certainly, but he felt suddenly tearful that his heart should jump at the sight of such a crankily dressed and unmistakably common fellow. It seemed to confirm finally that Cedric was a misfit and an outcast and would never be anything else. These pretty flirting girls with their strutting casanovas so full of the joy of youth – theirs would never be his world. His lot was to be forever cast, unless he chose to live a solitary life, with the likes of this fat apparition in ill-fitting black coat and shapeless grey slacks wobbling on tennis-shoe-shod feet towards him.

The 'Professor' and 'Tubby' Toebeck. What a team! A sort of Laurel and Hardy effort, Cedric reflected dismally. Because he himself was short of stature, Cedric liked James Cagney on the silver screen. He lived for the day when the cold water he bathed his eyes in every morning would have so improved his eyesight that he could dispense with his spectacles. Without his spectacles and clad in his pyjamas, Cedric could convince his looking-glass he had the makings of a tough character. Now he realized in a bitter flash he was cast to be one of the world's sad-looking little comic characters, like Stan Laurel. He felt damnably miserable. Mervyn looked more like a youthful Charles Laughton playing some disreputable role than Oliver Hardy though, Cedric thought. What an odd gait the fellow had: jaunty, splay-footed, and why were his hands clasped across his stomach as if he were concealing something under his coat?

"Follow me, old son," said Mervyn.

That Mervyn was concealing something under his coat or rather Martin Williamson's coat, he disclosed after Cedric followed him around a corner to a side street where it was comparatively quiet. Unbuttoning the coat, he produced a brand-new claw-hammer.

"For your father," he proclaimed triumphantly. "Isn't it a beauty? Old hawk-eye Toebeck noticed yesterday morning what a sick hammer your father's got. He was using the claw to pull out a nail and the head wobbled. As soon as you mentioned timber, I remembered. Boy, he'll be thrilled! Now, Cedric old son, that'll be your present to him. I've got him a box of Havana cigars – only the best, my child, only the best."

"But, gee whizz!"

"And for Granny I have some nice woollen stockings to go with the slippers I perceive you are carrying. Only Woolworth's, true, but conveniently displayed in a gift package."

"You shouldn't have, Merv, it musta cost you a fortune." "But a trifle, light as air," said Mervyn. "For a start I had the money which in my grief-stricken state I forgot to spend on a wreath. My old man would be glad to know it has gone to make someone happy. He would have spent it on methylated spirits. It takes all sorts to make a world, Cedric, my oath it does. For my own part I have a passion for condensed milk. The only reflection I can cast on your hospitality, old son, is that I haven't been able to find any condensed milk in your larder. But this state of affairs has been rectified. I have acquired a tin. Santa Claus could bring no better present." He patted a bulging pocket of the black coat.

"That hammer, though," Cedric protested. "You wouldn't buy a beaut hammer like that under ..."

"Hush, old son, you will tell dear Granny you have been saving up for it. Mundane matters like prices will not occur to your father, man of lofty ideals that he is."

Mervyn was bubbling over with good humour but, right then, as he extended his hand grandiloquently to drop the price ticket disdainfully on the footpath, a diminutive Christmas Eve reveller squirted him with a water pistol. Mervyn spun around, skipped forward and caught his youthful assassin in the seat of the pants with a mighty kick. "Take that, you little bastard," he hooted.

Cedric was startled but suddenly felt a lot better. Maybe he and Mervyn weren't a comedy team after all. Maybe they were men not to be trifled with. Who knew? Maybe, between them, they would make these good-looking show-offs with their flirting empty-headed girls sit up and take notice yet.

"Yuh, yuh, yuh," chortled Mervyn as he turned back to Cedric. "Pity I'm wearing sandshoes. On second thoughts though I'm glad. That was no way to treat a fellow pilgrim at a time of peace and goodwill. Yuh, yuh, yuh. Now look, Cedric, I suggest we return to your ancestral castle and hide these tokens of our esteem away until tomorrow. A man hardly fits into this festive scene going around brandishing a hammer."

"Will we come back?" asked Cedric.

"We shall see. I have an idea. Here, let's cross the road." They crossed the road and Mervyn stopped outside a doorway at the head of a flight of steps leading down to a basement billiard-saloon.

"You wait here, old son. This is only a venture, but I can't see the son of a metho king like Stanley Toebeck being repulsed."

When Mervyn came out on to the street again, Cedric knew he was carrying something else under the coat and was consumed with, curiosity but was obliged to keep on wondering until they were both sitting on the side of Mervyn's bed in the sleeping-porch. Mervyn took out two bottles, full to within an inch of the cork of a dark brown liquid, and thrust them between his legs under the bed.

"Sherry," he explained, "or so they allege. Anyway it isn't meths."

Cedric's heart sank. He glanced nervously at the closed door. The Williamsons had always been a staunch blue-ribbon family. Cedric's mother and Granny had played a big part in the campaign which had resulted in this part of the country becoming a prohibition area.

"They're not allowed to sell it," he said. "Gee, Merv, you can get into trouble for buying that. This is a no-licence district."

"You go and pinch a glass, old son. Your scruples will vanish like snow on the desert sand." Mervyn extricated a large tin of condensed milk and the box of cigars from his coat pockets and placed them on the dressing-table.

When Cedric came back with a glass in his pocket, steeling himself to refuse to imbibe, Mervyn said, "This quid your granny gave me sure bears a charmed life. The guy in the pool-room made me a present of this plonk." He said he felt bad about not turning up at the old man's send-off today. Bloody hypocrite. Think I can't see through that? He used to sell a lot of sherry to the old man. The old man was a bit of a sissy, y'know, and used sherry to break the meths down. Now Snip Hughes thinks he's lost one customer but he'll hook another one. That'll be the day."

Watching Mervyn half fill the glass with wine, Cedric felt degraded.

"I don't want any, "he said.

"Old son, the only reason I'm asking you to have a suck is because this is the night Jesus Christ was crucified."

"Born," corrected Cedric.

"Well, all right then, born. What difference does it make? The fact remains Jesus liked to get stuck into the plonk. Great man for getting a skinful. Nothing he liked better than sneaking away from the festive board and shooting the moon. I made a particular note of that at Sunday school."

"What Sunday school?" asked a shocked Cedric. "Which one did you go to?"

"I can't remember offhand," said Mervyn. "Here, have a swallow."

15

AFTER MIDNIGHT, with the house all dark, Cedric and Mervyn tiptoed out and lurched heavy-legged across the front lawn. The spectacle of the tower looming up against the night sky affected the drunken Cedric in an unexpected way. Normally the very thought of his father's tower flooded him with angry self-pity but tonight, strangely, it seemed symbolic of a simple decency: a sad thing but intrinsically virtuous. Its multi-type windows in the moonlight were reproachful eyes. "Oh baloney," hissed Cedric, to whom this new primrose path felt luxurious underfoot. Mervyn had suggested returning to the town with the express purpose of picking up dames and it was an idea that

Cedric had seen the merit of straight away. In fact he had acclaimed it as brilliant. The best part of a bottle of wine had given him a new slant on life altogether. All this mooning around, fighting off his evil, hah, hah, evil passions and murmuring 'as pure as the driven snow' and growing misty-eyed repeating Jasmine's name over and over like an echo until it faded away (a game he had invented himself) – all this stuff was so much bunkum. Action was the caper, and he would be eternally grateful to Mervyn Toebeck for yanking him out of his private morass of dreams before he sank from sight for ever.

"Dames!" bellowed Mervyn, when they were some distance away from Cedric's home. "Women! Wild women! That's what we want: Snatch. Yards of it. SNATCH. Where are yuh, yuh bitches? Come on out, yuh cunning bitches."

Cedric reeled along beside him. Every few yards they blundered into each other. Some larrikins in a prowling jalopy were rechristening the main street as a thoroughfare now that the barricades had been removed, but the people had all gone. The shops were closed and dark.

Cedric glimpsed a scrawny woman kicking through the litter on the road, and after they were past it dawned on his befuddled brain that this scavenger could have been the witchlike woman he had seen at the graveside. He stopped and peered owlishily back.

"Hey, Mervyn," he said, but Mervyn was well ahead by this time. Cedric stumbled on after him. He wondered vaguely if it was only his imagination or whether Mervyn really had walked faster at the sight of the mysterious woman.

"Well, this takes the cake," Mervyn groaned half-way along the deserted street. They stopped. "What a Godforsaken dump of a town! No likker and no snatch. Bet the bloody snobs've got plenty of likker in their cocktail cabinets. Bet the stuff's flowing like water out at the Pioneer Club. And there's plenty of snatch too but the dames've got it all. What a town! Don't even run to a cat-house. Cedric, old son, this is Christmas Eve and you can't tell me the Lord himself wants to see a man go to bed without dipping his wick."

Cedric, teetering to and fro, looked up and down the street. The moon, in a suspicious mood, peered at them over the dark buildings.

"Whoosh this coming?" mumbled Mervyn. "Don't tell me it's a cop. They don't need cops in this town. Girl Guides could control this burg. A town without a cat-house. It's a scandal."

The lone wayfarer approaching paused when he came abreast of them.

"Well, I'll be stuffed, "said Mervyn. "Old Winker." Cedric distinctly saw the man wink.

"Well, if it isn't Stan's boy," said the man, winking every so often in the craftiest way imaginable. "Stanley Toebeck, a white man if ever there was one. Didn't even go to old Stan's turn-out today. Big business. Daren't show myself. You know how hot it is, boy. A man's gotta lotta enemies in this game. Gotta play it pretty close to the chest. Sometimes a man needs eyes in the back of his head."

"Here," said the man, winking first at Mervyn and then at Cedric, "have a swig for Christmas. This is the real McCoy. A man isn't a big-time dropper for nothing."

He pulled a squat bottle out of a pocket and passed it around. Cedric only pretended to drink but the mouth of the bottle touched his lips accidentally. While the man and Mervyn were talking, he fished out his handkerchief, wiped his lips and spat silently.

"Look here, Winker," Mervyn was saying. "You couldn't put us on to a woman, could you? A man like you oughta know the ropes. We can pay, my mate and me. We got folding money."

The man gave the most gigantic wink of the whole series. Mervyn turned to Cedric and winked. Cedric winked. His heart began to thump. He felt evil but he knew he was going to see it through. When the man began to cross the road without saying another word, Mervyn leapt about a foot in the air in his excitement. He grabbed Cedric and they followed the man down an alley between two shops and across empty section, down another alley, across a side street, through a hole in a tin fence, across a yard at the back of a boarding house and so to gloomy sheds behind a tall warehouse. Here a terrible thing happened: the night swallowed up the winking man. Mervyn was distraught and ran about calling out hoarsely, "Winker, Winker," but Cedric was so tired and disgusted with himself and felt so sick that he just didn't care. He couldn't even bring himself to think about it. The man had hinted at enemies, powerful enemies, and Cedric assumed they had got him.

"Oh let's go home," he said, moving off, and Mervyn, speechless with chagrin, picked up a rock, threw it at a wall and tagged along.

Perhaps it was because they walked in silence that they became aware just when they came within sight of the tower that they were being followed. Mervyn stopped and took Cedric by the arm. They looked back: Cedric froze. What appeared to be a white, disembodied face loomed up out of the darkness. Cedric grabbed at Mervyn. The wine had worn off and his nerves were taut. The, floating head came closer and closer and stopped within a few feet. The white face belonged to a man as thin as a reed and dressed entirely in black.

"Jumping Jimmy Jackson," said, Mervyn. "The Spook!"

16

CEDRIC HAD little chance on that first meeting to see much of the mysterious stranger. He was left with an unreal impression of a long frail body that was little removed from a shadow and a face hovering above the shadow like a Halloween parsnip. In retrospect, the entire midnight excursion seemed a dreamlike experience, no part more so than the brief encounter with the person whom Mervyn had addressed as the Spook. Mervyn had not introduced the stranger to Cedric. He had shaken the newcomer by the hand and gabbled some disjointed greetings, perfunctory, agitated, punctuated by phony 'ha-hahs' and excuses. "Fancy seeing you, Merry Christmas, ha-hah, explain when I see you. Not supposed to be here, sorry to dash off, ta-ta, ha-hah ..." Still talking over his shoulder to the long white face in the night, Mervyn had taken Cedric by the arm and walked rapidly away, going right past the Williamson house. The lurching silhouette of the tower was left behind; ahead was the blue glitter of the neon sign above the new gas station.

"Do we have to use the front gate to get inside?" Mervyn whispered, urgently squeezing Cedric's arm as he bundled him along.

"No. Over the gate."

They scrambled over a five-bar gate. Half way along the grassy track leading to the meadow Cedric branched oft and led Mervyn through a shrubbery. They stole across the front lawn. Up close to the side of the house Mervyn stood still and listened. They tiptoed across the verandah and into the kitchen. Mervyn said, "Damn, damn, I'll bet we never shook him off. Not the Spook."

"Sssh," hissed Cedric. "Who is he? Crumbs, he frightened me."

"I'll tell you tomorrow," whispered Mervyn. "Look, Cedric, go to bed in the dark, will you? I'm not going to turn my light on. I'm just going to cut a piece of bread. I'm starving. I'll grab a spoon and tin-opener too while I'm at it. Nothing like condensed milk to soothe the old system."

17

MERVYN MADE further inroads into the condensed milk the next morning while he told Cedric about the Spook. Cedric declined to fetch a spoon and join him. They were sitting in the sleeping-porch. The previous night's indulgence in wine had left Cedric mildly feverish, sexually potent and faintly melancholic. Because it was a new experience he found his condition not unenjoyable. From the kitchen wafted the palate-titillating aroma of a joint roasting in the coal-range.

"The Spook is my old man of the sea," Mervyn told Cedric.

"His name is Fred Haunt, so you can see where this Spook business started. I don't think the poor devil is the full quid actual. It's childish the way he sneaks up on people in those rubber-sole shoes and tries to scare the tar out of them. He doesn't walk like other people: he's practised a sort of gliding movement. Ever since he got dubbed 'the Spook' at school he's never happy unless he's gum-shoeing around in the dark, gliding up to people and standing at their elbow and that sort of thing. It's pathetic. Not that it's not effective. Turning around and finding that dial of his leering at a man is enough to give anyone a dose of the creeps. He nearly got himself put away years ago going around at night pressing his nose up against windows. They didn't know whether he was a Peeping Tom or a moron. They let him off in the end. Later on he got in a real jam. I'll tell you about that in a minute. Poor old Spook. No wonder he's gone bald. He never did have much hair but it looked to me last night he's an egg-shell blond now."

"He's about three years older than me," continued Mervyn. "Makes him twenty-three or twenty-four. He's an absolute dunce and the last year I was at school caught him up. I was at the Tech where you are now. Took engineering. So did the Spook. I think he fancied himself as a mad inventor or something until he decided to go all mysterious. For years he was always pulling some crackpot blueprint out of his pocket, so they told me; but when I met him he'd reached the stage of carrying a test tube with some green muck in it and keeping on holding it up to the light and peering at it. Reckoned he was going to blow up the world or something. I'm a softhearted coot, Cedric, and I used to humour him and damn me if he didn't hook on to me. From then on I couldn't shake him off. I left school and got a job at the foundry, just stooging around while I made up my mind whether to sign up for a five-year apprenticeship, and the next day the Spook was working there too as a general rouseabout. He got in everybody's road: if anybody dropped anything the Spook was underneath it. He got fired but he still hung around the place like a bad smell. Every time I poked my nose out the door there he was, leaning up against the wall waiting for me."

Mervyn ate some condensed milk and licked his lips. He resumed, "A canary couldn't have lived on the wages they dished out at the foundry so I quit and got another job swinging a pick in a quarry. I was pretty hefty for my age and the ganger didn't know I'd only left school. Blow me down if the Spook didn't talk his way into a job there too: damned near killed the poor skinny blighter, but I gotta hand it to him, he stuck it out day after day with his hands dripping blood and his back nearly broken. They had to get rid of him of course. After that he used to sit up on the hillside and watch me work. He'd squat there even in the pouring rain. I used to feel an absolute heel having morning and afternoon tea in the hut with him up there in the rain chewing a straw."

Mervyn poked a large spoonful of condensed milk into his mouth. He rolled his piggy little eyes ecstatically.

"I'll say one thing for that job, tough at it was, they paid us. At night I used to shout the old Spook a meal. He used to sleep at his sister's place but she'd married a waster and she had no money to feed him. In the end she had twins on top of the brood she had already and they kicked him out. Now, Cedric, don't think I'm miserable but the idea of taking the Spook down to our shack was too much. It's what he wanted of course, but I painted a fearsome picture of my old man, not that I had to gild the lily very much, and scared him off."

Cedric made a careful mental note of the expression 'gild the lily'. He muttered it over to himself, a habit of his with phrases that took his fancy.

"I told him my old man'd slaughter anyone he found under our roof,"

Mervyn continued. "Apparently he started sleeping in the Domain and he got pneumonia in the end. I didn't know that for a long time. I didn't know until they took my old man up to the hospital in the rats and drained the fluid off his spine. I took the old scamp up some tobacco and I was walking through the ward and there was the Spook sitting up in bed looking better fed than he'd ever looked. From what I can make out they had one helluva job to get him to leave the hospital. He kept pretending he'd had a relapse. I felt so guilty about letting him sleep in the open I took him up some books and fags and tucker. When he came out he was a changed man, full of ambition, and I couldn't believe it when he borrowed a quid or two off me and told me he was heading north to the Big Smoke. He was going to be a big shot, he said. A big shot! What a laugh! He was a big shot all right. Y'know what happened to poor old Spook? I don't blame him, I'm just sorry for him. Actual, I blame the movies a lot. The old Spook used to just about live on gangster films when he had the price to get in, and he used to walk down the street afterwards with a fag hanging out of his mouth and his shoulders hunched up like he was Bogart or Cagney or someone."

Cedric winced.

"So what does he do after he's bummed around the city for a while and he's back to sleeping in a barrel or something, but pinch a gun out of a sport shop, no bullets, just a gun and he sticks up a little corner shop. The guy opens the till and throws the loot at him and what does the Spook do? He faints. Either he's weak from hunger or he couldn't believe there was that much money, but he faints. The big shot! They gave him two years in Borstal. I wouldn't have known about this either if I hadn't been reading an old newspaper in the dunny at the mill catching up on world events."

"Do you think he knows that you know where he's been all this time?"

"I don't suppose he does. On the other hand he might be kidding himself he's world famous. He's just the lad to be playing at Public Enemy No.1. Apparently he's just hit town and bludged his way in with his sister again. Well, we got rid of him, but I'm afraid that's not the last of him. He'll be back. You can rely on the Spook. He'll be back. The big thing to remember is to keep him from getting a foot in here at all costs. A big house like this is a bludger's paradise."

You should know, Cedric thought dryly.

18

THROUGH THE casement windows of the sleeping-porch the mellow sound of church bells drifted. Until Martin had begun to build the tower the Williamsons had never missed church services on a Sunday, let alone Christmas Day. Now they never attended. Cedric had not liked to ask Granny the reason. He knew it was something to do with the tower. He guessed that, although she hid it carefully, Granny was as sensitive to ridicule as he was himself. Granny rarely went anywhere away from home of late.

Because it was Christmas Day and also in honour of having company, no matter how undistinguished, Granny laid the table in the dining-room. From the cupboards of the great carved sideboard she brought forth a selection of beautiful old china dishes and silverware to adorn the white linen of the tablecloth.

The presents were a great success. As soon as Martin Williamson had mumbled grace his eyes flew immediately to the new hammer he had placed (reluctantly, at being summoned to the table) on the mantelpiece. As planned by Mervyn, Cedric took all the honour and glory of presenting the hammer. Granny, after scolding Mervyn and Cedric for buying such expensive presents, beamed happily. She had presented Mervyn, who had appeared overwhelmed, with a box of handkerchiefs. Cedric's presents had been at his bedside when he awoke (Santa Claus had never been allowed to perish in this house).

The noonday sun struck pleasantly into this gracious room through the tall windows. Not even the slack colonial summer attire of the menfolk, which unfortunately included Mervyn's check shirt, distracted much from the atmosphere of *haut monde*. Invisible servants seemed to wait in the wings. Cedric felt a sudden hunger for the wealth and the power necessary to maintain such a standard of living. He ate in silence for sometime, fiercely resolved to wave a golden wand over the house of Williamson. The wine had bequeathed to him a caloric surplus that metamorphosed the world from a grim taskmaster into an obliging mistress.

After the meal Martin Williamson lit and inhaled, with obvious enjoyment, one of the Havana cigars Mervyn had given him. Seeing this, Cedric felt very kindly disposed towards his friend. Mervyn, thought Cedric, may not be out of the top drawer but he is certainly a young man with bright ideas. He knew how to act on them too. That the poor chap had never dined before in such splendid style was a certainty. In fact it was not long before Mervyn made a statement to that effect

"Last Christmas ..." he began. "Yes, Mervyn," said Granny.

"Well, I don't know what you'll think. I'm only saying this to show what you've all done for me, but last Christmas dinner I had cold savs."

There was silence and then Mervyn added with a break in his voice, "*Saveloys*. And my old man dipped his in meths."

Cedric, despite his strengthening affection for Mervyn, winced a little. Surely this was gilding the lily a bit.

"You poor boy!" said Granny. "Try not to dwell on these things."

Mervyn had put his clenched fist down on the table and was staring at it. When Granny spoke he looked up and managed a smile that could only be described as brave.

"This is a good cigar," said Martin. "A marvellous cigar. I'd like to stand right upon top of the tower and smoke one of these cigars. Right on the very top."

19

SEVERAL TIMES over the last few days Mervyn had shown great interest in the upstairs of the big house but Cedric had ignored the hints. That afternoon, Cedric, his cageyness lulled by a mellow affability, conducted his guest up the wide handsome staircase.

"You'll have to excuse things being a bit dusty", he apologized. "We all sleep downstairs nowadays. Sorta more convenient.

There was nothing to be ashamed of, however. Although her heart was not in good shape, Granny never missed her weekly day upstairs, dusting, sweeping and airing, besieged the while by heaven knew how many bitter-sweet memories, a task that even without this last sentimental complication would have given many a strapping nubile young housemaid cause for much muttering.

Mervyn peered wonderingly into the many bedrooms with their bold, embossed period papers, dense pile rugs, velvet drapes and heavy Victorian furniture. When Cedric opened a full-length mirror door and showed how some of the bedrooms were connected by built-in wardrobes as large as many present-day rooms Mervyn was so intrigued he could only gape.

Finally he said, "If only the Spook could see this set-up. This joint would haunt beautifully. Cedric, old son, there's a fortune in this old house. You could have conducted tours at midnight, no half-price for children, scare the pants off people, get the idea? The Spook would run the show just for kicks. How do you go at maniacal peals of laughter, Cedric?"

Cedric peered rather crossly out through a rear window and his heart went out to Gus patiently champing at the grass in the peaceful tree-fringed meadow below. Mervyn had struck a sour note. Cedric could remember his father suggesting that he charge people sixpence to be shown 'up and over' the tower and how upset Granny had been. It was not often she put her foot down but she had that time. Martin had sulked like a little boy.

Mervyn redeemed himself by saying, "Y'know, Cedric this is a real honest-to-God mansion. It's mighty, boy. Compared to this the houses people build today are just hen-coops."

They wandered along a corridor towards the front of the house. Here was the first evidence that the inexorable finger of decay had, in speculatively prodding at pride, found poverty. The carpet had been rolled up showing boards bleached with moisture. Directly above was a circle of mildew in the ceiling.

"Place wants a new roof," explained Cedric. "Have to put some tins down when it pours. It'd cost a fortune. I'm afraid we're long way from rich, Mervyn."

"That makes two of us," said Mervyn. "Have you ever thought why we shouldn't be rich? Damn it to hell, we're young. The world's our oyster." He tapped Cedric lightly on the chest with his well upholstered knuckles.

They had just stepped over the rolled-up carpet runner.

They stopped and their eyes met.

"The world is our oyster," Mervyn repeated, putting great emphasis on each word.

Cedric realized he was expected to enter, histrionically anyway, if not comprehendingly, into the spirit of a moment pregnant with an amorphous greatness. He made his eyes narrow mysteriously, pressed his lips together, dropped his eyes to Mervyn's chin. Mervyn tapped Cedric on the chest again with the back of his half-closed hand. Their minds triumphantly blank they moved on down the corridor.

20

CEDRIC HAD hoped to avoid entering the master bedroom because of the distressing view of the tower it afforded, but the door was ajar and Mervyn peeped in.

"Some view, ain't it?" Cedric commented bitterly.

"Um," said Mervyn. Cedric had to admire the iron self-control thus displayed. Seen from the ground the tower was an eyeful, but some of the shock was absorbed by the backdrop of space and sky; but here, framed by the big windows, there was just the tower, ludicrous, insane, immense. Dwarfed by the tower, the big sycamore tree looked self-conscious and ashamed.

"Um," said Mervyn once more. "Aha! Got to hand it to your dad, Cedric."

Cedric, scowling, thought he detected the faintest of tremors in Mervyn's voice. "In lots of ways it's brilliant," Mervyn added.

"It's brilliant all right," said Cedric. "Come on." He led the way to the private sitting-room. The view from this room also depressed him, but this time it was the view from the side windows that offended more than the glimpse of the tower by those overlooking the front lawn. He said to Mervyn, "See all those new houses, those new streets?"

"What a classy room," said Mervyn. "Yeah, what about those houses?"

"Must look at them," said Cedric. "Hundreds of them and all rented for at least two-ten a week. More going up all the time. That land was all our land. Granny's land. A hundred acres of land right on the main street. The most valuable land in the town. You see that gully over at the back where they're ripping up all the earth? I used to play in that gully along the creek. I used to make huts in the willow trees. Look at those poor willows now. All uprooted and buried in clay. That was all our land. I went for a walk over there a week or two back and some cheeky sod told me to get the hell out of it. They're building roads on culverts over my creek. We got cheated out of all that land, Mervyn. Vernon Bramwell and Co. diddled my poor old Granny out of all that valuable land. See that big tall house that's just been built on the far side of the gully looking over the whole new suburb? That's Vernon Bramwell's. He's built that house for his second wife. They tell me she's young enough to be his granddaughter. What some dames won't do for money! Boy, how he must gloat looking over that land! It makes my blood boil."

"Bramwell, did you say?" said Mervyn perching himself on the arm of a chair covered with a dust sheet. "Tell me more."

Cedric obliged. The look of anger on the fat face of his audience deepened gratifyingly as he proceeded and became more and more vehement.

"Listen," said Mervyn after a while. "I knew that name Bramwell rang a bell. Is his son called Blair Bramwell? Bloke about twenty-four or twenty-five or so?"

"That's right. Real no-good playboy. Runs around in a dirty big Auburn roadster. Either that or his old man's Buick. Everyone in town knows he's a rotter but they all kowtow to him and the tarts all chase him. Makes me sick. Boy. There's only one God and that's money!"

"You're coming round to my way of thinking fast," said Mervyn. "Old son, you're starting to talk my lingo. Listen, I'll tell you something about this Blair Bramwell. You won't like it, but it wasn't my doing. It was my old man's."

"What was it?"

"Blair Bramwell ran a girl down on her bike once. Just a bit of a kid. Half crippled her."

"I remember that."

All right then. Well, he got off scot-free, didn't he? They said the girl had no light on her grid. It was just after sundown."

"Yeah, of course he got off. He's Vern Bramwell's son, isn't he? Look, boy, he duffed one of the maids up at his old man's house and she died having an abortion, but he got off, didn't he? Of course Blair had nothing to do with it. Not a nice pure sweet-natured kind-hearted stinking-with-gold boy like little Blairsy-wairsy."

Cedric's voice was muffled with rage. He hated Blair Bramwell not only because he was a Bramwell, but because he was tall and slick-haired and a playboy and ran around in an expensive open car and probably lounged around his home in a dressing-gown while Cedric, without his glasses, was groping his way around his bedroom swinging upper-cuts at a hulking guard who had just caught him (Jimmy Cagney) riding the rods.

"Calm yourself," said Mervyn. "Well, I want to tell you this. That kid that Blair Bramwell ran down had a light on her bike all right and a tail light too, but of course they got smashed up and there was no way of proving they were switched on. This Blair and some pal he had in the car with him swore she had no lights, so that was that. Well, for a start, Blair Bramwell had no pal with him in the car. That was a quick jack up. Another car pulled up behind just after the accident, some of Bramwell's boozy crowd, and one of them hopped in with Blair. They all belonged to the same set, been grogging on at some cocktail party."

"How do you know all this?" asked Cedric, his face taut with interest.   .

"Because my old man was the only witness of the whole thing. It was Bramwell's fault all the way. He was going hell for leather and he came around the corner in the middle of the road. Now you've probably gathered that my old man wasn't exactly a pillow of society."

Cedric frowned, but let the odd metaphor pass unchallenged.

Mervyn went on. "Awful thing to speak ill of the dead and all that, but, let's face it – he was a dead-beat old hophead. He said nothing to the police. If he'd spoken up, this Blair would have got a decent rap over the knuckles and the poor kid on the bike would've probably been compensated, but no, not my old man. Instead he puts the acid on the Bramwells and they slung some gold to keep his mouth shut. I don't know what he got out of it but for a while he was living like a lord. He thought he was going to keep on tapping the Bramwells but, of course, once the whole thing had been hushed up it was too late for him to speak and he got the bum's rush. That's how I found out. The old man sat banging on the table with his fist night after night damning the Bramwells to hell. One thing we can say about our families, Cedric old son, they had one thing in common: they sure hated the guts of this Bramwell push."

"My God," shouted Cedric, "I wish I could be a witness to something like that. By God, if there's one thing I'd like it'd be to see that Blair Bramwell stuck in jail! No money'd ever buy me off. Not when I think of poor old Granny. What I'd really like to see is his old man, that fat poufter, old Vernon Bramwell, behind bars. Ten thousand pounds wouldn't keep my mouth shut."

Mervyn uttered a shrill cry. Cedric paused. "What's wrong?"

"Can't you see," cried Mervyn. "That's it. Bleeding people like the Bramwells for some really big dough is the only way to get square. Sticking anybody in jail doesn't make you or me rich. If you want to, get the drop on them and bleed the bastards white."

"That's blackmail," said Cedric.

"Sure it's blackmail. So what? All right, so it's the dirtiest, lowest-down crime in the calendar, but what about the slinter they pulled on Granny? Did they show any mercy? What about the kid that got run over? What about this maid you said got duffed and died trying to get rid of it? Would you have any pity for a bunch like that?"

"No, damned if I would," Cedric spat out. "I'd see them shivering in the gutter first."

"Attaboy! It's dog eats dog in this world, and I'm glad you can see it."

"It's only a pipe dream anyway," said Cedric, going over to the mantelpiece and leaning dispiritedly against it.

Mervyn heaved himself up and went over to the window.

"Maybe, maybe not. It'd be damn interesting to keep an eye on the Bramwells anyway. I'll tell you something, old son. From this room we could watch that house through binoculars. We'd know every move they made. It'd be cat's meat to burgle that joint."

"You can count me out on that. Look Merv, I'm not a sissy but I've got poor old Granny to think of. If there's one thing she'd set her heart on it's my being a success. If I get into trouble it'd break her heart."

"I wouldn't ask you to get mixed up in anything like that," Mervyn said mildly. "Relax. Anyway burglary is a mug's game. People only keep chicken feed in their houses. I wouldn't stick my neck out unless it was for real dough. But you rather like this blackmail lurk, don't you? You like the idea of keeping an eye on them. It's only a shot in the dark, but what've we got to lose? Just say we did get the drop on them somehow? Boy! Oh boy! Things have happened before; they could happen again. If this Blair likes running around the servant girls maybe he's still at it. It's the sort of hobby I'd find fascinating myself. Yuh, just suppose we could catch this Blair canoodling with some flunkey. Be hard to sorta capitalize on though, wouldn't it?"

"Not if we had a camera," said Cedric, his eyes gleaming behind his glasses. "Get a photo. Nobody can argue with a photo."

"Now you're talking." Mervyn began to move around the room. "We should make this room our headquarters. This sort of a set-up brings on my delusions of grandeur something awful. I feel like a master criminal. I feel like a spider lurking in its web."

But Cedric's enthusiasm had already expired. One glance around at a world of cold, hard fact and it had died at birth. His eyes, as they rested on Mervyn examining the inlaid escritoire, held a hostile glimmer. What a cheek the fellow had to suggest appropriating this elegant room! With all the contrariness of the human mind, Cedric now pictured himself moving his books from his cosy downstairs den and taking over up here. It was years, he reflected, since a fire had crackled cheerfully in the fireplace against the surround of which he now leaned. In those days his father had sat, busy with plans or accounts, at the escritoire; his Granny ensconced in one of these chairs, now dust-sheet draped, reading happily in the flicker of the flames.

"So that's the General."

Mervyn's eyes were fixed on a point above Cedric's head. Cedric cast his eyes briefly up at the portrait of his grandfather, General Arnold Williamson, resplendent in the military attire and insignia of his rank. There was an even larger and more impressive one in the downstairs drawing-room. He nodded.

"You look despondent, old son," Mervyn said. "Never let it be said that a General's grandson let life get him down. To be a General you have to be a leader of men. You have to have resource, initiative, courage. I'm not kidding when I say this, but it wouldn't surprise me any if you've inherited some of those qualities I've just mentioned. There's something about you, old son. There's something intense and vital about you. I don't know what it is, but it's there. It's in your eyes, I think. A sort of brooding, determined look."

Cedric, flushing, jiggled around in his embarrassment. "My *four* eyes you mean, don't you?"

"No, I'm dead serious. Those spectacles suit you, Cedric. When I said all that, I didn't mean you're a military type actual. I meant you've got the look of a thinker about you. It's what's up top that counts in this world."

"Just as well for me," said Cedric who wasn't sure whether he was pleased or confused. "I mean, I'm only a little squirt."

"So was Napoleon. Anyway you're not so small. You're the wiry type. And brainy. That's what counts."

"Well, it's very nice of you to say so," mumbled Cedric.

"Here, yank the sheets off a couple of these chairs and let's spread out. I'm full of Christmas dinner."

"Me too," said Mervyn.

"I'll just cut downstairs first before I settle down." Cedric said, dumping a bundled-up dust-sheet on the carpet beside the chair he had chosen.

"Why not use that flash bathroom down the hall? Boy, I could dream rosy dreams sitting in solitary splendour in a dunny like that."

"No, I just want to see Granny for a moment," Cedric said, wincing a little as he frequently did at Mervyn's vulgar lapses. "I won't be a minute."

21

CEDRIC WASN'T really certain himself what prompted him to go downstairs, but it is significant that he went straight to his room, closed the door and went over to the mirror. Usually, when he did this, he removed his glasses and squared his shoulders. This afternoon he did neither. If anything he allowed his shoulders to slump even more than was natural. No doubt about it, he did look the intellectual type. There was something brooding and mysterious about his eyes. Perhaps Mervyn was right. After all, to see oneself through the eyes of another was a real vital clue to establishing a personality. How much easier to throw this James Cagney stuff away and just be himself. Well, *cultivate* himself. Be tough by all means, but be brilliant with it. Mysteriously tough, laconic, enigmatic, a thinker. No reason why the girls shouldn't fall for him, glasses and all, if he played it right. Cedric Williamson, the brains of the gang.

Scratching himself lightly under the nipples, Cedric sauntered thoughtfully, nonchalantly, around the room. "Is everyone here?" he said softly (but with an undertone of menace) to his brawny henchmen lounging around the walls. There was a murmur of assent. "Be seated, gentlemen."

Cedric sat down on the bed. He sighed. On the bedside table were his Christmas presents. An open card read:

'To Cedric from his loving Dad and Granny.'

There was a tie, a shirt, a fountain pen and a propelling pencil in a velvet-lined case; a box of handkerchiefs (bigger and better than Mervyn's); a box of chocolates, books, wonderful books, nothing highbrow. Good old Granny, for it was her, Cedric knew, who had done all the choosing. Granny was very ambitious for Cedric, forever encouraging him to study but, at the same time, she worried about him overdoing it and she often said he should relax more, especially near bedtime, with some light reading. Cedric had once reflected to himself wryly that perhaps she was frightened he too, reeling from an onslaught of irregular verbs and quadratic equations, would begin to build a tower.

Cedric picked up the book on the top of the pile and fingered it lovingly. He opened it and smelt the new print and the new paper. Then he stroked the other books. There were two sets of companion volumes. *The Mystery of Nameless Island* by John Hunter, and *The Quest of The Pirate Gold* by Peter Martin; and, both by Lindsay Thompson, *Blue Brander* and *The Gang on Wheels*. There were also copies of J. B. Priestley's *The Good Companions*; *Very Good, Jeeves* by P. G. Wodehouse, and a *Greyfriars Holiday Annual*.

"Books is nice ole fings," Cedric said sadly under his breath. He sensed the tears of self-pity, spawn of solitude and frustration, welling up behind his eyes anti he bounced off the bed. Mervyn was right. He *must not* let life get him down. The looking-glass of the dressing-table drew him again like a magnet.

"Who am I?" he asked the image.

Pisa Williamson? God forbid!

The Professor?

Cedric peered at his reflection intently. The Professor? Happiness stirred, stretched, rubbed its eyes. Thoughts, shapeless but unmistakably the bearers of good tidings, began to crowd in on him. As if he had been lost in a cave for a long time and now, from some vent, some escape, the cold fresh air of the outside world fanned his face, so his heartbeats quickened.

The Professor. Of course! His schoolmates had seen it: Mervyn had seen it. It was his role in life. Was it really so bad? No, now he had seen it for himself, recognized it, ushered it in, it was good. He felt a glow of joy. He breathed deeply. He could see quite clearly be had been slamming the door in the face of his own personality. Now that his real self was safe inside, at home, he could develop, expand, accentuate the positive. Not everyone could look like Blair Bramwell. An imp tried to sneer its way into Cedric's new-found joy at the thought of tall slick-haired Blair Bramwell, but it was pounced on, torn to pieces. The world of glamour, glitter, girls, money, open cars, why! It would be Cedric's too. Now? Soon? Somehow? Cedric didn't want to think too much about it. He had been miserable for so long he dared not risk exposing his new buoyancy to the corrosive action of thought. He just wanted to feel.

Only a few moments before he had been near to sprawling on the bed with his face in the pillow; now, borne on a wave of exultation, he was on his way back upstairs to Mervyn; he was closing the door behind him on the bedroom and its ghosts of countless yesterdays. The only question that nagged at him now was whether 'Pisa' had quite ousted 'Professor'. He almost laughed aloud remembering how he had hated both nicknames. Well, he was certainly going to encourage this 'Professor' stuff from now on.

Jesus, he thought, strolling slowly along the corridor and inhaling deeply as if he could almost smell his new-found happiness, Jesus, he wasn't an outcast after all; thank you, Jesus, thank you! He frowned. He wasn't too sure where he stood with God and Jesus. One of the few friends he had made at school and been close enough to enjoy serious conversation with, a very deep bloke called Tomblinson who had now gone away, had been an out and out atheist. His arguments had very nearly convinced Cedric. Tomblinson had lent Cedric several books and left town without calling to retrieve them. The only one of these books Cedric had not choked on (because of dryness, not heretical content) was Anatole France's satirical masterpiece *Thaïs*. The writing, the language had intrigued him. Less to his credit was the way he had wallowed in the description of orgies – the lovers coupling in their vomit, the philosophers pouring wine on the nipples of their courtesans. Cedric's heavy switchback of blond hair had bristled like the armour of a wary hedgehog. Three doors opened off the side veranda: one into the sleeping-porch occupied by Mervyn, one into the kitchen and one into a short passage which branched off at a right angle from the corridor along which the re-born Cedric now passed. At that precise moment someone rapped against this latter door. Cedric swung off down this short passage and opened the door.

22

WHEN CEDRIC looked out there was nobody there. He frowned and stepped out. His hands flew up and he only just choked back a yell: leaning close against the wall was 'the Spook'. It couldn't possibly have been anyone else, but it was a few speechless seconds before Cedric had collected his wits sufficiently to arrive at this conclusion.

The Spook had one hand, the fingers bright copper with tobacco stain and a cigarette protruding between two of them, cupped across the lower half of his flour-white face like a mask. Smoke drifted up in front of his eyes and curled back over his head as if following the few wisps of hair switched back over the nearly bald pate. With the other hand he held the lapel of his coat across his throat so that from chin to toe there was no colour to be glimpsed but black. The hand holding the cigarette now dropped down and Cedric saw clearly for the first time the face that was to dog him through a thousand nightmares.

"Mervyn anywhere about?" the apparition inquired with a minimum of lip movement. Cedric was trapped. The familiar and assured way in which the question had been spoken made it rhetorical. The Spook knew full well that Mervyn was 'about'. A direct lie was not practical politics. On the other hand surely Cedric, the master-mind, was not going to fumble his first awkward situation. He must stall for time.

"Could you hang on for a minute?" he gabbled and dived back into the house. He had given the impression, he hoped, that a sudden urgent recollection such as a kettle boiling or a tub overflowing had called him away. He clenched his fists going down the corridor and furrowed his brow but, much as desired to handle this unexpected development himself, his brain refused point-blank to work. Nothing else for it but to have a fast council of war with Mervyn. He went up the stairs. He paused on the landing and thought hard but no solution presented itself. He carried on up to the private sitting-room and went in.

"Merv," he said urgently.

Mervyn looked sharply up but his eyes by-passed him. Cedric wheeled about. In the doorway, the lower half of his face masked by the cupped cigarette-holding hand, was the silent-footed Spook. Cedric felt his face going red with anger. What sort of a cheeky, insufferable imbecile was this! He glared at the Spook and then down at Mervyn who sighed and looked at Cedric with the shadow of an amused smile and then said, "Hi, Spook! Well, now you're here, come in sit down." But Mervyn's eyes said to Cedric, "We'll fix this somehow."

"Fred Haunt, Cedric Williamson," said Mervyn.

"Hi," said the Spook.

"How do you do," said Cedric coldly.

The Spook subsided into the chair Cedric had undraped for himself. Cedric sat down on the extreme edge of the dust-sheeted chesterfield couch and folded his arms. Mervyn kept casting veiled conspiratorial looks across at him. By maintaining an aloof silence Cedric hoped he was salvaging some of his aplomb. He would not be outwitted like that again, he vowed to himself.

"Well, have you made your first million yet?" Mervyn asked. "How did you get on in the Big Smoke?"

"Not so hot," said the Spook.

Mervyn coughed. Cedric fished out a handkerchief and blew a snigger into it. He'd have to learn to fight that weak giggle of his if he was going to be a leader of men. The Professor! He sat, only half listening to the conversation, nursing the new Cedric like a film projectionist with a faulty machine.

The Spook chain-smoked, tossing ash on to the hearth and the butts into the fireplace. All the time he talked he wagged whichever of his black-trousered legs that was resting across the other knee. He hinted at schemes he had evolved which would result in making a fortune. There was a carburettor, for instance, which he had in mind that would enable automobiles to do something like one hundred miles to the gallon. There would be big companies, oil companies, interested in purchasing this revolutionary device just to destroy it. By dropping hints in the right quarters he would soon have some big combines shaking in their shoes. There was also a perpetual-motion machine. This would have to be faked, the Spook admitted, but it could be faked convincingly. For a million he would be prepared to burn the blueprint. Big vested interests would breathe again. They could consider themselves lucky to get off so cheaply.

The Spook re-crossed his legs without missing a single wag from the knee. He'd discovered perpetual motion all right, Cedric reflected irritably. Not only did Cedric consider the Spook the most infuriating numbskull he had ever been closeted with, but he felt downright insulted by the way all the conversation was addressed to Mervyn with barely a glance in his, the host's, direction.

Probably, however, the Spook continued, the most brilliant of all his schemes was his very latest. He had hit upon this idea at a time of his life when he had been undergoing a spell of enforced idleness. The actual phrase he employed was 'doing bugger-all'. The idea had been lying 'dominant' in his brain for some time. Cedric missed some of the conversation about here while his mind hunted for the word the Spook *should* have used. It finally came up with 'dormant'.

"It dates back to when I was sleeping in the Domain," the Spook said, blowing smoke through his copper-coloured fingers and wagging his leg. "It's been lying dominant all that time."

"Did you hear that, Cedric?" Mervyn said. "Blow me down if that isn't a coincidence. Now isn't that something like we were discussing ourselves this very afternoon?"

Cedric could see that Mervyn was really interested now and not just kidding the Spook along.

"I missed a bit of that," Cedric said.

Mervyn sprang up and walked around the room. "Blackmail!" he exclaimed. "What a coincidence! All we need is a flashlight camera. I wonder what one would cost?"

"What's all this about?" Cedric said petulantly.

"Tell him, Spook." The Spook now favoured Cedric with a fishy gaze. Cedric listened.

The Spook explained that during the month or so a summer-house in the Domain had been his dwelling and his slumber had been interrupted night after night by couples intent on finding a quiet spot suitable for love-making.

"They weren't just kids neither," said the Spook. "They were all sorts of people. Men with other guys' wives and all sorts. Boy, did I hear some conversations! And did I see some sights! Right up close. They never knew I was there. I used to get a silly on," the Spook sniggered nastily. "I reckon if I'd fallen down I'd've pole vaulted into the lake."

Distaste mounted in Cedric, but neck and neck with it mounted also an erotic passion. He turned to Mervyn.

"But, Mervyn, these people aren't people like – you know who we're after." He nodded towards the window. "You can't imagine people like You-Know-Who taking girls into the Domain at night. Not rich people with cars."

"You'd be surprised," said the Spook.

"Oh, bunkum."

"You're missing the general idea," said Mervyn. "Look, Cedric, old son, you have to crawl before you walk. You could think of this as a dummy run – experience. We could have a prowl around this Domain of the Spook's just for kicks, but we might move on to the grounds of, say, the Pioneer Club."

Cedric looked up sharply.

"That got in amongst you, didn't it?" grinned Mervyn. "Boy, that's got you thinking. There's no telling where this might lead to. With a bit of luck we could hold some of the most influential people in this town in the hollow of our hand. And with no risk. Strike like shadows in the night. And all we need is a flashlight camera."

"Same old trouble," said the Spook. "Always capital holding a man back."

"Damn," said Mervyn. "By God, we'll get one somewhere even if we have to steal it."

Cedric wasn't ever sure where the inspiration came from, but he recognized immediately the opportunity to dazzle his company. As far as he was concerned this blackmail business was just a lot of tommy-rot, just a game to fill in time, but here was an opportunity to impress people with his ingenuity and prove that he really was a leader by virtue of superior intelligence. He arose from the chesterfield and began to stroll around the room scratching himself lightly underneath his nipples as he had down in his bedroom.

"Well, gentlemen," he said. "I fail to see the necessity for a flashlight camera. Maybe later on, but not immediately. The flash should suffice. A nice bright flash from a big torch. Curiously enough I have just the one for the job. It'll never cross our victims' minds that it's just a colossal bluff. They'll think they've been photographed and that's all that matters."

Through the corner of an eye he saw Mervyn's mouth fall open. He leaned forward to peer out of the window across the new housing development to where, above the gully, the late afternoon sun lit up the tall pretentious Bramwell residence. He himself basked in the reverent silence that had fallen behind his narrow stooping shoulders.

23

IN THE upstairs bathroom, tiled, ornate, which had so taken Mervyn's fancy, Mervyn, having followed Cedric down the hall, impressed firmly on him that he must on no account, in a weak moment, ask the Spook to stay over for the evening meal.

Cedric had never imagined for a moment when he first met the Spook that he would ever find himself actually enjoying his company, but Granny's call up the stairs that tea had been prepared came all too soon. Mellowed by the praise heaped upon him for his resourcefulness and cunning and never really visualising the venture as anything but a theoretical exercise, a game to while away an idle half-hour, Cedric had entered whole-heartedly into the atmosphere of conspiracy. He had made several further suggestions which had been hailed as 'brilliant'. He became more and more convinced as time passed that these two fellows, so much older than himself, were looking to him as their leader. He seemed to be speaking more fluently. He was avoiding the 'sorta' and 'kinda' style of speaking which for so long had rescued him from many an inarticulate corner. The extensive vocabulary he called on so readily in his essay writing was no longer playing hide-and-seek with his tongue. When he moved thoughtfully around the room it was with a slouching assurance. He was learning to stifle his nervous giggle with a thin-lipped, twisted, superior smile. It was amazing, he reflected, how his real personality, once recognized and made welcome, could almost be felt growing to stature within him.

When the call came that tea was ready (Cedric had explained to his grandmother, when he had gone downstairs to find the torch, that he was entertaining two friends in the private sitting-room) they had all the drapes drawn and were practising operating the switch of the torch, pressing it and releasing it quickly as if it were a button, to try and get the desired effect in the dark room. It was a torch powered by four cells and its lens was about three inches in diameter. Cedric and the Spook were happy with the flash produced but Mervyn was not convinced it was bright enough.

"This has got to look like the real thing, chaps," Mervyn said. "It's got to be really dazzling and there ought to be a sort of pop. Don't get the idea I don't appreciate this brainwave of yours, Cedric old son, but we can't leave any stone unturned to get results. The biggest whiz-banger aspect of your suggestion is that we don't have to invest in a camera. I don't think this flash is going to bother us much. I know an old guy who works at the mill who's a real shutterbug and I can remember him talking about taking flashlight photos."

"I don't like the idea of going around asking questions," said Cedric anxiously. "I want this to be the perfect crime."

"You can forget worrying about this guy," said Mervyn. "He's a doddery old coot but he knows his onions when it comes to photography. I've only got to get him talking. I wish I'd listened to him yakking away at smoko now. I'm sure you can get magnesium foil tubes or something nowadays instead of magnesium powder. They're probably not very dear."

"You still have to be seen buying them," put in the Spook. "Hang on," said Cedric excitedly. "I was looking through a magazine only last week and I'll swear I saw an ad for something like that. I wonder if I can find it. I'll nip downstairs. Better pull those curtains back in case Granny comes right up this time."

Downstairs Cedric found the weekly magazine without any bother and opened it up right at the advertisement. He was so elated he tripped and nearly fell going back up the stairs.

The advertisement, inserted by the Kodak people, was headed up 'THE SASHALITE'. There was a picture of a small box with the lid open to reveal the compact contents.

Under the picture was the wording:

The Sashalite consists of a sealed glass bulb, containing oxygen, in which there is a quantity of metal foil. On passing a small electric current through the bulb, an intense flash of soft light is produced, lasting about 1/75th second. There is no smoke, no dirt, no noise, no mess. The flash is entirely confined within the glass bulb, so that there is no risk of fire. It is entirely independent of the weather: outdoor pictures can be made in the wind or rain, if necessary. The complete amateur outfit consists of a Baby Bulb, collapsible cardboard reflector, adapter and battery, packed in a strong cardboard box.

The listed price was seven shillings and sixpence. The Baby Bulbs were tenpence halfpenny each.

Mervyn slapped Cedric on the back and performed a sort of hula grotesque around the room.

"Even *we* should be able to afford that," said the Spook. "A camera would set us back a packet," said Mervyn. "In fact we'd've had to wait for months to raise the wind. Not only that but we'd've had to learn something about developing. Now we're in. Cheap." He chortled. "Thanks to your brilliance, Cedric, we're in. When shall we meet to further our plan?"

"Tomorrow afternoon," said Cedric, adding smoothly, "if you gentlemen can see your way clear to attend a little conference."

"It wouldn't have surprised Cedric if they had clicked their heels. The Spook looked pathetically happy and excited, but Cedric steeled himself. "And now, if you will excuse us, Fred."

Mervyn took the Spook by an elbow and conducted him away. It was the next thing to a physical eviction. Alone in the private sitting-room, Cedric rubbed his hands together and chuckled.

24

DOWN AT the gate, still holding the Spook's elbow, Mervyn was saying, "So you see how it is, old son. You don't mind being shoved off like this? One false move here could throw a spanner in the whole works. Right now, I'm sitting pretty. This Cedric's a good kid, but I've got an idea he's not such a Simple Simon as he looks. We've got to kid him along a bit. The way I see it is, if I'm O.K. with young Cedric, I'm O.K. with the old lady. Right now I've got her eating out of my hand. The old boy doesn't count. He's as cracked as a second-hand jerry. All he ever thinks about is this screwy old tower."

"Jeez," said the Spook looking up at the tower. "Did you ever see something like it. When I walked down the street I thought I was seeing things. It's the funniest thing that's happened to the old town all the time I bin away in the Big Smoke."

"Don't laugh, you sap," Mervyn said, shaking the Spook's arm roughly. "They can see you from the house. I'll tell you this; they're pretty sensitive about this tower around here. Well, now you've got the picture, O.K.?"

"O.K.," said the Spook. "See you tomorrow afternoon."

"They must sell dozens of them to make them worth handling. If we whip up about ten bob between us I'll buy it and a couple of spare bulbs tomorrow."

On the Friday afternoon they again drew the drapes of the private sitting-room and pressed the button on their new toy.

The flash was intense, blinding.

"By God," said Cedric. "You were right, Merv. There's no mistaking the real thing when you see it."

The Spook seemed stunned. They looked at the Sashalite reverently. Reluctantly they hid it away, reloaded, in the ottoman-type window seat.

On the Monday afternoon at about four o'clock, Mervyn said, "Well, we're doing a lot of sitting around gas, gas, gas, but it seems to me we've got everything there is to nut out, nutted out. How about we move in? What's wrong with tonight? There wasn't much moon last night so tonight would be just right. Tomorrow night's New Year's Eve. Let's strike tonight. We've gotta start sooner or later. We could go on guessing for years. It may work and it may not but one thing's for sure: we're not going to prove anything one way or the other sitting up here on our chuffers."

"I'm easy," said the Spook. "In fact, I'm all for it."

They both looked at Cedric whose heart had been sinking throughout Mervyn's outburst. That action should be mooted so suddenly and on such unassailable grounds put him in a spot. He had fondly imagined that all this comfortable plotting and play-acting was as doomed to be as indefinitely pigeon-holed as the Spook's carburettor and the perpetual-motion machine.

"Well," said Mervyn, "you're the mastermind, old son. Going to give it the green light?"

Feeling sick and frightened, Cedric nodded.

25

THE EGG had been laid and each afternoon for the rest of that week Cedric, Mervyn and the Spook sprawled around the upstairs sitting-room generating the heat necessary for the evil wretched embryo to open its hooded eyes.

On Boxing Day the shops were all closed but Mervyn went off window shopping, taking Cedric's bicycle. He came back with the information that a chemist handling Kodak equipment actually had a Sashalite apparatus in his window display.

Cedric didn't like the idea of buying it locally, but Mervyn overruled the objection. "They didn't know me," he said.

26

BY EVENING, putting on his navy-blue suit in his bed, Cedric didn't feel quite so uneasy. Little things like the Christmas presents beside his bed made him feel guilty, but he frowned such ideas away. He was as good as certain it would turn out to be a fiasco. It was just an excuse to prowl around the Domain at night and that was better than just hanging around. He had told Granny another lie, that he and Mervyn were going to see a film, and he felt pretty bad about that but he couldn't spend all his life wrapped in cotton wool.

They left the house at twenty minutes to eight. Mervyn was wearing Martin Williamson's black coat. In one pocket he had the Sashalite. There was nothing they could do about his grey flannel trousers. They had agreed that grey was probably nearly as good as black on a really dark night anyway. Mervyn's ancient tennis shoes were indeterminate enough a shade to be invisible.

They waited for nightfall in the reading-room of the public library. A few people came and went: pages rustled. Mervyn winked at Cedric across the room. At long last it became dark enough outside, beyond the frosted panes of the windows, for the night to mirror the yellow lamps of the reading-room. Mervyn, without a glance at Cedric, left. Cedric looked up at the clock, which ticked in dignified contentment between the 'No Smoking' and the 'Silence' notice. Twenty-five minutes to nine. At twenty to nine Cedric left. He took the back streets.

It was a good hike, a full mile at least, to the bus shelter where the conspirators had agreed to meet, but Cedric was nearly there before he saw anybody at all. The man was standing under a corner street-lamp smoking a cigarette. Cedric jay-walked across the road to avoid passing him directly under the street-lamp. Cedric felt sure he had seen the man before. He was young, in his early twenties, a slim-waisted big-shouldered six-footer, dark-haired, good looking, wearing a leather jacket. Adolescence had been, and still was, the stamping ground of many jealousies for Cedric and he hung on tightly to the image of himself as the stoop-shouldered (but dangerous) intellectual, lest the sight of this lounging, handsome fellow release in his bosom an envious dissatisfaction, that old feeling of insignificance, to sabotage the new-found but precariously perched complacency with his own endowments.

The glow of the Spook's cigarette greeted Cedric when he peered into the gloom of the bus shelter. Mervyn's bulky shadow loomed up. He whispered, "Let's get moving while there's no one around."

Cedric had planned to say, "Well gentlemen, shall we open our offensive?" He had spent a considerable time working out how to strike just the right note, facetiousness veiling a command, and he now swallowed the perfected remark resentfully.

It was barely a hundred yards from the bus shelter to a stile set in the high hedge, which would take them into the Domain. The main gates – where stood, complete with a dried-up leaf-choked fountain, the statue of a pioneer settler – were several hundred yards further along. They were nearly at the stile when they heard approaching footsteps.

In the still night the click of high-heeled shoes was unmistakeable.

They stopped, irresolute. Mervyn, who was in the centre, grabbed both Cedric and the Spook by an arm. They stood still, listening to the rapid tap-tap-scrape-tap. To their relief the lone walker was on the opposite footpath. Then they heard the motor of a vehicle down the road behind them.

"Quick," said Cedric. They sprinted for the stile, clambered over and crouched down. The lights of the car swept past, clearly illuminating the girl who was, by this time, right across the road from the stile. Out of school uniform, tight and wobbling along in high-heeled shoes, she looked different – but Cedric recognized her immediately as Maybelle Zimmerman, a girl in his own form. Rumour had it she was a hot number and this Cedric had always been only too willing to believe. On sports days, when the girls wore brief rompers, her chubby but shapely legs, not white, not suntanned, but ruddy with rude health (just how rude only the inside story of Cedric's private war with his 'evil passions' could reveal) had always drawn his virgin gaze, glasses and all, like a magnet.

The car lights became two glaring eyes and then went out. The tap-tap scrape-tap faded away.

Mervyn had been wrong in prophesying no moonlight. There were two half-moons, one in the sky and the other in the lake, both to be capriciously glimpsed through tangled boughs and black and silver leaves, one by peering upwards and the other sideways as they trod the mossy path, veined with gnarled roots, down into the basin.

The lake was long and formed like an exclamation mark with the dot provided by an oval splash of shadowed water where the lake narrowed and shallowed. Between this pond and the main lake the piers of a rustic bridge capitalized on amalgamating promontories of mud.

They crossed the bridge and began to ascend again. The moon on high about-faced, but its twin sister still played pale Ophelia among the reeds. The path was steep and they paused for breath. On either side the trees leaned towards them.

"The lake is bottomless," the Spook informed them in a sepulchral voice. Cedric had to concede the guy had a flair. The disembodied voice sounded most eerie. The Spook's Halloween parsnip of a face (Mervyn's face was the pumpkin) hovered against a background of limp deformed trunks hanging from the gibbets of their own branches.

They resumed the climb. On their right they passed several paths winding down to the lakeside. Proudly the Spook pointed out the roof of the summer-house which had once been his bedroom. It was situated in a dell about half-way down the wooded slope to the lake.

"It's probably as good a place as anywhere to use for a look-out," Mervyn commented. "But we'd better have a snoop around first."

Cedric decided to assert himself. "I really do think you should extinguish that cigarette, Spook," he said.

"Quite right," said Mervyn. The Spook complied.

They decided not to sit in the summer-house itself in case it was the very place their victims chose. They sat on an overgrown log under the trees about fifteen feet from the hut. From here, as the Spook pointed out, they had the view they wanted and also a choice of several paths, either down or up, to effect their departure from the dell.

They had just sat down when Mervyn, who was sitting in the middle, grabbed the Spook and Cedric. There was a slithering sound just behind and above them, and a voice, a man's voice, uttered a rude expletive.

Then a girl's voice gave vent to the same expletive followed by, "Look out, this path's all slippery."

The couple came running off the steep path into the centre of the clearing. The girl stood looking out over the lake and the man, a big man, came up behind and held her tightly. He kissed the nape of her neck.

"Leave my tits alone," the girl said.

She sounded angry, but then she giggled.

In front of the summer-house was a round concrete picnic table with a circular seat. There was a clinking sound and a mumble of voices. Cedric made out the word 'gin'.

"Did you mix it up?" the girl asked.

Further mumbling. Another giggle. The girl climbed up and sat on the table with her back to the lake and her right side to the tense watchers. Liquor splashed into a glass. The silhouette of the girl's head tilted back as she drank. She emitted the sound one makes when one shudders. The man's deep voice asked her something.

"Nah," she said. "It's good: beaut-ee-e. Just a goose walked over my grave. Hey! this table's cold on my bum. Gis' a smoke."

"Haven't you got no panties on, darling?" the man said. She slapped him playfully. The man struck a match for her cigarette. By the light of the match, Cedric saw it was Maybelle Zimmerman. He felt positively ill with passion, jealousy, disgust. He passed a hand over his face feeling each feature carefully. Why was he passing his hand over his face, he wondered? He knew there was some reason, and its elusiveness tormented him. Between his spread fingers as he passed his hand over his forehead and eyes again, he saw Maybelle's lover pushing her skirt up to her hips and he couldn't think clearly about anything. She leaned forward so that her breasts rested on the top of his head and she held his wrists, but there was no real resistance. She was giggling and in the dim moonlight her thighs were revealed completely uncovered.

"You better watch my stockings," she said. Now the man was kissing the upper reaches of her legs.

"Let's have another guzzle," she said. "I like to get a bit high first."

"Oh darling," the man was saying. "Sweetheart, honey, I love you."

"I wanna drink, lover," Maybelle said.

The man clinked the bottle against the glass. Maybelle left her skirt up. She muzzled the top of his head as he poured. She took the glass from him and drank, returned the glass and, as he poured out his own drink, lay right back across the table with her hands supporting her head and stared up at the night sky. The man began kissing her legs again.

"Honey, honey," he kept saying huskily. "I want you, honey."

"Ooooh-kayee," she said. "Let's get down. This table's cold." She wriggled around off the table and stood on the seat pulling her skirt down. He went around and put his hands on her hips. Standing up there on the seat she was an inch or so taller than him. He lifted her down and with an arm around her shoulders drawing her in close to him they began to walk awkwardly towards the summer-house.

Once she paused.

"You gotta be careful, Ernie," she said. "Promise you'll be careful."

"Sure, I'll be careful, sweetheart," Ernie said.

Now Cedric was sure it was the chap in the leather jacket he had seen lounging under the street-lamp near the bus shelter.

"Don't you duff me, for Chrissake," Maybelle enjoined Ernie. "I don't want to start the New Year with a bellyful of arms and legs. I've always been scared of letting any of the other boys play around, but I sorta trust you. I love you, Ernie, but you will be careful, wontcha?"

"Sure I will, baby. I didn't come down in the last shower."

"You got a froggy?" Maybelle said.

His answer was inaudible because by then they were in the summer-house.

27

MERVYN WAS almost beside himself with excitement. He hissed, "Listen, now listen, Spook, you musn't hash this up. You gotta move fast but wait 'til they're right in the middle of it. You know what we planned. Make a sound and shoot just as they look around. Get 'em staring right into the light.

"I know, I know," the Spook said. He was shaking badly. "I'll see you back outside the house. Don't you lose them."

Bent double, Mervyn and Cedric slipped up the path. A few yards along Mervyn stopped and grabbed him. Cedric could only just discern his outline in the gloom. They were breathing hard, their hearts thundering.

"This is tougher than I thought," Mervyn whispered urgently. "Where can we get to hide? If that guy catches either of us, God help us."

"Listen," Cedric croaked. "I know the dame. Let's just clear out."

"Good, good. But we still gotta track that guy to his lair. Which way'll they go, I wonder."

"I don't know."

"Let's creep down in these trees just above the hut and lie dead still," Mervyn said. He squeezed Cedric's arm. They stood listening. Mervyn crouched down on his finger-tips and knees and began to crawl away down the bank under fronds of fern and a curtain of clematis entwined around tangled supple-jacks. Cedric followed. It seemed to him that Mervyn was making more noise than a wild buffalo. Then he was silent. Cedric moved forward and one of his knees sank deep in the dead leaves. A twig snapped under his knee. He felt in front of him and his hand touched Mervyn's hefty rump. Now he could see the summer-house in the moonlit clearing. They were just above where they had been sitting.

Mervyn wriggled back and put his mouth against Cedric's ear. "Whatever happens, lie dead still."

Cedric was supporting his whole weight on one unnaturally twisted wrist but he dared not move. He stuck it out for a few minutes and then managed to lower himself into a more comfortable position.

"Ssh!"

They hadn't long to wait.

Plotting that afternoon Cedric had suggested that the Spook should make a noise of some sort, clear his throat or something, before he pressed the button of the Sashalite so the subjects would realize, in their guilty fear-stricken reconstruction, how clearly their identities must have been revealed as they looked up into the flash of light. The suggestion had been acclaimed as brilliant. The Spook had privately improved on it. When he now spoke up, he said, with all the inflexion of a polite and patient photographer addressing a nervous child, "Say cheese".

Two seconds later the summer-house was fleetingly illuminated by an intense glare. Cedric and Mervyn heard footsteps scampering up the path on the other side of the plateau and realized the Spook must have worked his way around to the far side of the summer-house to get a better focus.

The big chap, Ernie, was fast. He came stumbling out of the summer-house still pulling up his trousers, stopped, listened, and then away he went with frightening speed up the path the Spook had taken.

Maybelle came out and stood by the picnic table. "Ernie," she called in a frightened voice. She went back into the summer-house and she seemed to be whimpering.

"Serve you right, you slut," Cedric mouthed silently.

Maybelle emerged again, half running, carrying her shoes. She put them on using the seat around the table to elevate each foot in turn.

"Ernie," she quavered. She looked over her shoulder and all around in obvious terror. When Ernie came slithering back down the path she ran to him.

"Who was it?"

"I don't know. They got away. Some kids. I'd've broken their bloody necks if I'd got 'em."

"Let's get outa here," said Maybelle.

"I'm gunna have a drink," said Ernie. "Damn and blast! Fancy some damn kids spoiling it all just when we were getting cracking."

"Oh shut up!" said Maybelle. "Look, were you careful?"

"Don't be silly. I'd only just got going. Look, Maybelle, honey, let's go somewhere else, please baby, that's sheer murder getting interrupted half-way, a man can't stand ..."

"I'm not in the mood," said Maybelle. "I shouldn't have come here. Hey, what'd that kid yell out?"

"Say cheese," said Ernie. "What was that supposed to mean?"

"You dumb-cluck!" Maybelle said angrily and loudly. "He took a photo. That's what. A flashlight photo. How do you know it was a kid?

What kid'd have a flashlight camera? We're in the cart good and proper. Jesus, if Dad or Mum see that photo! I looked right up into the light."

"Me too," said Ernie. "For crying out aloud! How old are you?"

"Fifteen," said Maybelle viciously. "Are you in the cart too, brother! You knew I was under age."

Ernie lit a smoke.

Maybelle snapped, "No, I don't want one. I wanna get outa here."

"Listen," said Ernie. He lowered his voice. Cedric and Mervyn strained their ears but couldn't make out what he was saying.

Maybelle said, "But they'll know who we are from the pitcher they took."

More muttering. While he was talking Maybelle listened, sulkily pulling up her short tight skirt and fixing her suspenders. Lying in the darkness Cedric's emotions were in a turmoil. The passion which had shaken him had been slain by disgust. How shallow and dirty this sex business looked in all its dismayed aftermath.

"C'mon," Ernie said. He took hold of Maybelle's hand and they started up the path.

Cedric and Mervyn lay very still. A minute later, close behind them when the guilty party reached the spot where the paths leading from each side of the plateau met, they heard Maybelle saying, "I'll be shaking in my shoes for months now thanks to you, Ernie Fox."

"Don't use my name," Ernie said. "We gotta split up and sneak out."

"That's all right for you isn't it, you coward." Their voices faded away.

Mervyn and Cedric now permitted themselves the luxury of having silent hysterics and then Mervyn said, "Well, we know his name and you say you know the girl. Do you think we oughta follow them? Find out where he lives? Perhaps we ought to. He may not be in the telephone directory. He might live out of town."

"Can't see it," Cedric said, realizing full well that all be really wanted was to go home. "I'd know that guy anywhere. I've seen him around town lots of times. We'll track him down all right. Anyway he's on the alert tonight. It'd be damned risky following him."

"You can say that again. O.K. then. Brother, have we had luck tonight! The girl's under age and I'll bet he's twenty-four or twenty-five. That's a twelve-month rap for carnal knowledge. I hope he's got plenty of gold."

"Say cheese," Cedric said. He chuckled. He had to admit to himself that, although he felt soiled, it was an adventure he wouldn't have wanted to miss.

"We'll have to watch our step leaving the Domain," Mervyn said. "But once we're on the street we could be anybody."

"We don't want to be seen," Cedric warned. "Not even on the street."

They took a roundabout route to the Williamson house, meeting no one. They walked fast.

"That damn show tonight's upset me," Mervyn puffed.

Cedric didn't get what he implied until Mervyn went on. "It's made me as randy as an old tom-cat. I've got enough dirty water on my chest to sink a boat. Boy, it's enough to make a guy understand what sends some blokes to old Rita."

"Who's old Rita?" Cedric asked.

"No one," said Mervyn hastily. "A mere figure of speech, old son." Cedric, whose private war with his pubertal passions made everybody else suspect, now misconstrued this 'old Rita' business. He imagined he had learned a new sophisticated term to describe a shameful solitary act. Mentally he congratulated himself on being affected very differently from Mervyn by the night's adventure. He felt as pure as the driven snow (a favourite battle slogan of Cedric's good fairies). Sex, he now saw quite plainly, was a revolting business.

In the shadow of the tower the Spook, a sinister but triumphant figure, awaited them. They congratulated him warmly.

"It was brilliant," said Cedric.

It was the Spook's hour of glory and it was obvious he would have stayed all night, but as soon as the theatre traffic began to roll past, Mervyn suggested they break it up and meet the following afternoon. It was the sensible thing to do, Cedric had to admit, but he sympathized with the silence that failed to conceal the Spook's disappointment. In the sleeping-porch it was Cedric's turn to be let down. Mervyn yawned and stretched. "I think I'll hit the sack, old son. Work well done has earned a night's repose."

28

IN HIS own room, sitting on the side of the bed regarding his bare feet, Cedric heard the ghostly giggling of Maybelle. That their scheme had gone without a hitch seemed unbelievable. Maybelle Zimmerman! The awful little bitch! Just to think!" He caught himself passing his hand over his face again as he had done in the Domain. Why? Some reason for this odd compulsion eluded Cedric. He passed his hand over his face again, this time deliberately, in an attempt to flush the tantalizing will-o'-the-wisp. It declined to reveal itself. Damn it; what did this business of passing his hand over his face mean? He put out, the light and rolled into bed. There was no need to read about adventure tonight. He was living it now. Somehow he knew he would have to wriggle out of going ahead with this filthy racket, but he would consider that problem tomorrow.

For a long time Cedric was unable to fall asleep. Much later, after much tossing and turning, he was so close to slumber that he was not sure whether he actually heard a suspicious sound in the night or dreamed it. Then it came again – the creaking of a wheel. Cedric slid out of bed quietly, turned up the edge of the blind an inch or so and was just in time to see the dark bulky figure of Mervyn Toebeck wheeling Cedric's bicycle around the end of the house.

"Well, well, well," murmured Cedric. Where the devil could Mervyn have been? he wondered. Perhaps he and the Spook were pulling some sort of a double-cross. Had that quick break-up tonight just been an act? Cedric, mulling it over, squinted out at the pale lawn until the cold struck through the soles of his feet.

He was just lifting one leg back into bed when a thought came from nowhere. He switched on his bedside light. He went over to his too his bookcase and peered into the untidy contents of the shelves. There it was – *Thaïs,* the book the atheistic Tomblinson had lent him. Where before there was dark mystery in his mind there was now certainty. Without hesitation he turned to the last page in the book.

Paphnutious, the monk whose desire to redeem the soul of Thaïs had been but a distortion of his lust for her, turns blindly away from the harlot. Death has transfigured her. Eyelids have closed for the last time on the violet orbs of allure. The full curving lips pressed by a thousand gallants are forever silent. The voluptuous form that hinted of word-*less* ecstasy is still. The features that taunted mad desire are a mask of spiritual serenity. The burning carnal beauty of the *living* Thaïs is no more. And Paphnutious, alone in his empty world, passed his hand over his face even as Cedric ...

It was Cedric's first inkling of the mysterious double life led by his mind. Mouth agape, the little book only an inch from the tip of his nose – for he had neglected to put on his spectacles – he read the final paragraph of *Thaïs,* the very paragraph he had read and re-read and lipped silently to himself some months before, so intrigued had he been with the stark power of the writing:

> He had become so repulsive, that passing his hand over face, he felt his own hideousness.

29

THE SPOOK arrived the next afternoon, the last afternoon of the old year, with the information that there were four numbers listed in the telephone directory which might lead them to the Ernie Fox they had caught in their snare. He had written them down, as well as the street numbers. One of the names was spelt with an 'e' at the end.

"Fox-e," said Mervyn. "Not too foxy, I hope."

Covertly Cedric watched the Spook and Mervyn for the slightest sign of any secret agreement between them, but could only conclude in the face of their innocent enthusiasm that he was barking up the wrong tree. An explanation of Mervyn's midnight excursion now occurred to him. The fat libertine had been out looking for the odious Winker to ask, more successfully this time, to be introduced to some low woman.

"As I see it, today is out," said Mervyn. "Let him sweat it out today. He can imagine we're developing the negative. Anyway he'll be at work through the day most likely and up town with the crowd tonight. We know he drinks, so tomorrow he'll probably have a thick head and feel really low. We'll catch him at his lowest ebb. A mysterious phone call, say tomorrow night will scare seven bells out of him. I wish we knew what sort of a job he's got. We must find out his financial position before we put the bite on."

Cedric had woken up that morning frightened. He still was, but didn't want the Spook or Mervyn to guess. Things had got out of control. How was he going to wriggle out of this mess? He said, "I suppose you realize Fox might go to the police rather than pay? He might give himself up and then they'll lay a trap for us. I think I heard once the police encourage people to give themselves up rather than pay blackmail. They go easy on anyone who does that."

"Sure, sure," said Mervyn. "But you can forget it. This Ernie Fox is in a spot. I'd say he'd be well over twenty-one and we know the girl is only fifteen. Even if he doesn't care about doing a stretch in jail he's got to think of the girl. We'll make it plain that these photos are going to be widely distributed if he doesn't fork up. For all we know he might be a married man on top of everything. There's not one chance in a thousand he'll run to the law."

"What if he did?" said Cedric. "I don't want to be a pessimist but I like to think ahead and be ready."

"And a very sensible attitude too, I'm sure," said Mervyn.

"Well, we agreed the other day that the only real risk we run is picking up the money. If, by some remote chance, this Ernie Fox is crazy enough to drag in the bulls, that's the angle they'll work on. In fact, it's their only chance. Put yourself in their shoes. Until we make a move to pick up the money we're just shadows, a voice over the wire."

"That means," said Cedric, "that if we do what we arranged, that is get this Ernie Fox to post the money addressed to a phony name care of the post office, the police could be watching the letter counter."

"More likely to wise up the post office clerk," said the Spook. He threw the butt of his cigarette into the fireplace and lit another cigarette. "Stands to reason," he added. "Umm," mused Mervyn. "Yeah, you've got a point there, Spook. After all, post office employees are government servants just like the cops."

"That's the one thing I don't like," said Cedric. "Picking up this money."

"That's the one thing I *do* like," said Mervyn. "But I will admit I wish we could think of some better scheme of doing it. Come on Cedric, you're the mastermind."

"Look here," said Cedric, who found it impossible to resist airing his knowledge, "this isn't actually original, I think I read something along these lines, but how about he's told to wait by his phone at a certain time? Over the phone we tell him where to go. When he gets there, he's to open a note. The note is made up of printed letters cut out of a newspaper. It tells him the next place to go. When he gets there he's told to walk down such and such a street, throw the money in an envelope over a certain gate or something like that and keep walking."

"By God, I believe you've hit it," said Mervyn. He sat down on the chesterfield beside Cedric.

Cedric was still frightened and he knew he was getting more involved all the time but the academic aspect of the campaign did intrigue him. He wished it were only a game they were playing so he could enjoy thinking it out without fear of the consequences if anything went wrong.

"All right then," Mervyn said. "Let's take it step by step. First he's told over the phone that we've got the photo of him and Maybelle right in the act. We tell him that for a certain sum of money we'll post him the negative and he can breathe easy again."

Cedric endeavoured to hide a worried frown. He could see complications setting in badly.

Mervyn resumed, "O.K. then he's to wait by the phone at, say, half-past eight. We'll make it some night after he's had a chance to raise the wind. We tell him to go some place where he finds a note made up of letters cut out of a newspaper," (did Cedric detect the faintest sarcastic inflexion?) "and the note tells him where to go to put the money. If he doesn't do what we say or he's followed by anyone, the photos go in the mail all over town or so we'll tell him. We'll warn him we mean business. One false move from him and he's had it. Suppose we tell him the note is in the public phone box, say the one opposite the library? One of us could be watching. It's well lit all around there and if anyone's following him it'll be obvious. Can you hide a note in a phone box?"

"What if someone is watching?" asked the Spook through his smoke-wreathed hand.

Cedric, in spite of his distaste for the whole business, didn't like Mervyn taking over the brain work. He said, "Hang on, I've got it. In the phone book, between certain pages, Ernie Fox'll find a note pinned. It'll tell him to go to, say, the primary school. Yeah, that's it, the primary school. Hang on, hang on …"

"I've got it," said Cedric, quite carried away. "It's foolproof. Look, we can forget about watching him at the library phone box. Whichever of us was there couldn't get in touch with the others anyway. The note pinned between certain pages in the directory'll say quite simply: '*Walk down*

Fenton Street, put the money on the sundial inside the school gates and walk away down Fenton Street in the middle of the road. Keep walking.' Boy, that's solved it, I reckon. There's street lamps all along Fenton Street and from wherever we're hiding we can see he doesn't double back. If one of his friends or a policeman is following him they won't know what to do. By the time they've worked it out it'll be all over. One of you, er … us can make a dash for the sundial and away we go. Exit singing and dancing. There's a dozen ways out of those school grounds and I know them all."

"So do I," said Mervyn. "Y'know something? I took a penny to school every Friday to help buy that sundial."

"You're going to get 'em all back now," said the Spook.

"Old son, you're a little wizard," said Mervyn. He slapped Cedric on the knee. "What do you reckon, Spook? Ain't he a wizard?"

"Sure is," said the Spook. "Someone's calling you, Cedric."

"Cedric sprang up, crossed to the door, opened it, and went out into the passage. Granny was standing by the head of the stairs. Cedric went along to her. She was only a little old lady and Cedric was the taller by an inch or so.

"What is it, Granny?"

She began to descend the stairs beckoning him to follow her. On the landing where Granny paused, Cedric repeated, "What is it, Granny?"

"I'm worried, Cedric," the old lady said. "I don't mind Mervyn but who is that thin man in those black clothes? He looked as if he might be consumptive or something. They're both too old for you, Cedric. I hope they're not talking about nasty things."

Cedric felt terrible. He laughed lightly.

"Who, the old Spook? He's an old friend of Mervyn's. He's harmless, Granny."

"You all seem so quiet and secretive," Granny said, "locking yourselves upstairs all day with the sun shining outside. That thin man, he doesn't look healthy."

"Ssssh," said Cedric. "Nothing's wrong, Granny. I'm going to be stuck into my swot again as soon as New Year's over. Just sitting around having a yarn, that's all."

Cedric couldn't meet the faded blue eyes. From the tower came the sound of hammering.

"I don't want you to work all the time, Cedric," Granny said sadly. "I think you've worked very hard and been a very good boy."

A vision of ink-blotted examination papers swamped with faulty spelling and miscalculations flitted before Cedric's mind's eye. A grunt of spiritual anguish escaped him.

"Oh, Granny," he said. "I've done my best. Do cheer up."

"You're such a good boy, Cedric. I don't want any nasty older people leading you into mischief."

Cedric achieved his light, airy laugh again. "Why, Granny, what nonsense! We're just having an old talk. There's not much a guy can do outside, y'know."

"All right then, Cedric. I don't want to spoil your holidays. I'm only a poor old woman, and I've seen a lot of trouble. You run along back to your friends." She smiled at him and began her way slowly down, holding on firmly to the handrail.

Cedric started to go up but stopped after a few steps.

He felt so miserable he couldn't bear it. "Granny," he called. He ran down and caught her up. "I'll get rid of old Mervyn and his mate. What say we go up town for a while this afternoon, just you and me? Look at the shops."

"Do you really want to, Cedric?" Granny asked. The tired eyes were suddenly bright and hopeful. Cedric kissed her on the temple.

"It's what I want to do more than anything else in the world," he said, his arms around the frail bent shoulders. He squeezed her.

Cedric stood on the landing watching his grandmother descend the stairs slowly and carefully. His eyes narrowed tenderly. When she reached the floor she looked back at him and they smiled at each other.

30

THAT AFTERNOON, pottering sedately around the town with Granny, Cedric was greeted with one 'Pisa', two 'Professors' and (incredible) several 'Cedrics'. He presumed this formality was a concession to his grandmother's presence. He tried hard to nurse the elation he had at first felt on accepting his role in life as that of 'the Professor', but all the time he could feel it slipping away like a handful of sand trickling through his fingers.

Sitting with his grandmother at a table in a tea-shop and staring out at the jostling shoppers in the main street, Cedric abruptly faced up to the fact that the whole notion was ridiculous. The Professor, indeed! Cedric Williamson, mastermind! On a day like this with everybody lounging around in the sunshine whistling and calling out to each other – happy, normal people, suntanned people, wearing sandals and shortsleeved shirts; young people like himself, but *they* were all enjoying themselves on their holiday while he felt old and jealous and melancholy. He smiled brightly across the table to Granny. On no account would anything be allowed to spoil this afternoon for her he vowed.

Granny daringly poured herself some more tea. Cedric saw her look around the crowded tea-shop, nervously, eagerly. To her this is a wonderful adventure he thought, and he closed his eyes tightly for a pitying, loving second. Right then all he wanted were his books and his old humdrum happiness. Dull that way of life might be, but at least it was safe and honourable. Mervyn and the Spook were just figments of a bad dream. An old man who gassed himself in a sinister, tumbledown house (those blank staring windows); the winking man, the nether world of 'Snip' Hughes and illicit liquor, a woman like a witch among the grey tombstones; the depraved giggling of Maybelle Zimmerman – it was all a bad dream. But to what did he awake? His father's tower, a botched exam, another year of being little, short-sighted 'Pisa' Williamson, scoffed at by boys and girls alike. Lost in bitter thoughts his face set grimly.

"Cedric! Cedric," Granny said in alarm, touching his hand.

"What is it? Who did you see?"

Cedric realized he had been staring blindly out the door of the tea-shop. He snapped out of it and tried to smile.

"I was just thinking," he said.

"You looked as if you'd seen someone you hated," Granny said. "Oh dear, you worried me. You're not unhappy are you?"

Cedric shook his head. "Of course not, Gran."

Walking along the main street he fought a losing battle with a resolve not to steal sideways glances at his reflection in mirrors in shop windows and doorways. One mirror revealed him mercilessly as a pimply-faced, bespectacled shrimp of a chap, so short his long trousers only looked ridiculous, and – horror of horrors – with the shoulders of his blue blazer white with dandruff. Frantically he flailed at his collar and shoulders. Granny should have noticed that and told him before they left home, he thought furiously. He knew his face had gone crimson. He knew that Granny was as short-sighted as he was himself and that his fury was most unreasonable but he had to take it out on someone and he began to walk so fast, dodging through the crowds, that he left the old lady behind. When he came to his senses he about-faced and began to weave his way back.

He saw a man looking at him curiously and he realized his face must reveal something of his inner turmoil. Surely he hadn't been muttering to himself! Crimson faced again he tried to remember if his lips had been moving. He was a freak all right, he thought savagely. Just then the worst thought of any struck him: a thought so awful he stopped in his tracks. His father was nuts; maybe he, Cedric, had inherited the streak of insanity. People bumped into him and he moved over and stood on the edge of the gutter, feeling nauseated. My God, he had to shut ideas like that out of his head! Making his mind a blank he hurried back along the street looking wildly around for his grandmother.

She didn't appear alarmed by his disappearance. She was peering at the dishes displayed in the window of a delicatessen shop. He stood beside her and stared, at first unseeingly, into the window also. Then, gradually, in spite of his misery, frustration, mortification, fear, rage, perplexity, his digestive juices began to clamour out within him exactly as if he were a normal human being. His eyes devoured puddings, black and white, plump pink hams, sausages seasoned by every conceivable means, tripe and onion pies, bacon and egg pies, cuts of cold chicken, exotic cheeses, pork, glazed, stuffed and pressed, duck eggs, jars of pickles, savoury mince, calf's-foot jelly.

Slyly Granny produced a small purse. "If there's anything you'd like, Cedric? It doesn't matter how much it costs. I've been saving up. After all, it's New Year."

And so, as countless thousands of other disconsolate wanderers on life's lonely shore have done down through the ages, Cedric found respite and nepenthe in good old food.

And books. In a bookshop window they passed, or rather did not pass, on their way home, Cedric saw a copy of *Huckleberry Finn*. He had read *Tom Sawyer,* but not the adventures of Huck. He stared at it eagerly.

"You want that nice book?" Granny said happily.

"No, no, you've given me so many books now, Gran ..."

Out came the little purse again.

The evening meal was made even more enjoyable by the non-appearance of Mervyn.

After tea Cedric sat and read quietly. At a quarter to nine he laid down *Huckleberry Finn,* too happy to read further at the moment. His eyes were misty with happiness. As he had hoped, but had not dared to admit even to himself, the solution to all his problems had stolen softly up to him.

Cedric was beginning to respect the machinations of his subconscious more and more with every day that passed. *He would be an author.* It was perfect. His essays as school proved he had a flair for writing. It was a noble ambition. It would bring pleasure to tens of thousands of generations. It fitted in with being 'the Professor'. It would give a zest to his studies that the goal of passing a mere examination could never give. From now on he would read even fiction analytically. And if he were different from other boys, so what? A writer was supposed to be eccentric. He would be famous. Granny would be happy. He wouldn't have to teach and handle tittering girls and fierce louts bigger than himself. He wouldn't have to take an interest in football and cricket so he could manage sports periods. He wouldn't have to *sing.* It was these fears which had made Cedric, originally resigned to becoming a schoolmaster, change his mind lately in favour of studying law. Granny had liked the idea but Cedric knew she was worried about the money involved. Well, now he wouldn't have to be a stodgy old lawyer either. He could carry on with the teaching idea and then suddenly produce a novel that would stagger the world. Sitting in his armchair Cedric sighed contentedly. On top of all the other blessings, it now occurred to him he would be rich. Everyone knew that authors were simply lousy with money. He decided to take a walk in the balmy night by way of celebration. Even the sight of the tower failed to throw him. "My father was an eccentric too, y'know." At the gate he could hear the sounds of revelry drifting down the main street. He walked in the other direction. As a thinker and a writer it was only fitting he should remain aloof from the common herd.

31

THE GAS station was still ablaze with lights. Cedric on his happy New Year's night stroll saw a tall burly young man, handsome in spite of his sullen expression, standing by the hoist in the lubritorium and wiping his hands on a piece of waste. It was Ernie Fox.

Gulping, Cedric walked past. He crossed the road and waited in a garage doorway. Within ten minutes the sliding doors of the lubritorium banged shut. The lights of the gas station went out one by one until there was just the neon sign glowing against the sky.

Ernie Fox and another man – smaller and, Cedric guessed, older – left together. Cedric followed them. He didn't know whether he was doing the right thing or the wrong thing, but it seemed as if destiny intended it this way. Also, he couldn't resist stealing a march on Mervyn and the Spook. They would find out where Ernie Fox lived sooner or later. It might as well be sooner and Cedric get the credit. Then if he played sick later on they could hardly suspect him of chickening out. But, he thought, even if he did play sick and Mervyn and the Spook went ahead and got caught he still wasn't safe. He'd be dragged into it somehow. The thought chilled him. The disgrace! It would kill Granny. Perhaps the best thing to do now he had gone this far was to see it through and make damn well certain nothing *did* go wrong. Anyway a bit of detective work like following Ernie Fox was all in the day's work to a writer. Cedric cheered up a little. He'd think something out.

A block short of the noisy, brightly lit shopping area the two men parted. Cedric was relieved when Ernie Fox turned away from the town and went in the direction of the railway station. Keeping his distance and realizing that detective work was not as simple as it sounded in books, Cedric tagged along. Suppose Ernie Fox was shrewd enough to guess that someone would be keeping an eye on him? Cedric swallowed hard. Suppose the big fellow guessed he was being shadowed, and slipped into a gateway and waited? Cedric crossed over. He fell further back.

Ernie Fox crossed the four sets of railway tracks. This was risky. Cedric turned right, ducked across the road, slipped through a wire fence and crossed the railway. On the other side of the line he sped back, in the shadow of the bank, towards the signal lights at the level crossing. He stood for a few seconds close to a telegraph pole. Ernie Fox crossed over and turned down a side street, away from the mill. Suppose it was only a ruse and he was waiting by the corner? Cedric crossed over the road again. This part of the town was called Grant's Fields. The Grant family had been the original mill owners. It had grown into a typical 'across the tracks' settlement. There was no one abroad, but many of the houses had lights and Cedric felt as conspicuous as a giraffe at a pet show. He reached the corner in time to see Ernie Fox turn into a gateway. In the still of the night he even heard the click of the gate.

Cedric was able to count the houses down the street as far as the place where his quarry had gone to ground. Five. Allowing for that empty section and the skip-a-number system, even numbers one side, uneven the other, that would be right. On the Spook's list Cedric could recall the address, No. 11 Collett Street. He smiled. He felt pretty smart in spite of all his worries. He hurried home.

The sleeping-porch was empty. Cedric read in his room for some time, listening for some sound indicating Mervyn's return. In the end, yawning, he switched out the light. Even this dabbling in crime, he reflected, fitted in with being a writer. It was all experience.

32

THERE WAS a public phone box one block from the hospital and it was from here, at nine on the first night of the new year, that the conspirators rang Ernie Fox. The streets were dark and deserted.

A voice which sounded as if it were that of an elderly woman, a tired voice not unlike Granny's, answered. The line was very clear and Cedric, his ear by Mervyn's shoulder, heard quite clearly her slow footsteps departing. "Ernie", she called.

Ernie Fox asked gruffly, "Who's speaking?"

"Wouldn't you like to know," said Mervyn blandly. "Now listen." He began to speak rapidly, but with careful enunciation. "It's very important that you listen to every word I say. If you hang up we won't ring again and you'll be in big trouble. If you listen quietly and sensibly, everything'll work out all right."

There was silence at the other end and then Ernie Fox said in a desperately polite voice, "Just a moment, please ... just wait a minute ..."

It was obvious there was someone close by at his end and he wanted privacy badly.

Mervyn closed one eye in a viciously triumphant wink. Otherwise his full-moon face was impassive, inexorable.

"Yes. Go on. What do you want? I think you've got the wrong number."

"We haven't got the wrong number, Mr Fox," Mervyn said briskly. "We have just developed a perfect picture of yourself and Maybelle Zimmerman misbehaving yourselves. It's a very rude picture, Mr Fox. There's no mistaking who either of you is or what you're doing. Miss Zimmerman is only a schoolgirl and that's carnal knowledge, Mr Fox."

"I don't know what you're talking about."

"You know all right. Two nights ago in the Domain. The flashlight photo turned out beautifully."

Ernie Fox was either spluttering or whimpering or both. "Look here, this is awful. This could ruin May – this girl's life. Please, mister, whoever you are, have a heart, please, please."

"It won't only ruin Miss Zimmerman's life," Mervyn said in a fierce but controlled voice, "it's going to ruin yours as well unless you do exactly what we tell you. You could get anything from three to seven years' hard labour for carnal knowledge. If a judge sees this picture, you're as good as up the river. For a long time. When you come out you won't be a young man any more."

"Oh for God's sake," Ernie Fox's voice sobbed along the wire. "Please wait. This'll kill my old mother. Haven't you got a mother, mister? Look, please, I'll do anything but please have a heart."

Cedric's hand had flown up to his face. He felt again his Paphnutian hideousness. Right then, a spark struck in abysmal darkness, the thought appeared: I've got to *do* something, I can't be a party to this.

"There's no sentiment in business," Mervyn's voice resumed implacably. "You've asked for this and you've got it. Now, don't get hysterical. If you listen to every word I say you'll see things aren't so bad. We want to sell you this picture. Not only the picture but the negative. We'll send you the negative through the post and you can burn it and forget the whole business. You'll never hear about it again. If you don't buy the picture we'll send some lovely post-card size reproductions to Maybelle's father, to your mother, to your employer, to different people around the town, the headmaster of the high school for one, and a special one with some details on the back to the police. Don't try to get in touch with the police. They won't help you. If you do anything silly like that we'll just send out the pictures and vanish. You'll end up in jail. If you try to skip town the same thing will happen. There's nothing you can do except buy the picture. We're being very fair. You buy the negative and that's the end of the whole thing. You'll be able to sleep easy again. And don't be a naughty boy in the future. Now isn't that a fair deal?"

Some of the Spook's cigarette smoke drifted into Cedric's eyes. He felt too spiritually nauseated to wave it away. He stared down at the three pairs of shoes grouped together in a sinister pentacle on the concrete floor. Six or seven blocks away there was another pair of shoes, or even slippers, with another pair of human feet inside them – not smug rejoicing feet but the feet of a person sick and frozen with fear, the feet of a young man who had whimpered, "Haven't you got a mother, mister?"

"How much?" Ernie Fox's voice croaked out loudly in the phone box.

Mervyn could hardly speak without betraying his elation. "Cheap. We'll give you a few days to collect it. I don't know if you've got any money or not. You may have to sell something. You may have to borrow it. We're not going to haggle.

This is our price and that's the finish. You'll never hear from us again. You'll get the negative in the mail next day."

"How do I know I will. What about the photos? For God's sake! Anyway you haven't said how much. I tell you I've got nothing. I'm broke. I've only got my wages. I only get four pounds ten a week. I've only just started a new job. I've got to pay Mum some board. I owe a lot of money."

"Other bills can wait," Mervyn cut in. "We won't. Exactly one week from tonight, Wednesday night, we're going to ring your place, just like tonight. At nine o'clock sharp. You be waiting by the phone. Got it? Nine o'clock, tonight week. No monkey business. You'll have the money in your pocket in an envelope, sealed down. Better put a small weight like a few pennies in the envelope as well, to weigh it down in case it's a windy night. On the phone we'll tell you where to go. Have your shoes on. Walk straight out of the house and go where we tell you and do what we say."

"Look here, I want to think this out. How do I know I can trust you? How do I know you won't go on torturing me?"

"There's nothing to think out. You're not in a position to ask questions. You just start walking with the money in your pocket and everything will be hunky-dory. You mustn't tell a living soul. Now listen again. Tonight week, that's next Wednesday, at nine the phone rings. Money in a weighted envelope in your pocket. I'll tell you where to go with it."

"You – dirty – rotten – blackmailing – bastard," Ernie Fox said.

"Now, now, now," said Mervyn, grinning. "You're caught and you know it. It's cheap not to do five years in the boob. That is if Mr Zimmerman doesn't kill you first."

"Cheap," snarled Ernie Fox. "All right, let's have it now. How much?"

Mervyn put his mouth close to the mouthpiece, "Fifty quid: not a penny less; not a penny more."

"Are you mad? I haven't got fifty shillings."

"Beg, borrow or steal it," said Mervyn. "There will be no second warning. *This is your last chance.*"

He cradled the receiver on a sound like someone chattering with the cold.

33

AT ONE o'clock in the morning, four hours after the phone call, Cedric, pyjama clad, tiptoed from his bedroom to his den and closed the door carefully behind him. His conscience had triumphed after a long, bitter, sleepless struggle. Just exactly who or what its real opponent or opponents had been was obscure. Not greed – of that at least Cedric was positive. A one-third share of fifty pounds, even to the impoverished Cedric, even by the monetary standards of those pre-war days, was hardly a sum to distort all perspective. Even Mervyn and the Spook had admitted it was just the beginning, just a 'feeler'.

"We shall soon have a nice full net of wriggling, squirming fellow-pilgrims," Mervyn rejoiced. "By God, but we'll make them sweat blood!"

He had slapped Cedric, who was confused and feeling ill but smiling a sickly smile, on the back. "And we owe it all to you, old son, you and your ingenuity. That no camera idea was a honey. We're in a business with no overheads. And we're in a business where there's no question of the demand and supply drying up. It's not as if we were dependent on some passing whim of the public, some current fashion. This dirty sexy business is here to stay, my beloved 'earers. They'll never stamp it out."

"We'll hook bigger fish than Ernie Fox too," said the Spook.

"You're dern tooting we will," said Mervyn. "I've got my sights on the Pioneer Club and the likes of Cedric's pal Blair Bramwell. Eh, old son?"

In his bedroom, head in hands, Cedric had wished to heaven that it were Blair Bramwell in their snare and not Ernie Fox. Far Blair Bramwell, Cedric thought fiercely, he would feel no pity. He would not have the slightest compunction at turning up the heat to full blast. Bramwell was a skunk. Not only that but they wouldn't be playing for a petty fifty pounds: the stake would be thousands of pounds. Blair Bramwell would be able to raise big money even if he had to crawl to his father. If it were really old Vernon Bramwell's money it would be all the better. The rustle of each note in Cedric's fingers would be the music of revenge. It would be money that rightly belonged to the Williamsons. And he, Cedric, would have no qualms of conscience in using extortion to secure its return. But the fact remained that this Blair Bramwell business was but a pipe-dream and it was poor misguided Ernie Fox they had in the vice. Cedric kept on hearing in his mind the slow footsteps of an old lady walking away from the phone and her tired voice calling her son. He could hear Ernie Fox's pleading voice.

Cedric had put out his light. He lay in the dark and stared ceilingwards – just exactly, he guessed, what Ernie Fox would be doing. Fifty pounds was a lot of money to raise in a week, Cedric thought. How would he, himself, in Ernie Fox's plight, set about it? Quite impossible. Whom could he approach? No one. Burglary? That, Cedric guessed was just about the stage Ernie Fox's thoughts would have reached by this time. Unless of course he did have some possessions, such as a motor-bike, he could dispose of. And if he did in desperation attempt burglary he would probably be caught and the disgrace and shock of that would kill his mother. Whatever happened, Cedric would always hold himself responsible, he knew. Even if everything went smoothly he doubted if ever he would be able to sleep easy again. It was in his hands to rescue this Ernie Fox, this human being like himself, this fellow pilgrim (Cedric suddenly hated Mervyn) from his mental anguish. Cedric knew what a ghastly thing it was to have a worried mind, to have some awful fate hanging over one's head.

Once, after school, Cedric and the atheistic Tomblinson had descended from their philosophical pedestals for the time necessary to raid an orchard wherein a tree famous for its deliciously sweet and juicy apples grew. They had only snatched an apple apiece, but as they departed, a gang of barefoot boys from another school had come wriggling through the hedge and descended upon the orchard like crazed pillagers in full cry. One horrified backward look had made plain to Cedric and Tomblinson that this gang was there to strip the trees bare. Out in the street they had heard the shatter of some of the glass panes of the greenhouse and then, as they took to their heels, a man's voice yelling out angrily.

That the police would be called in was a moral certainty and Cedric had palpitated with fear all through the long night. The next day, through a classroom window, a policeman who looked as if he might make a little extra money by doubling as the public hangman had been glimpsed crossing the quadrangle and entering the main building, intent, it was to be surmised, on interviewing the headmaster and instigating some sort of a line-up. Tomblinson's magnificent contempt for the hereafter was only, apparently, matched by his respect for temporal consequences: in the singing class he fainted. Whether it was a genuine faint or merely another aspect of Tomblinson's deepness, Cedric never found out, but, be it fortuitous or inspired, Tomblinson was packed off home and Cedric sweated out the day alone. The strain was so great he nearly gave himself up. The following dawn revealed a Cedric haggard with apprehension and fatigue. Weeks were to pass before he was able to convince himself that the danger was really past.

Recalling that time of mental torment; reliving it; remembering how, in spite of Tomblinson's philosophy, he had gone on his knees and prayed; remembering how it had broken his heart to watch Granny pottering innocently around unaware that detectives were closing in – Cedric's heart went out to the miserable Ernie Fox. He wriggled his feet into his slippers and stole along the passage to his den.

34

CEDRIC KNEW just what he was going to do. In his den he sorted out an envelope and then tore from a scribbling pad a piece of blank unlined paper. Before he put pencil to paper a confused loyalty to both Mervyn and the Spook, and – an even stronger voice – loyalty to the unbelievable, miraculous success of a plot which was in a way his own brain-child, challenged his resolve. Finally he began to print on the blank unlined page:

> I happen to know you are being blackmailed. I also know it is just a bluff. The flashlight picture is just a blur. Tell him when he rings you up you have no money and are going to the police if he rings again. For my sake do not mention this message. If you do I will write to Maybelle's father. I mean that. I am only doing this because I feel sorry for you. I hope you are grateful to me. Burn this. Now you can get some sleep.

Cedric printed on the envelope: Mr Ernie Fox No. 11 ... Then he paused. An idea which obviated looking through the house for a stamp presented itself. He crossed out the No. 11 and printed instead: 'Garage attendant. Private and confidential'. He re-read his note, smiling grimly, and put it in the envelope which he sealed down.

In the hall his overcoat hung from a stag's horns. He slipped it on, opened the front door quietly and left it wide open. It was a very dark night. The tired old moon was finding it harder to drag itself up from its couch of clouds each night. The tower could have been a tree, an inky cloud, an ogre of the night, anything like that. Against the black sky beyond the Williamson shrubbery Cedric saw the misty bluish glare that haloed the new neon sign. So it glowed all night! Cedric had often wondered.

There was a street lamp just past the gas-station and Cedric stood still for some time in the shadow, listening, peering, before he pulled his overcoat collar up over his face and walked briskly to the cover provided by the row of gasolene pumps.

A realization of the enormity of his treachery now smote him. Holding the envelope tightly by his thumb and forefinger he rapped it in an agony of indecision against his chin. He knew that to stand still like this at the most incriminating point of the entire furtive mission was absolute folly. Yet to abort his great nocturnal effort by returning to his sleepless bed with the letter undelivered was humiliating. He crouched down and pushed the letter under the office door.

Before he reached the gate of his home a thought turned him clammy with fear. Finger prints! He stood still biting his nails. If Ernie Fox had contacted the police already the envelope was a real windfall for them. Cedric could have wept with vexation and apprehension. He looked up and saw the dark outline of the family mansion. Poor Granny! He thought of old Gus in his dark innocent meadow. Gus would be dead when his young master was released from prison. He would find the noble creature's grave and weep on it. The world would spurn Cedric Williamson, a blackmailer and, most contemptible of all, a blackmailer whose spinelessness had betrayed him.

Already his mind was tumultuous with arguing voices, some pooh-poohing his fears, others just as quickly reiterating that these same fears were far from groundless. The peace of mind he craved was further away than ever. The thought of the days that lay ahead in all their complex duplicity and perplexity drew a whimper from him.

My *holidays,* he thought bitterly. He looked up at his father's tower, dark against the sky, and his sanity teetered. The prospect of being alone once more in his bedroom affected him almost claustrophobically, but there was nowhere else to go.

Full of stifled misery, he opened the gate, stepped off the path and began to slink wearily across the springy turf. He stopped. There was a light in the sleeping-porch – that had to be the explanation of the shaft of light that lay across the side lawn.

Peeping around the corner of the house with the big bay windows of the drawing-room behind him, and between him and the front porch where the front door stood open, Cedric confirmed that the light actually did stream from the sleeping-porch at the end of the side veranda.

That it must be nearing two o'clock in the morning Cedric knew, but he also realized there could be quite a simple explanation for Mervyn's light to be still burning. Had not he himself been unable to sleep? Mervyn might be reading. He might be eating condensed milk with a spoon. Every time Mervyn went up to town for anything at all he must purchase a tin of condensed milk, Cedric had deduced, because there were always freshly opened and emptied tins ranged along the dressing-table in the sleeping-porch. A puzzling thought now crossed Cedric's mind. It amazed him that it had not presented itself sooner. Where did Mervyn get money to buy condensed milk? He had no pocket money,

Cedric was certain. Was he borrowing from the Spook? Did the Spook have any money? It was all very odd.

Now that his suspicions had been aroused Cedric recalled other incidents that were at loggerheads with their circumstances. The expensive presents – the hammer, the cigars, the stockings – that Mervyn had purchased on Christmas Eve. Purchased or acquired? None of these items had been wrapped up, Cedric remembered. Very significant. And had not Mervyn said, when they were back from town and he had produced the sherry he had been given by Snip Hughes at the billiard saloon, that Granny's pound note for the wreath bore a charmed life? The only explanation Cedric could think of was that he was a thief. A shoplifter. Of course! 'How naive I am', Cedric rebuked himself.

More to postpone an encounter with the gloomy thoughts that he knew awaited him in his bedroom than out of curiosity, Cedric decided to sneak along the side lawn and see if he could peep through some chink in the blinds.

When he was about six feet distant from the lighted windows, Cedric crouched down and peeped around over first one shoulder and then the other in sudden apprehension. He told himself angrily that it was ridiculous, but he couldn't shake off a strange feeling that he was being watched, silently laughed at, as if Mervyn Toebeck knew perfectly well he was being spied upon. It was a mad notion and Cedric couldn't even have begun to explain it in a way that would have made sense. But right then, crouching there in the darkness to one side of the unwinking shaft of light, he felt, with an unnerving certainty, that Mervyn was omniscient. It must be some evil power he possessed, Cedric thought, stiff with fear.

The old familiar outline of the sleeping-porch, such a pleasant room in the shade of the overhanging lilac tree, looked very different to him tonight. Even his old friend, the lilac tree, silent and dark, seemed sinister. Cedric by an effort of will forced his numb limbs to move. Still crouching he began to back very slowly and cautiously and then, as his panic mounted, he made a wild dash for the corner of the house. He pressed his back against the wall. His heart pounded as if he had run a mile instead of a dozen yards.

Staring across the gloomy lawn, Cedric felt all confused.

Although this new disturbing fear of Mervyn was uppermost in his mind, his earlier worries clamoured for attention. Most coherent among them was the little voice upbraiding him for his unbelievable stupidity in not seeing the danger of dispatching the fingerprint-smothered note until one minute after the deed had been irrevocably accomplished. And if one minute could reveal that aspect, what fresh complications would the hours and days ahead bring? Could Mervyn already know of his treachery? Preposterous! He must be overwrought. That was it, Cedric decided. He was over-tired, over-excited, and his brain was playing tricks on him. The real Mervyn was the Mervyn of the daylight hours, the fat, genial, vulgar but likeable Mervyn, not the shapeless, huge slug-like omniscient shadow into which Cedric's delirious weariness had transformed him.

He shut his eyes and tried to conjure up a sane picture of Mervyn's beaming pumpkin of a face. Eyes only, faceless, stared back at him, eyes which grew and grew until they were great square, black sockets – the windows of the dwelling in which Stanley Toebeck had taken his own life.

Now, uninvited, there began to move across the screen behind Cedric's closed eyelids a picture of himself and Mervyn walking along the narrow-gauge railway in the mill-yard. Again he saw Mervyn emptying the stolen blocks of firewood from his shirt and again heard his high-pitched humbugging voice saying, "My strength is as the strength of ten because my heart is pure." Worse, he had known his father was dead: *there would be no more fires in the house behind the mill.*

Cedric's eyes opened wide as the terrible inference exploded. *He may have killed his father; he wanted me with him when the body was found.*

Cedric thought brokenly of his Granny sleeping so innocently within. Poor Granny! Her own son, Martin, building a tower that made them the laughing stock of the town, and now her stupid grandson had brought a murderer into the house – a fat, cunning, oily-tongued murderer. Worse than a murderer: what did you call a monster that slew his own father?

'In my grief stricken state …'

Cedric sneered. But the sneer was superimposed on a face taut with anxiety. It seemed to him that forces beyond his control and bent on his destruction were insidiously encircling him. He cast his eyes upwards, imploringly, and his face became transfixed in a mask of terror.

35

HE WAS being watched. The moon, emaciated and bleary-eyed, had parted the grey curtains of its chambers and, by its light, Cedric saw a shadowy figure standing on the very top of the tower. Slowly the curtains drew together again.

Cedric couldn't remember the journey on trembling knees to his bedroom. So Mervyn had been watching him! Who else could it be? A moan escaped Cedric. He felt sick.

His bedroom was on the opposite end of the long veranda to the sleeping-porch but, unlike the porch, did not open on to the veranda. He bent back an edge of his blind and pressed the corner of his eye against the cold glass. The pathway of light still fell across the side lawn. But as Cedric watched it went out. What in the Devil's name ...? Cedric knew it was an absolute physical impossibility to have shinned down all those crazy ladders in the tower and be back in the sleeping-porch in such a short time. Cedric collapsed on the side of his bed. It dawned on him now whom he must have seen. The Spook!

Cedric did a very childish thing. He crawled into bed and drew the sheets right over his head.

With his mind in such a state it was small wonder that when he did doze off, his sleep was troubled. One part of his nightmare was so vivid that again he found himself awake. He propped himself up on one elbow, listening, but the slow frightening footfalls of some dread monster shambling along the hall outside and past his door had ceased with the opening of his eyelids. Cedric had a strange feeling that he had dreamed this dream before.

36

CEDRIC'S SLEEP was short and failed to refresh him, but, without actually dispersing the chimeras of the small hours, it was sufficient to have built up a protective wall of stubborn unreasoning disbelief to keep them at bay. The nightmarish figure on the tower top he attempted to dismiss from mind as just some freak effect of the moonlight. He arose, dressed and washed like an automaton, deliberately nursing the vacant state of his mind. He even remembered to get the eyeglass from the medicine chest and bathe his eyes. He took a deep breath before he entered the kitchen, frightened that Mervyn would sense something different in his demeanour, but breakfast went over smoothly. When Mervyn winked at him across the table Cedric surprised himself by being able to return the wink easily and naturally.

However, he was glad when Mervyn announced that if there was no little household chore Granny could find him, he would stretch out on his bed for awhile and read.

"This P. G. Wodehouse of yours is a card," he chuckled. "There's some real characters in this yarn I'm reading. I'm glad you've got a collection of these, Cedric."

So the explanation of the late burning light was as simple as that. Mervyn had been beguiled by the inanities of Bertie Wooster and the machinations of the imperturbable Jeeves.

In his bedroom Cedric selected one of his new books to read. Book in hand he stood pondering. Even assuming it had not been just an hallucination and the Spook had actually been on the tower top, there was one place where Cedric had been completely private and that was in his den when he wrote the note. The note had been out of sight in his overcoat pocket when he had gone to the gas station. And Cedric was as good as positive that no one had followed him there. He had been very wary and looked up and down the street several times. So, at the very worst, the Spook would tell Mervyn that Cedric had gone for a late stroll and on his return crept up close to the sleeping-porch. What could they make of that? Damn them anyway.

Cedric took his book to the meadow but found he was unable to concentrate. Out here, with the sun shining and birds twittering in the pines and blue gums, his dark suspicions seemed ridiculous, and the watcher on the tower, crazy. Now that he had things more in perspective he wasn't particularly concerned about the note to Ernie Fox either. The aspect that consoled him most was the time element. It was unthinkable that Ernie Fox would have gone to the police last night after receiving the phone call and just as improbable that he would have done soon his way to work this morning. In his tricky position he would be absolutely fat-headed to approach the police. And with the police out of it, thought Cedric, what is there to worry about? Nothing.

The mad idea that Mervyn had some uncanny power of knowing

what was going on was just that – a mad idea. And, Cedric told himself: I did the right thing, of course I did. I'm a good decent, kind-hearted bloke with an eminent career ahead of me as a novelist, not a crook. Furthermore, he reasoned, the collapse of the campaign against Ernie Fox would put the kybosh on any further blackmailing ventures and would also lead to the breaking up of his association with the unprincipled Mervyn and the imbecile Spook. He would soon find a way to get shot of Mervyn. Mervyn wouldn't last long after Cedric began locking himself away in his den to study.

Cedric opened his book again. Before he had read a few lines he looked up and made a face. Suppose, he thought, Ernie Fox isn't at work today? Suppose he's changed his job?

Cedric went and ran his fingers through Gus's mane and had a bright idea. He put his book away in his bedroom and fetched his bicycle out of the little woodshed. The sleeping-porch and the lilac tree looked quite normal this morning. He propped the bicycle against the veranda steps and went along to the open door of the sleeping-porch. Mervyn was sprawled out on his bed holding a book.

"Going for a bit of a spin on my grid," Cedric said.

Mervyn, on the verge of chortling over something he was reading, lowered the book and said, "Eh? Oh good."

As Cedric wheeled his bicycle away from the steps a shiver ran down his back. Damn it, he thought, I've got to cut this nonsense out; the fellow's just as easily hoodwinked as anyone else. There's nothing creepy about him. It's some nonsense I've invented myself. He felt vexed with himself for even bothering to explain where he was going. The chap was only a parasite, all said and done.

Outside the gate, Cedric, ignoring a young couple sitting in a little car and gawking up at the tower where his father was working, squeezed the tyres of his bicycle. They were both spongy. He wheeled the bicycle down to the gas station.

Ernie Fox and another man, smaller and older, each clutching tyre levers, were standing glaring down at a split-rim car wheel which was obviously putting up a fight over parting with its tube.

Ernie Fox looked down at Cedric and said, "Yeah? Right oh. Wheel it over there." He followed Cedric over to the air-hose, took the hose from Cedric's uncertain hand and, crouching down, unscrewed the valve cap on Cedric's front tyre.

"It's all right, I'll do it," Cedric said. "Thanks very much."

As he swung his leg over the bar and rode off he felt elated. Ernie Fox was in a good mood. That must indicate he had got the note as planned. And Ernie Fox was an easy-going, good-natured guy who hadn't minded blowing up a schoolboy's tyres. Somehow, he didn't feel jealous of Ernie Fox's good looks any more, or even spiteful about Maybelle. The whole business only seemed sordid.

He felt a little sad to realize his adventure was a thing of the past but he reminded himself firmly that he had done the right thing. Getting tangled up with types like Mervyn and the Spook, who saw no wickedness in trading in human misery, simply wasn't good enough for a General's grandson. This brooding sinister stuff was finished: The fact that for a whole day and a half now the ambition to become a famous and wealthy writer had burned steadily within him had sustained him, proved to Cedric he was on the right lines at last.

As he neared his own home he saw that the young man and his girl-friend who had been sitting in the little car staring up at the tower were now on the footpath. The young man must have called out a question because Cedric heard his father's voice wafting down from the tower: "C'mon in. I'll show you up and over."

The girl seemed reluctant but the young man took her by the hand and led her giggling through the gate.

"Can't miss this," Cedric heard him say.

"Is it safe?" the girl asked and Cedric caught the word 'nuts'.

Ears red, Cedric cycled steadily on. Nuts. Yes, might as well face it, his father was nuts. Stark, staring crackers. The tower now loomed in his thoughts as an even bigger incubus than Mervyn Toebeck. Somehow he would rid himself of Mervyn and the Spook, but he would have to live with that confounded tower. All his life, famous author or not, he would be 'Pisa' Williamson. These days that should be golden, the days of his boyhood, would turn leaden one by one in the shadow of his mad father's tower. He wished his father would fall off the tower and break his neck. A pity he hadn't died when he had fallen that first time from some scaffolding. Cedric pedalled faster to leave such thoughts behind. I don't really mean it, he thought, but Jesus! it's enough to make *anyone* bitter. And then, he thought, did Mervyn kill his father? He didn't want to think about it.

He stood up on the pedals to pick up even more speed. He coasted in by the cinema and peered gloomily at a poster from which a frilly-skirted Shirley Temple, leaning over a gate, smiled a winsome smile at him just as if he were like other boys. Cedric reflected that in real life she would giggle derisively at 'Pisa' Williamson as all the other winsome dimply maidens did.

37

THAT AFTERNOON, shut up in his den, Cedric found himself unable to run away any longer from speculation about Mervyn and his father. Mervyn and the Spook were in the upstairs room. They had given no sign they were ganging up on him behind his back. He had left them alone for ten minutes but there had been no indication on his return that the Spook had said anything to Mervyn to make him suspicious. This convinced Cedric that the figure on the tower had only existed in his imagination. At three o'clock Cedric had told Mervyn and the Spook that he had to do some study, "To keep Granny happy." Having sabotaged their castles in the air, he found it unbearable to sit around with them and feign enthusiasm. Mervyn had suggested that if they were really going to operate in a big way they should strike again in the Domain, but Cedric had managed to veto this by saying he considered it dangerous. Ernie Fox, he said, might possibly have rounded up a gang to lie in wait. He would be quite desperate, Cedric pointed out.

In his den, unable to keep his mind fixed on his textbooks, Cedric began to chew over any suspicious behaviour of Mervyn's that he could recall. The disgorging of the pilfered firewood from his shirt didn't impress Cedric as an argument half as much as it had in the stilly night. It was a vagary, certainly, but it might have easily been that Mervyn sensed his new friend's disapproval. Cedric's mind strayed to the police station. His eyes narrowed thoughtfully. Now that he came to think of it …

Yes, now that he was so much wiser if not so very much older, there had been more to that interrogation the police had put Cedric through than, in his smug self-importance, he had noticed. What had appeared to be mere routine questions had, in fact, been very probing questions cunningly couched. Cedric, staring unseeingly across his book-cluttered table, relived the scene.

A very old constable Cedric had seen around the streets of the town for as long as he could remember, but whom he had never expected to be closeted with in his lair, had sat at the typewriter looking different without his helmet. The also venerable, but far more imposing-looking Detective-Sergeant Huggins had beamed at Cedric in a reassuring, fatherly way.

"Now then, Eric; it is Eric?" "Cedric."

"Yes, yes, Cedric. Mrs Beatrice Williamson's grandson. I remember your grandfather, the General, Cedric. Wonderful man. Now then, Cedric you say you met this chap Toebeck on the road behind the station? Never seen him before?"

"Never."

"What were you doing yourself, Cedric? You understand we have to ask all these silly questions."

"Oh that's quite all right. I don't mind. I was out for a bike ride. I sat down on the bank over by the mill and Merv came along. He came across the railway lines."

"Where had Toebeck been, did he say?"

"No, I think he was just mooching around. Bit like me, I think he was bored. Anyway we got yarning."

"Whose suggestion was it that you both go to his house?" "Oh, his. I said we could go for a ride if he had a grid, but he said to come around home."

"Do you usually go home with any old stranger? That's not very sensible, young man."

"I suppose it isn't, Sir. I don't suppose I would normally." "Normally?" The detective had seemed to pounce on this.

"Why wasn't this just normal? Did he seem particularly anxious for you to go with him?"

Cedric hadn't wanted to bring Mervyn's interest in his father's tower into this, especially after the detective had mentioned his exalted grandfather in such a respectful way. He didn't want to say that Mervyn had virtually offered to swop a view of a drunken father for the view of a mentally unbalanced father's work.

"Oh, it's hard to say, Sir" Cedric had floundered. "I wouldn't say so. It just sorta happened. He said they just lived around the corner and then he said, 'Come on round'. I just wandered along with him. It was something to do, I suppose."

"Now, Cedric," said Detective-Sergeant Huggins, "I don't want you to repeat this to your friend, but would you say that Mervyn Toebeck had any sort of a home to be proud of? Would you ask a friend home to a slum like that? This is just between us, Cedric."

"No, I jolly well wouldn't."

"Um. And yet he seemed keen for you to come. It was his suggestion? You're sure of that?"

"Oh yes, Sir. Definitely."

"Did you perhaps refuse, at first?"

"I believe I did, Sir. Not really refuse but sorta." "You weren't very keen?"

"No Sir. That's sorta the way it was."

"But he insisted?"

"Well yes, I suppose he did."

"It wouldn't have struck me that a young chap like you would have seen much to cultivate in a fellow like this Toebeck. He's quite a lot older."

"Yes, I suppose he is. I can't sorta explain it. I was just bored."

"Quite so, so you went to Toebeck's place. What did you think of the house?"

"I was a bit shocked, to tell you the truth, Sir. I didn't really want to go in."

"Did you demur?"

"I beg your pardon, Sir."

"Did you decline to go in? Did you say to Toebeck that you'd rather not, or anything like that?"

"Well, I think, let's see, I think I said, 'let's skip it' or something like that."

"But he insisted?"

"Well, he was sorta inside by then and halfway down the path so I just followed him."

"I see. And you followed him inside?"

"Well, no. I smelt that funny smell right at the back door. I thought, help, what's that? And then I thought, gas, it's gas."

And so it went on, with Cedric enjoying every minute of it and Detective-Sergeant Huggins running the tips of his fingers through his silver-grey hair every so often as he framed old questions in new ways and took Cedric through it all again step by step.

38

"WHAT A sucker I am," Cedric muttered to the desk in his den. He could see plainly now that the detective had been suspicious. He could follow his train of thought. If Mervyn had had, say a fight with his father and knocked him out – he was big and hefty enough and his father had just looked a long-legged, skinny old blighter – and then hauled him over to the gas oven, he would then naturally have cleared out of the house. And what would look more innocent than to return with company? But why had the police stated quite bluntly that there were no suspicious circumstances? With a jolt Cedric remembered Mervyn's strange chuckle when he had read that sentence from the newspaper out aloud. He jumped up and began to pace around his den. He felt frightened and this time he knew it wasn't imagination. There was something creepy about Mervyn. This big house with just himself, a boy; his father, a nut; his Granny, a little frail old lady; and Mervyn Toebeck – a murderer. By God!

39

THAT NIGHT, at midnight, lying awake, Cedric heard the creaking wheel. The sound grew fainter as it went away towards the front gate. Mervyn had left the house on another of his nocturnal excursions.

40

THE NEXT afternoon Cedric again excused himself from Mervyn and the Spook's company and repaired to his den. Again he tried to study and again he failed. At about four o'clock it struck him that it might be beginning to be obvious that he was avoiding their company. He would put in an appearance, he decided, yawning and rubbing his eyes and cursing algebra and pretend to enter into the spirit of their conversation. After all, he consoled himself, it's not long to wait before Ernie Fox hangs up on Mervyn and then I can make a stand and tell them straight I'm throwing in the sponge.

The upstairs room was empty. It was as fogged up as an opium den. Angrily, Cedric opened the side windows and then went across to the front windows intending to throw one open and create a draught. He saw Mervyn and the Spook going up the street towards the town. He must have only just missed them on the stairs.

Impulsively Cedric padded down the stairs and darted through the kitchen out on to the veranda. The sleeping-porch door was closed. Again, even in the broad daylight, he had the feeling of being watched. "Well, that's so much bally rubbish," Cedric told himself. "Haven't I just seen the blighter going up the street."

He opened the door cautiously and called softly, "Mervyn."

He entered, leaving the door half open. His heart began to thump. He didn't know what he was looking for. Mervyn had made his bed very neatly. On the bedside table there was a pile of books and some tins, some empty, two unopened, bearing the condensed milk label. The only possible place to hide anything in this small, skimpily furnished room was in the one drawer of the little dressing-table. Cedric pulled the drawer open a few inches: it was stacked with piles of money, pennies, threepences, sixpences and shillings, nothing any larger as far as Cedric's rapid examination could tell, but it must have amounted to several pounds in value all told. He shut the drawer and left the room, carefully closing the door.

He went to his bedroom to think. He stared out his window across the lawn. The only explanation for that drawerful of copper and silver he could hit on was that Mervyn was taking it off the Spook at the snooker games they played. Cedric knew nothing about the game but it seemed reasonable to suppose they played for money. For that matter it didn't necessarily have to be the Spook that Mervyn was winning from. But why, he puzzled, wasn't there a single half-crown or florin in the whole accumulation. Not one ten-shilling note. It was baffling. More likely, Cedric thought grimly, these night trips are to rifle some small merchant's till. Even then, surely, he would take some money larger than a shilling?

Absolutely nonplussed, Cedric sank down on the side of his bed. All he could hang on to was the thought that he did not have long to wait before he could set the machinery in motion to end this perplexing and, he felt sure, dangerous association. He counted out the days, or rather nights, on his fingers. This was Friday afternoon. In six night's time, counting the night ahead, they would be ringing Ernie Fox.

Six more nights ...

41

THE FIRST of the six nights passed uneventfully.

But on the second or, more precisely, the morning of Sunday, for it must have been well after midnight, Cedric heard the footsteps. He lifted his head from the pillow, vaguely aware that some sound had awakened him. Had he been dreaming? Then, a few yards along the hall from his bedroom door something slithered down the wall and hit the floor with a muffled thump. Immediately afterwards a floor board creaked and then another under what were unmistakably slow, measured footfalls. The eerie, deliberate strides continued and Cedric's hair rose from his scalp as they seemed to stop directly outside his door. But it was only the long pause between the steps that gave the impression of each being the last. The zombie-like walker paced the full length of the long hall until at last the awful footfalls faded away somewhere in the heart of the great house.

Cedric knew his duty was plain. Granny's bedroom was at the far end of the corridor and, if there were a stalking killer abroad he had to act and act fast. Although he was near petrified with fright he scrambled out of bed. His father's bedroom was in a distant wing of the house that ran behind the side shrubbery and situated moreover at the very end, which made yelling out for Martin Williamson futile. He thought, perhaps it *was* Mervyn, *is* Mervyn, Mervyn Jekyll and Hyde Toebeck; Mervyn who had sold his soul to the devil when he slew his father.

In his haste and jittery state Cedric knocked over his bedside lamp. He fumbled for it frantically and righted it, hoping fervently the globe had not smashed. The friendly rose-coloured shade lit up as he thumbed the switch. Stumbling around the end of the bed pulling tight the cord of his pyjama trousers, Cedric saw propped in a corner the weapon he needed – an old hockey stick he had only ever used as an improvised putter in a childish back-lawn golf game. He seized it.

He flung his door open and both he and Granny emitted startled yelps together. In her long night-dress and illuminated only by the light streaming from her bedroom door at the far end of the hall she could have been a little ghost.

Cedric lowered the hockey stick and put a hand over his heart. "Help, you scared me. Granny, did you hear something? Who was that walking along the hall?"

"The curtain fell down." Granny pointed past Cedric in the direction of the front door. He looked around and saw that the heavy velvet drapes and the round rod they were attached to had fallen from the pillars of the archway opening into the vestibule. Cedric could remember dislodging that rod himself on several occasions when he had pushed carelessly through the drapes and dragged one or both of them after him with his shoulders.

"Granny, listen, someone walked down the hall. They went down past your room. You must have heard the footsteps. Such *slow heavy* footsteps, Granny. I'm scared."

"There's nothing to be frightened of, Cedric."

"But there is, there is. Granny, I didn't dream it. I tell you I heard them."

Granny shuffled past Cedric. She looked very old and feeble.

"Don't bother with the curtain," Cedric said. "I'll just shift it to one side."

"It doesn't make sense," Cedric said, following her. "A burglar would try to keep quiet. It was like somebody deliberately trying to scare the wits out of us."

The Spook, Cedric thought. Some evil conspiracy? Rage joined forces with his fear.

"Look, Granny, whoever it was went on into the house somewhere. They must be still there. Granny, I tell you I'm scared."

And Cedric was scared, terribly so. If anything, his fear was mounting. Someone lurking in the house! In the huge old house with many never-used rooms. Granny so old and weak and his father so far away. Cedric knew he didn't have the courage, hockey stick or no hockey stick, to negotiate the two long, dark doorway-lined corridors beyond this hall to Martin Williamson's room.

"Is that front door locked?" he said. Ashamed of the quaver in his voice, he cleared his throat. He felt further ashamed when his grandmother entered the dark vestibule. A tug of war team wouldn't have dragged him past that archway.

"Yes, it's locked."

"Look," Cedric said. "I'll get out through the kitchen. I'll cut around the lawn to Dad's room. I'll have to wake him up. Whoever that was may attack Dad in his bed."

"Your father locks his door," Granny said. "He doesn't, does he?"

"Yes, we mustn't wake him, Cedric. He's not at all well." "I didn't know he was sick." As soon as he had spoken Cedric realized that Granny had been delicately referring to his father's mental illness.

"He takes tablets at night," Granny said in a voice that was nearly a whimper. Why was Granny so peculiar? Cedric was positive his father didn't lock his bedroom door. It was a thing no one in their right mind would do in their own house. 'In their right mind,' a cynical mental voice echoed. Cedric felt confused, frustrated.

"I tell you I heard someone. There's someone in this house."

"These old houses," said Granny. "Sometimes, lying awake, I hear footsteps on the stairs. First one stair creaks and then another just like someone coming down. But it's only the timber. As the atmosphere cools, the wood contracts."

"*The wood contracts*," said Cedric in disgust. "And that's how the curtain fell down, I suppose?"

"It's a wooden rod," his grandmother said mildly. "But it's not even cold," Cedric argued.

"I'm cold and I'm going back to bed."

"You're not going back to that room along there," Cedric said. But his mind was wandering. Those footfalls! There had been something familiar about them. This thought struck a frightening chord. And then Cedric remembered the footfalls in his nightmare of three nights previously – the night he had seen the watcher on the tower.

"I'll lock my door," Granny said. "Now you get some sleep, Cedric. We'll talk about it tomorrow."

But the subject was not pursued.

42

A GUSTY wind had arrived with first light, flinging fistfulls of raindrops and leaves about as if they were confetti, conditions which made the meadow unsuitable for cerebration. In his den, Cedric sat at his table, deep in scowling thought.

He pulled across a pad, opened it and headed up a blank page. By dinner-time the document read:

Q. Was my meeting with Mervyn accidental?

A. Yes.

Q. Did Mervyn invite me to his place innocently?

A. On the face of it, yes. But in the light of his funny laugh when he read out 'No suspicious circumstances'; the fact that there was really no point in inviting me; the fact that no normal person would have wanted to show a stranger a filthy old house and a boozy father: the odd look that crossed his face two or three times when we first met; the way he gripped the handle-bars as we left the police station and he asked me if the police were suspicious; the way he emptied out his shirtful of firewood (Why? If he did it to impress me, why take me to his slum home?): the fact that he got angry when I said it was awful for him to say 'that the quicker drink killed his father the better': these things all add up to make the answer: *No*.

Q. If the answer to the last question is no, does that mean that Mervyn knew his father was dead?

A. Yes, or dying. His father may have threatened to gas himself and Mervyn may have deliberately left him to it.

Q. Does this make Mervyn a murderer?

A. Yes, as good as. On the other hand he may have knocked his father out and stuck his head in the oven.

Q. Do you think that is what actually happened?

A. I don't know what to think.

Q. Is there any way of finding out?

A. I can only try. I am in a better position than the police. I can talk with him and try to trap him. I feel that I won't rest until I know for certain.

Q. Suppose you never find out?

A. Well, that's just too bad.

Q. Suppose you do find out and you're right. Would you go to the police?

A. I don't suppose I could ever get any real proof. Even if he told me, he would subsequently deny it. It would be my word against his. I would have made a dangerous enemy. No, I don't think I would go to the police. I don't think Mervyn's father was much loss to the community. But, in certain circumstances, I would write an anonymous letter to the police.

Q. What are these circumstances?

A. If it became desperately urgent for my safety and Granny's to get rid of Mervyn and Spook. I don't like the way they are starting to take this place over. There are some funny things going on around here.

Q. Funny things such as?

A. Mervyn takes my bike, saying nothing to me, and sneaks away about midnight some nights. He has a drawer full of pennies, threepences, sixpences and shillings. Nothing larger. I am now sure I saw someone standing on the top of the tower at nearly two in the morning. (It doesn't seem possible that it was Mervyn. The light went out in his room too soon for him to have come down.) Last night I heard footsteps coming from the front and going the full length of the hall. They were loud, slow footsteps. Definitely not a burglar. Definitely a man I would say probably a big man. Not only that, but I have dreamed of these footsteps other nights. This would seem to indicate that the walker has walked before.

Q. Could you have imagined these last two queer happenings?

A. The figure on the tower? Just a chance I may have. The footsteps? Don't hand me that. Granny tried to (Why?). I heard them all right.

Q. Why should Granny treat it so lightly?

A. All I can think of is that she only just woke up as the footsteps died away. I think she had a look around, saw the curtains had fallen down and put the sound down to that.

Q. Could she possibly know or guess it was Mervyn or the Spook, and not want to frighten you by telling you?

A. Bunkum!

Q. Have you any plan of action?

A. Yes. I am going to spring some questions and watch Mervyn's reaction. I am going to pluck up my courage and eavesdrop on Mervyn and the Spook when they are in the private silting-room this afternoon. I know a secret about this house that nobody knows. And I am going to try and find out who the woman who looks like a witch really is. I can't get it out of my head that she is connected with this affair somehow. It's fishy the way Mervyn pretends never to see her.

Cedric locked the pad away in the table drawer and hid the key in the dry writing-stand well provided for red ink.

43

CEDRIC MADE his plans quickly but carefully. There wasn't long to go before lunch and the Spook would arrive shortly after that. He walked past the sleeping-porch and glimpsed Mervyn's stockinged feet – he was lying on his bed, presumably reading. Cedric went straight to the woodshed, picked up the step-ladder, leaped up the back steps carrying the ladder and lugged it up the stairs. The ladder was nine or ten feet long and he banged one end against the wall as he manoeuvred it across the landing. He put the ladder in one of the built-in wardrobes which could be used as connecting passages between the upstairs bedrooms.

44

AFTER LUNCH Cedric followed Mervyn out of the kitchen on to the veranda and they both sat down on weather-bleached cane chairs. The wind reached them even here and leaves flipped across the chamfered flooring past their feet.

"Well," Mervyn said softly. "Not long now. I hope this character Fox has raised the money. It'll be good to feel some real money in our pockets. Folding money."

Cedric entertained a mental glimpse of a drawer full of small change. He looked around the veranda, making sure that Mervyn noticed this display of caution. He swallowed hard before he spoke. He reminded himself that, although his coming remark was an out-and-out lie, there was no possible way of Mervyn proving it to be.

"Mervyn," he said, glancing carefully around again. "Yeah."

"Can you think of any mistakes we might have made? I'm hanged if I can. I mean we've completely covered our tracks, haven't we?"

"What are you getting at?"

"This morning," said Cedric, "I saw Detective Huggins." Mervyn turned his full-moon face slowly to focus his gaze on Cedric. "You what?"

He wasn't imagining this, Cedric told himself: there was menace, wariness, immediately beneath that genial mask. Mervyn's little piggy eyes had turned cold and dangerous.

"Detective Huggins. I saw him. Just before lunch. I haven't had a chance to speak to you. Look, Merv, I tell you he was watching this house."

Mervyn's eyes, small enough at any time, were mere splinters of glass now. Cedric forced himself to keep very calm. There was nothing gullible about this Mervyn Toebeck. There was a big difference between the theory and the practice of tripping him. Cedric realized now that there was a vast gulf between Mervyn's worldly education and upbringing and his own almost cloistered life. Cedric was a naive youngster, a bookworm, clever, yes, but not shrewd and cagey and vicious: his was not the wisdom of the jungle.

"You saw Huggins watching this house?"

"He was standing across the road," Cedric said. A branch of the lilac tree scraped in the guttering. "He crossed over. I thought he was coming in. I nearly died. I was standing in the front porch. He looked over our gate. He didn't see me."

"Was he looking at the tower?" Mervyn asked.

"He never even looked at it. He looked straight at the house."

"It's a big house," said Mervyn. "You look at big houses if you're out walking on a Sunday."

"It's been here a long time. So's Detective Huggins. But hang on. He only walked past the gate a few yards. Then he came back and had another look. A real long look. I stood well back out of sight. Gee, my heart was thumping!"

A few minutes passed in silence. "What do you reckon, Mervyn?" Mervyn said nothing.

Cedric decided to follow through. "I've thought of everything. I don't see how it could possibly be anything to do with Ernie Fox. Do you think it could?"

Mervyn shook his head slowly. "As I see it, that's impossible. No."

"Mervyn," said Cedric diffidently. "I don't like to mention this but I couldn't help remembering that awful grilling Detective Huggins gave me at the police station. It couldn't be anything to do with your father, could it?"

Cedric didn't want to meet Mervyn's eyes, but just studying the lower half of the fat face he was sure the shot hit the magazine.

"How the devil could it have anything to do with my father?" But the voice was shaky and the fat face pale.

They were so engrossed that the Spook scored one of his little triumphs. They both started up out of their cane chairs when he coughed.

He had already seated himself on the edge of the veranda and was leaning back against one of the posts. With his long white face and black clothes, the buckled, skinny, inert form could have been that of a corpse between the lifeless lips of which some profane prankster had poked a limply hanging cigarette.

"By God, Spook," snarled Mervyn. "You'll be the death of me." He sank back in the cane chair and then pulled himself abruptly to his feet.

"Let's go up."

They trooped upstairs. At the door of the upstairs sitting-room, Mervyn said to the Spook, "You go in. I just want to ask Cedric a private question."

Mervyn and Cedric walked along and stopped within a few feet of the stained-glass window at the end of the passage.

Mervyn said, "What's all this about a grilling at the police station? You never said they grilled you. I want to hear about this."

Cedric knew he had gone all shifty-eyed. He tried to master it, look frank and open. "Oh, I thought you knew. There didn't seem any point in talking about it. You said the police always made a mountain out of a molehill. I just thought they'd put both of us through the hoop the same way."

"What I want to know," Mervyn said, "is what they asked you. "Damn it, old son, it's not very nice to feel a man's being treated like a criminal just because he has been born under an unlucky star. It's bad enough to have your father do himself in without the police looking at you sideways. What were these questions?"

"Well, I just can't remember offhand but they went over and over how we met and the way you asked me home and all that. They kept on saying, did you look as if you'd had a fight or a scuffle or anything like that?"

"What! What!" shouted Mervyn, seizing Cedric by the arm. "They asked you that, the nosey bastards? A man ought to sue them. What were they insinuating?"

"Well, to be honest, Mervyn, that's why I didn't mention it to you. It just made me feel all sick inside for the dirty dogs to try and turn things around and make it look as if you might've ..."

"Might've what?"

"Well," Cedric grinned his weak grin. "Look, Merv, you're my good friend now. I know you must have had a helluva life with an old man that drank meths all the time. I'm one guy that does understand. Look at, well, my father. How do you think I feel about that damned old tower and the kids all chucking off at me? Sometimes ..." Cedric looked down at the floor. "Sometimes I wish he were dead," he blurted out.

There was a long silence and then Mervyn said, "You don't know what you're talking about." He began to pace about restlessly. "You don't know how lucky you are. Has your father ever bashed you around the house with his fists? Has he ever put the boot into you? Have you had to crawl down the road to wash yourself in a stagnant pond because the old tin bath is full of piss and spew? Did you have to get a paper run so you'd have enough money to eat? Did you ever come home and find your old man trying to shag an old whore on a sack in front of the fire? Both too pissed to stand up. Ever been too frightened to dry your eyes on a towel in case you got the clap and went blind? Did your old man ever get you drunk and help you on board an old prostitute when you were fourteen and tell you it'd turn you into a man? Stanley Toebeck, a real white man! But boys grow up, Cedric, they grow up. There comes a time when they're bigger and stronger than their old man. Oh Christ yes, and smarter. Smarter than the fuckin' police too." He advanced on Cedric, his little eyes glittering. "You hear me, old son: smarter. A lot smarter." He put his hand on Cedric's shoulder.

Cedric didn't think he would be capable of calling out even if Mervyn attacked him. But Mervyn said softly, almost pleadingly, "You're my pal, ain't you, old son? You'n me are going to be smart, eh?"

A white-faced Cedric nodded. "Yes," he croaked. "I'm sorry, Mervyn."

"Forget it," said Mervyn. He slapped Cedric affectionately.

"Let's get back to the Spook. Don't mention that police business. It's my guess that means nothing. No sense in undermining morale. Next week we're going to get our first taste of easy money. And, by Jesus, we're not looking back."

45

FOR THE next hour they went over and over, detail by detail, the modus operandi of picking up the blackmail money. Cedric, anxious to drive away any faint shadow of suspicion, threw himself so heart and soul into the conference he almost convinced himself he was genuinely concerned by the time he felt he could make his daily pretence about retiring to study. To fit in with his plan, however, he felt he should make some remark that would put the cat among the pigeons before excusing himself. He sauntered across to the side windows while he dreamed up something.

A maroon Auburn roadster, its white canvas hood drawn snuggly up into position, its exhaust hoses glittering in the afternoon sunlight, was stealing along Dale Lane.

"Hey," said Cedric. "Quick, you fellows!" He was joined at the window by Mervyn and the Spook. He pointed and said, "Blair Bramwell. Better remember that car. It shouldn't be hard. It's the only one like it around." Even as he spoke he wondered why he was bothering. At least, he thought, it makes me look enthusiastic.

"A car like that means money," said Mervyn. "And money is going to be our hobby, fellows. As soon as we've got the gold in our pocket from this first go of ours, we'll really open the campaign. You can't tell me it's some ordinary couple that sneaks out of the Pioneer Club when they're having one of their boozy socials, to have a jump. If they have to sneak and can't wait 'til they get home to bed, that means intrigue, and intrigue's our business. The night has a thousand eyes, comrades."

"I only hope we can be lucky again," said Cedric, turning away from the window. "Well, I'm afraid I'll have to leave you. I'll have to get back to those books of mine even if it's only to keep Granny from grizzling."

46

CEDRIC CLOSED the door behind him and moved quickly towards the head of the stairs, but, instead of descending, darted on tiptoe down a passage on his left. In the dark wardrobe between the two bedrooms he struck a match. He laid it down to burn out on one of the steps of the ladder, and lifted the ladder into the middle of the floor. He opened the legs of the ladder so that it stood firmly with its top ledge a few feet below a trapdoor in the ceiling. Quickly he mounted until he could push up the trapdoor with the palm of his hand. He struck another match and laid it down on the ladder. By the flickering feeble light he reached through the opening in the ceiling and hooked the fingers of both hands over the nearest joist. One spring and he was hanging by his elbows with his head and shoulders in the gloomy loft between ceiling and roof. Another effort and he was right up, standing not quite erect with his feet braced on parallel joists.

A draught blew out the first match he struck. Except for a ribbon of wan daylight, which marked the entire perimeter at ceiling level, and a few chinks of light where the iron seemed to have sprung from the rafters, it was quite dark, much too dark to proceed without a big risk of falling. For him to fall would be disastrous, he realized only too well. It would sound like an earthquake. He might even go through the ceiling. In addition there was the danger of rupturing some of the conduit pipes which housed the electric wiring and being electrocuted. Again was brought home to Cedric a concept of the depressing gulf between theory and practice.

He struck another match and shielded it with his cupped hands. It continued to burn but he could not step, bent forward from the waist, from joist to joist without support from his hands, either by resting them on his knees or stretching out to the rafters above. His knees shook with the strain of maintaining balance. Finally he decided to try to cover the distance in darkness by getting down on his haunches. Every few feet he struck a match to take his bearings. The going was slow and Cedric, feeling the tremendous strain of moving in absolute silence, was tempted to quit. Even the scratch and flare of a match sounded as loud as a squib exploding. But before he was halfway his eyes had grown accustomed to the dark and he could see quite plainly the outline of the chimney which rose out of the private sitting-room. He knew, from a boyish exploration that, at a corner of the chimney boxing, there was a gap in the ceiling moulding which provided a peep-hole. He had been ten years old when he last put an eye to that peep-hole. His mother had been alive then and he had looked down upon her as she sat at the escritoire engrossed in letter writing.

Applying his eye again, this grey windy Sunday afternoon, to that same peep-hole he experienced not excitement but an unexpected lurching sensation of emptiness, self-pity and sadness, shot, as the light in the bevel of a mirror is shot with exquisite colours, with a nameless hope. But his mother was not seated at the escritoire, and the little boy in the short trousers who had innocently explored the loft of his home was gone forever as well. There was a small shower of leaves or raindrops directly above his head. A sheet of iron shuddered. Far away the lilac tree scraped along the guttering.

Seen from above like this, the private sitting-room seemed strangely deep and all odd angles like a room in a dream. The top of his grandfather's portrait was thick with dust. The only signs of life he could see were the Spook's black-trousered crossed legs, one shoe clear of the floor, and that leg wagging steadily from the knee cap. Smoke drifted across the room. There was no conversation. Minutes passed and still the skinny leg wagged on. Still no voices. A frightening idea occurred to Cedric: perhaps Mervyn, the strange, evil, all-knowing Mervyn, had hunted through the upstairs bedrooms and found the stepladder? Perhaps right at this minute he was waiting in the dark closet watching the trapdoor? Desperately trying to preserve stealth even under fire from such agitation, Cedric began the return journey.

At one stage of the trip the roof was hipped sharply and he had to lean well back, hands outstretched behind, to wriggle beneath the rafters. Sweating and begrimed with dust and cobwebs he paused here, glad of the fresh air which fanned his face. Right before his eyes was one of the places where the iron had lifted. Through a row of rusted nails semi-wrenched from the rafters, Cedric, as if looking through bars, stared down at a big expanse of sloping roof and, beyond that, the meadow.

Behind a blue-gum tree, Mervyn Toebeck, looking very small from this height and distance, was lowering a partly filled sugar bag into a hole. He picked up a spade and filled in the hole. With his hands he began to scoop up blue-gum leaves and pine-needles and cones and sprinkle them artistically over the freshly-turned earth.

47

NOT UNTIL Tuesday afternoon did Cedric get the chance to peep into the drawer of Mervyn's dressing table. The money was gone. Cedric had expected it to be. He congratulated himself.

The afternoons in the private sitting room, now that there was nothing left to discuss and it only remained to be patient, had become futile and boring. The Spook and Mervyn had gone to town without even bothering to go upstairs first. This gave Cedric plenty of time. He took the spade and headed for the meadow.

"You tell me if anyone's coming, Gus," Cedric ordered as he put his foot to the shoulder of the spade.

The sack was buried only a few inches under the surface.

Cedric was proved right again. It contained a great pile of pennies, threepences, sixpences and shillings.

He chuckled. "Now it's my turn to give you something to think about, Mr Toebeck," he muttered.

He took off his blazer, spread it on the ground and onto it tipped the money. Into the sack – one of the two sugar bags he guessed that Mervyn had used to transport his belongings – he tipped several spade loads of pine-needles and blue gum leaves. He re-buried it in exactly the same place leaving everything looking just as he had found it. The great heap of change wrapped in his blazer made a hefty bundle. He took it to his den, arranged it in piles on the table and counted it. It amounted to only a few pennies short of six pounds.

Cedric found a square cardboard carton and packed the money into it. He had several of these cartons in his den. He stored different things in them. They were part of his 'system'. There was only one hiding place he could think of and that was the loft between the ceiling and the rafters. The step-ladder was still in the wardrobe between the upstairs bedrooms. He had been waiting for an opportunity to smuggle it down, but on the way up he found Granny waxing the balustrade of the staircase, so he knew it would have to be left in the wardrobe. He had the laden carton under his arm beneath his blazer.

"Do you have to work all the time, Granny?" he said as he manoeuvred past.

Back in his den Cedric unlocked the table drawer and took out the document he had earlier drawn up. He now added:

Q. Why did Mervyn bury the money in the meadow?

A. Obviously because I invented that story about Detective Huggins watching the house. This can only mean the money is stolen.

Q. Do you think you are on the track of solving this mysterious business?

A. I have learnt this – attack is the best defence. I am going to keep on throwing spanners in the works. When the machinery jams maybe the truth will come to light.

Q. Does the fact that Mervyn imagines Detective Huggins is more interested in the stolen money than in clearing up the mystery of Stanley Toebeck's death mean that he is innocent concerning his father's death?

A. Definitely not, I should say. I think the last question is inaccurately phrased. What proof have we that Mervyn knows just what Detective Huggins is interested in? He may be guilty of both theft and murder. He may feel secure about having covered up his tracks after committing …

Cedric broke off here to look up in his dictionary a word he felt sure existed that began with pater or something like that. He found it and resumed writing.

… patricide, but having possession of all that small change is a complete give-away concerning the theft angle. So the fact he took precautions to hide the money definitely does nothing to exonerate him from patricide.

Q. This confounded money! Why is it all in small change?

A. I have no answer. I admit I'm stumped. My theory that he may have won it in the billiard-room – which still didn't explain why it contains nothing larger than a shilling – went by the board when be buried it. It *has* to be stolen. Has he perhaps been stealing it from the billiard-room and been frightened to 'take it to a shop and change it for anything larger?

Q. If the above suggestion is correct, are his midnight trips unconnected with the thieving?

A. Your guess is as good as mine. He may break into the billiard-room after it is closed at night.

Q. How do you propose to find out?

A. I think I had better have a look at Snip's billiard-room.

Cedric read the document right through. It pleased him.

This author business was the answer all right. And playing detective went hand in glove with being a writer. These holidays were turning out to be fun after all.

Having had the foresight to keep back fifteen shillings in silver from Mervyn's hoard, Cedric left for town feeling buoyantly rich.

48

THE WIND had spent itself and the day was hot and still. Cycling slowly along the eastern end of the main street Cedric could smell exhausted gasolene, newly-mown grass and melting tar. There had been a big holiday exodus from the town so that the shopping area, although many of the businesses had reopened their doors after the Christmas and New Year interlude, looked forlorn to Cedric as he pedalled languidly along.

He turned off the main street, coasted into the kerb and parked his bicycle in the stand almost opposite the doorway of the basement billiard saloon. He had the entire side street to himself. There was not even a parked automobile. He stood in the shadow of the balcony of the old Empire Hotel which had been a private boarding house ever since liquor licences had been withdrawn. But there were still empty hogsheads to be glimpsed if one peered down through the iron grating, not far from Cedric's feet, into the gloomy dusty cellar.

Cedric crossed the street towards the big expanse of windowless wall on which huge faded lettering spelled out: SNIP'S POOL PARLOUR – BILLIARDS – SNOOKER – TWELVE TABLES. There was no veranda on this side of the street and the sunlight bounced off the bitumen and the concrete wall. His mop of switched-back hair felt as hot as a compost heap. Back across the road the balconied Empire Hotel standing in its pool of shadow, its venetian blinds drawn, looked cool and silent. From the basement below the doorway before which the undecided Cedric loitered, came the snick-snick of clashing balls.

Cedric had a vague idea that there was some age restriction applying to billiard parlours. Was one required to be sixteen, eighteen, or twenty-one? he wondered. Detective work was hard enough, he fumed, without fat-headed obstacles like that presenting themselves. Well, he could always plead ignorance. He could say he was looking for a friend – which would be near enough to the truth. He had his long trousers on: he had money in his pocket. To hell with it! He went down the wide, bare concrete steps.

At the foot of the steps another flight of stairs, much narrower than those down from the street and dirty, dark and damp, fell away on his left, leading, it could be imagined, to hell itself. On the right was a short passage ending in a match-lining partition with a curtained opening. From beyond this opening drifted the snick of ball meeting ball followed by an occasional curse.

Diffident but determined, Cedric peeped around the curtain. He beheld a basement, low-ceilinged, but in other respects vast. The twelve billiard tables had been arranged longitudinally in three rows of four. The three end tables nearest the entrance and one at the far right-hand corner had been uncovered but the rest were draped. The bottom table and the top table of the furthermost row from where Cedric stood were in use. Three lights in their big round shades hanging low over the emerald green beds of these tables and the small pilot lights on the wall above the score-marking boards were the only means of illumination fighting the gloom of the great cellar.

There was a group of young men playing at the distant table. They were obviously enjoying themselves, but their language would have startled the driver of a bullock team. Cedric winced at the stream of blasphemy and four-letter words addressed both to the balls and the players – and not only the rival players but to the player himself in self-condemnation of his own ineptness – which echoed down the room after nearly every stroke of a cue.

In contrast, only an occasional comment and a quietly spoken one was uttered by either of the men at the top table, just along from the match-lining partition, against which a nervous, but outwardly nonchalant Cedric now leaned.

If either of the men playing at the top table or the elderly man ensconced on the nearby leather couch watching the game had spared Cedric a glance, it was casual enough to be discounted. Emboldened, he peered hard at the group of players at the deep end. Neither Mervyn nor the Spook was among them. His gaze returned to the top table. A gleaming blue ball stole across the green cloth and disappeared into a corner pocket.

"Looks like I've let you in this time," said the short, chubby man dressed in sandals, khaki shorts and opennecked shirt.

The man who had just played was immaculately and, considering the summer heat, conspicuously attired in the trousers and waistcoat of a dark striped suit. His collar was stiff and white; his white sleeves were gripped at each elbow by silver garters; he wore a green eye-shade; thinning hair was brushed straight back. Deep lines curved from the corner of each nostril to the sides of his unsmiling mouth: the face was hard, hawk-like. Cedric knew – although he had imagined a much less impressive person, someone dissipated looking and down at heel (someone a little like Mervyn's father or the winking man) – that this was 'Snip' Hughes. It had to be.

The man played another shot, and a red ball whistled into a pocket with a distinct thud. The white ball returned spinning backwards – so quickly that it impressed Cedric as miraculous – over the course it had just travelled, to end up at the very tip of the still extended cue. Taking his time, a picture of icy concentration, the man struck the white ball again very gently. Its object, a black ball, was deflected towards an end pocket on the very edge of which it teetered before tumbling in.

"You haven't lost your touch, Snip," said the man sitting on the leather couch. "Look at that position. You'll clear the deck."

"I'll put my cue away," said the man in the khaki shorts. Red ball after red ball Snip Hughes proceeded to sink, each one followed by a successful pocketing of the glittering black ball. Then he potted a yellow ball, followed by a green. The brown ball, when he turned his attention to it, proved stubborn. It hovered on the edge of a pocket but defied gravity.

Snip Hughes said, "Well, cut off my penis and call me Venus."

"Hard luck," said Snip's opponent. "You would leave a sitter. It's no use to me, though; I need about forty snookers and with your knowledge of angles I'll be wasting my time."

49

CEDRIC DRIFTED silently and inconspicuously down the length of the room, keeping on the side furthest from the two lighted tables. He wondered if perhaps one of these tables had come from his own home. Some years earlier Granny had sold the equipment in the Williamson billiard room. He peered at the racks full of cues and various rests.

He wondered what the big basement parlour would look like with all twelve tables in full swing. He guessed it was probably a good business normally and that this afternoon it was only suffering a spell of summer holiday doldrums like the rest of the town.

He sauntered past a doorway marked 'Men', behind which plumbing dripped and burbled, then sat down on one of the long leather-upholstered seats and stared across two covered tables at the table where the group of profane young men were playing a game in which all the balls were painted different designs and colours and bore a different number in a circle.

Cedric listened with great interest to the rugged conversationalists across the way. His vocabulary increased by leaps and bounds. Whatever would Granny think? he wondered. He decided he would buy a packet of cigarettes sometime. If, he reasoned, he could, in the manner of the bad hats of Greyfriars and Highcliff Public Schools, bounders like Vernon Smith and Ponsonby, 'put on a fag', it would do much to conceal his youth and purity when duty called him to investigate places of this nature.

Cedric was just on the point of standing up and making his way back to the outside world when a man emerged from the latrine and walked across towards the street end of the room.

"Snip," the new arrival called out, "Where the hell's Winker?"

It was gloomy and until he heard the high-pitched voice, Cedric had not realized that the bulky sloppy shape was none other than that of Mervyn Toebeck. Cedric's head shrunk down between his shoulders as if he were trying to disappear within himself. Should he call out and brazen it out, saying, "I thought I'd find you down here, Mervyn"? No, he'd never discover anything that way. Quickly he stooped down and crawled between the huge carved legs of the nearest billiard table. Even for the pint-size Cedric it was uncomfortably close quarters. He wriggled around so he could stick his head out and listen. He saw two figures coming down beside the tables in the direction of the latrine door. One of the figures appeared to be bent and stumbling; the other had the jaunty splay-footed gait of Mervyn Toebeck. Cedric pulled his head in fast.

"You old scamp," Mervyn was saying. "I thought you'd cleared out."

"I musta dozed off in the office," said the other voice.

"They're here, eh? The truck's here, eh? They musta sprung off their tails this trip, just as well I gave you a job as lookout. I knew I was due for a snore-off. A man gets pretty stuffed in this racket."

Mervyn pushed the latrine door open and stood aside to let his companion enter, whom Cedric now recognized as the winking man. Before Mervyn followed him through he called back, "Keep your thumb near that buzzer, Snip."

Cedric emerged and brushed down the knees of his trousers. He took a handkerchief and mopped the sweat off his face. He sauntered along, keeping his eyes fixed on the top table: neither of the players was looking his way. He couldn't see which way the man sitting on the leather seat was looking. Quietly he pushed open the high heavy door marked 'Men' and peeped inside. No one to be seen. He entered.

50

THE LATRINE was more like a cave than a room: a cave or a fissure in a grey dripping cliff-face. No ray of sunshine had ever alighted even for an instant in this dismal hole. The walls, the floor, even the ceiling glistened with moisture. It was cold. There was a draught from slat ventilators which opened on to some eternal night. The floors of the two doorless cubicles were paper strewn. The cisterns gurgled and mumbled like Skid Row sleepers. The one electric bulb, which was supported by an iron pipe sticking out from the wall, was of low wattage and further enfeebled by grime but it was sufficient to confound Cedric with his greatest puzzle so far there appeared to be no further exit.

Beyond the cubicles, the latrine became a storage space for brooms and mops and buckets and drums almost full of paper and refuse. Cedric began to get a queer, unreal feeling as if he were in the middle of a nightmare – and then he saw the iron ladder set into the concrete of the end wall. Up close to the ceiling was a small door which, just as Cedric's eyes sought it out, was opened an inch or so by the draught. It bumped gently back into position. Cedric took out his handkerchief again and mopped his face.

He glanced over his shoulder. He could hear nothing from the billiard room. The thick walls and the heavy door were apparently as good as sound-proof. But anyone might enter at any moment and he would get no warning. What if it were Snip Hughes? The thought of that man frightened him mightily. He could easily be a murderer. No one knew Cedric was here. He would vanish without a trace. The police would find his bicycle in the grid-rack over by the Empire. Or would Mervyn beat them to it and ride it airily away to some place where it would never be seen again? Cedric felt convinced he was throwing down the gauntlet to the forces of evil. He very nearly beat a retreat. 'It's the sensible thing to do,' an inner voice pointed out. 'Go on, beat it'.

He began to climb the ladder.

51

THE LITTLE door opened out to reveal a tunnel-like passage for Lilliputians. The tunnel was about four feet high and two-feet-six wide and extended for some fifty feet. Cedric was able to discern this because halfway along there was an opening through which daylight filtered. There was also light at the far end.

He swallowed. This could well be a corridor of no return. Hopeless to try and brazen out an encounter with Mervyn. He was a spy and even a fool would see it immediately.

But Cedric's mind was working overtime. "I had to see you, Mervyn. Detective Huggins" – no, not Detective Huggins again – who then? I know – "the Witch, that witch-like woman, y'know, she was at the cemetery; I saw her peering out of the shrubbery at our house, I'm sure it was her. She scared me. Who is she? I had to see you. Just as I came into the billiard room I saw you going into the lav. Sorry to bother you, Merv ..."

By now the crouching Cedric was halfway down the tunnel. The daylight was admitted by an iron-bar grating. At some time there had been a window as well, but now only jagged triangles of glass jutted from the iron sash set in the concrete surround of the aperture. The only view afforded by the opening was a blank brick wall two feet or so distant. A tree had grown between the buildings and a branch bearing leaves and clusters of tiny green berries was buckled against the bars.

There was no door at the other end. He looked down into a blackberry-overgrown section some fifteen feet square. It was bounded an all four sides by high walls, completely hemmed in, with the exception of a two-feet-wide gap running parallel with the tunnel between the concrete wall of this building and the brick wall of the adjoining property. There was a wooden ladder leaning against the wall just below the opening of the tunnel. Cedric descended. It was do or die now.

That the gap between the buildings was never used and therefore most probably led nowhere was easy to deduce because the blackberry bushes had piled up against all four walls and across this one opening. But along the centre of the square of ground a pathway had been kept clear of blackberry. It led to a wide wooden door in the wall of the building, the rear of which stared at the back concrete wall of the building he had just left. Cedric was back again at basement-floor level.

The buildings were all two-storeyed, and he felt as if he were standing at the bottom of a well. If some one came out through that door he knew he would be trapped. Anyone trying to hide in that tangle of blackberry bushes would be ripped to ribbons by the thorns. Quickly Cedric crossed to the wooden door. The top of it fitted into a rusted iron track. It was easy to tell by the overlapping length of track which way the door slid. Cedric pushed, closing his eyes at the squeal emitted by the rollers. He only opened it wide enough to slip through.

He peered in before entering. This was no basement proper, only the underneath of same large building. The floor was hard dirt, cracked and uneven, littered with bottles, bones, worm-eaten planks and half-buried rotten sacks. It was gloomy but far from pitch dark: light filtered in right around the enormous cavern through ventilation boards and places where boards had rotted away. Cedric knew he must be underneath some very old building. The stout piles were all of wood.

He tried to puzzle out just what building it was. He remembered the shops in the main street that must be located at its front at ground level but, native of the town notwithstanding, he had never thought to look beyond those show windows or above those verandas. He squeezed inside and jerked the door shut an inch at a time. Again the feeling descended upon him that this was all some strange dream. Frightened, but grimly determined, he began to move forward, gingerly testing the uneven ground with the toe of his shoe with each step he took.

He had progressed about fifty yards when he heard voices.

He crouched down. Not far from his feet was the shrivelled up, fang-bared remains of some animal – a cat? His flesh crawled. He skirted the skeleton and pressed on. There was a wall ahead of him but it did not quite meet the one on his left to which he had been staying close. Nor did this wall continue. If he went through the opening on his left he saw immediately, by the rising terrain and the long line of light beyond, he would escape to the outside world. He almost smiled. He was going to get away with this. He heard the voices again. He mustn't get caught now. But he had to know.

He peered around the gap in the wall ahead. The Spook and Mervyn were only a short stone's throw distant. Mervyn was standing with his arms supporting a wooden crate, his knees buckled with the weight. The Spook was endeavouring to free from a wire around the crate a hook at the end of a length of rope by which means the crate had been lowered down through a trap-door six feet above their heads.

"For God's sake," Mervyn rasped. "This thing's heavy. I can't stand here like a half-sucked blackball much longer. Get it out, you ape!"

"It's out," squawked the Spook. He took an end of the crate and he and Mervyn lugged it off behind a great pile of timber. Cedric now perceived the winking man standing a little back, his thumbs in his braces. The hook was drawn up. By the time the Spook and Mervyn returned, another crate had commenced its swinging descent.

Cedric saw it all now. Mervyn and the Spook had been roped into the illicit liquor racket. He had actually solved none of his problems but nevertheless he felt excited and triumphant. He was one smart cookie, sure enough. He knew more about the underworld goings-on in this town than Detective Huggins.

Now that he was fairly confident he could escape by taking the route under the building on his left and would not have to make the perilous trip via the billiard parlour, Cedric felt there was nothing to be lost by staying longer and learning all he could.

By crouching low he could make out the dual rear wheels of a heavy lorry parked above and beside the open trapdoor. He guessed it was backed into a shed. The driver looked down through the trapdoor once and spoke to the winking man, but the light was behind him and Cedric couldn't make out his features. All he could recall of him were two out-spread corduroy-trousered legs on either side of the rope. When the buzzer sounded it was as faint a sound to Cedric's ears as a fly caught in a web and he was not alarmed – not, that is, until the winking man called out, "Listen! It's Snip buzzing. Snowy must be in the room."

The buzzing ceased. "Shitabrick," said the Spook.

The winking man held up his hand. "Don't panic. He's probably just nosing around. Hurry up and stow the crate away."

The Spook and Mervyn tottered off with the last crate. The winking man called up through the trapdoor, "How many to go?"

"About ten."

"O.K. Start swinging 'em down at the double. Huggins is in Snip's room, but it's probably nothing. Hit the track as soon as you're unloaded."

Mervyn and the Spook were coming back. The winking man was peeling off his coat. "It's a crate apiece from now on. We gotta tramp. Fred, you head back and yank that ladder down. Pull it under the building and get on back here, fast as you can."

Before Cedric had really grasped what was happening the Spook was nearly around the end of the wall and on top of him. The fright Cedric got was like the white flash of an explosion behind the eyes. He had been crouching for so long the strength had ebbed from his knees and they only just managed to catapult him upright and on his way through the opening on his left. He kicked a tin and it went flying to strike a pile with a loud bang.

He heard the Spook's startled shout. The ground rose sharply now and he was bent double before he could reach the line of daylight. He fell on his side and rolled out. Another cry followed him, a hollow echoing cry.

52

CEDRIC WASN'T in open country yet. He knew where the place was, though. It was the Borough sheds. Even had he not been here once before as a nosey kid, he would have known it by the great silent steamroller, the old carts tipped up on their shafts and the black Thornycroft tar lorry. Half the corrugated iron walls were gone and half the roof was open to the blue sky. Cedric soared over piles of coke and coils of hose like an antelope.

Through the great, lurching doorway he broadsided into the open. The section was a storing place for timber, telegraph poles, railway lines, drums, great wooden spools of cable, and there were elderberry trees and clumps of fennel and blackberry, but nothing close provided any real cover.

He skidded around the end of the rambling network of corrugated iron sheds. Pressing himself against the wall, he peeped back. The Spook came tumbling into view, but looking in the wrong direction.

Cedric swung himself over a sagging, twanging barbed-wire fence and jumped a ditch. There was a low coop in the long grass and a startled bantam mother with pale chickens nearly as big as herself clucked indignantly at him as he panted past. He ducked through a gap left by two missing boards and he was in Burton Street.

If the town had a low quarter it was Burton Street. The side on which he had emerged was respectable enough, a place of commerce, the warehouses of grain and implement importers; but the far side, the railway side, was the oldest part of the town and the little neglected hovels were the homes of the dregs of the population. It wasn't enough to be poor to live in Burton Street – it was essential to be low as well as broke. Cedric had nothing against Burton Street except that it was too long to cover in one spurt without being seen if he were still being pursued. He made a fifty-yard dash and then turned into the office doorway of a warehouse. He had a bad stitch and he couldn't have run farther anyway.

He straightened up and rubbed his side. He hoped fervently that a glance along the deserted street would discourage pursuit. But that the quarry would be hiding in a doorway seemed an elementary deduction. He went up the steps and tried the stout door – it was fast, naturally. He looked through the letter slot. A filing cabinet and the end of a desk was all he could see. Well, he thought, if they come, they come …

53

CONCEALED BY the warehouse doorway, Cedric sighted, diagonally across the road, a little old church some obscure religious group had built among the squalid, disreputable houses. If only he'd had the sense, he reproached himself, to cross the road to that church! There was probably some back way out of the church grounds into the wastelands which stretched to the railway. But it was too late to risk crossing the road now.

He wondered if anyone was watching him hiding in this doorway. Were there eyes behind those dirty rags that passed for curtains in the front windows of the almost derelict houses? It was hard to credit the buildings were inhabited. The roofs were flaking away in rust. The weatherboards were grey with age and neglect. Some sort of yellow-flowering weed had taken over the unkempt ground between the houses. In places the tallest sprouts were nearly as high as the drainpipes from the gutterings.

Cedric strained his eyes to read the partially obliterated writing on the sign-board tacked above the portals of the high narrow church. He finally decided that it announced: '*The Most Holy House of Worship of Believers in the Ancient Order of Martyrs.*'

He repeated it over to himself several times. For some reason some of the new words he had learned in the billiard room crept into his pointless soliloquy. But because (before his father had begun to build the tower and Granny had feared the congregation were whispering behind her back) Cedric had been taken to church regularly, he now couldn't quite bring himself to say these awful words in a religious, however vaguely religious, context even to himself. He compromised. He mumbled: 'The most Holy House of bee Worship of bee Believers in the Ancient feffing Order of bee Martyrs. The most feffing Holy be feffing House of Stupid Goddamned Believers in the feffing Ancient bee Order of feffing great big cees.'

This lowly form of diversion passed the time quite efficiently. His gaze was drawn to the sky. The spire of the church seemed to be pointed directly at a crescent moon – a mere wisp of a crescent moon pale and only just visible in the deep blue of the afternoon sky. It was not, however, the moon which intrigued Cedric but the star. And such a big bright star. Never, even by night, had Cedric ever seen a star in such close attendance on the moon. The crescent moon and the bright star below looked like the flag of some far-away mythical land.

Cedric heard voices and froze. He soon relaxed. The voices were coming from the other direction – from the town end of Burton Street. There was a burst of maudlin song. Cedric made out a man's voice and then a woman's. The man appeared to be walking or staggering out on the roadway. Drunks! thought Cedric, typical Burton Street drunks; as soon as they're past I'll scram.

The woman drew level with the doorway. Cedric caught his breath. It was the Witch. She saw him just as quickly and stopped. She came close to the bottom step and peered up at him. He had never had a close-up of her face before. The scrawny features were dead looking, the colour of a cameo brooch. The eyes were weird. She raised her hands and, sure enough, the fingers were like talons.

Cedric gulped. She was a witch, for sure. Her jutting chin was long and thin. The nose was thin and sharp too and a shade of blue grey. Cedric's eyes moved fearfully to her companion who had stopped also and was standing in the middle of the road, swaying backwards and forwards. The man was short and fat, with a round, red face as if his collar were throttling him.

"C'mon, dearie," the man said in a thick, boozy voice.

"Doesn't get a nice new hat every day, eh?"

Cedric felt pretty safe. The chap was harmless, anyway.

But he felt less sure of himself when he met the Witch's unmistakable mad gaze again. Then he nearly laughed in her face when he saw the price ticket hanging from the side of her hat.

"You're the boy," she said. "You're Mervyn's friend."

"C'mon, dearie," the man said. He pulled a bottle out of his pocket and tilted it up.

"You're the boy, aren't you?" the Witch said.

"I dunno," said Cedric.

"I'm in the grip of the grape," the man said. "C'mon dearie. Not every day a nice man buys um a new hat, diddum."

The Witch took a step closer. Cedric recoiled.

"Where is he?" she hissed. One yellow tooth jutted up from her lower gum. "Mervyn Toebeck. The fat boy that killed my Stanley. Stanley would've never killed himself. His father, his own father! Wicked! Wicked! Don't tell me Stanley did for himself. I knew Stanley too well to believe that. The fights they had! I told Stanley that fat lazy good-for-nothing would do him one day. And I know. I've read it all in the cards. Where is he? Tell me, boy."

"I dunno," said Cedric desperately.

"You know!" she screeched. She took a step up towards him. She wore an ancient brown costume that only reached her knobs of knees. The new black straw hat with its floating price ticket completed a ludicrous ensemble.

"Don't you touch me," said Cedric from the top of the steps. "Don't you dare touch me. I'll kick you in the stomach."

She stopped. "Let's be friends," she said cunningly.

"C'mon, dearie," the man said. He sat down suddenly in the middle of the road. "Awright then, awright. You can stick your new hat up your arse."

"Let's be friends," the Witch said again. "You don't want to be friendly with a murderer, do you? I tell you he killed Stanley. He thinks he's got away with it, but he won't. You know where he is, don't you?"

"Yes, actually I do," said Cedric.

"Will you help me?" the Witch said. Her eyes gleamed.

Cedric knew she was quite mad. He thought: In for a penny, in for a pound.

"Yes, I'll help you."

54

ON THE evening of the same day that Cedric had fled from the bootleggers and subsequently been confronted by the Witch, Vernon Bramwell, sipping an aperitif in the lounge of his tall home across the gully, remarked disparagingly about a certain Mr Gerard Hemingway: "Chap apparently thinks he would find nothing to interest him at the Pioneer Club. He won't be asked to join again. Fellow would be better off concerning himself in local affairs than chasing around the wilds of Africa."

"He's got his photograph in the *Record*, here," said Vernon.

"Oh," said Blair. "Hemingway? Heard of him somewhere."

He looked hard at Margot Bramwell, one of his eyelids flickering, but she stared fixedly into her cocktail.

"May I see it?" asked Blair.

The newspaper was handed over.

Small black print under the photograph read:

> Mr Gerard Hemingway who leaves for Africa on a big game hunting Safari today being interviewed at his apartment by a *Record* reporter. Mr Hemingway is holding his Wesley Richards rifle. The bejewelled scimitar to be seen in the background is only one item in the priceless collection of souvenirs which Mr Hemingway has amassed in his career as explorer, archaeologist and hunter and which adorns the walls of his luxury apartment. Mr Hemingway is well known to readers ...'

Looking at the *Record* in his own house, Cedric had taken little notice of the Gerard Hemingway write-up. Gerard Hemingway could go to Timbuktu and stay there for all he cared. He didn't mind if there were thousands of bejewelled scimitars in Mr Hemingway's luxury apartment. Cedric was interested in another article on the same page as the photograph of the globe-trotter. The article concerned the unusual spectacle of the crescent moon and the bright star. Cedric, reading the newspaper over his evening meal, learned he was not the only person in whom the sight had aroused interest. It was, indeed a phenomenon.

The heading read:

AMAZED AT BEAUTY IN AFTERNOON SKY

> The brilliantly clear spectacle of the planet Venus close to the lower edge of the crescent moon delighted and astonished people glancing heavenwards in the early part of this afternoon. The Director of the Observatory, Mr R. W. Mather, said the occurrence was far from unheard of, but that the clarity of the moon and planet in such proximity in broad daylight was most etc. etc ...

Cedric had read the article with great interest. In a way he wished that no one else had seen the sign in the sky. Anyway, he thought, nobody else saw it from a doorway in Burton Street while they were hiding from bootleggers. No one else was up to his chin in an adventure as he was. And such a mysterious adventure, complete with characters like the Spook and the Witch. The moon and the star above that lonely spire had appealed to Cedric as some celestial symbol of his private war with the forces of evil.

In the den that evening after tea, Cedric took out his document. At the top of the first page he inexpertly drew the spire of a church and sketched in above it the sign of the crescent moon and the star.

Cedric decided to abandon his question and answer system.

He made a side heading:

8 p.m. Tuesday 7/1/36.

Well, I am in the thick of an adventure now. I nearly got my throat cut today. It is hard to imagine what the rum runners would have done if they had caught me. Yes, Mervyn and the Spook are helping the winking man to run his booze into the town. I imagine that Snip Hughes is the master-mind. Apparently Detective Huggins keeps an eye on the billiard room. The crooks call him 'Snowy'. I don't know if they got away with it today. My guess is they did. They seem to be pretty well organized. But I am as good as certain I escaped without the Spook catching sight of me.

I am now convinced that Mervyn killed his father. The Witch is quite sure. She is mad as a snake, but these people can be very shrewd. She says that Stanley Toebeck was not a man who would have ever committed suicide. She has told Detective Huggins all this, but apparently she had no evidence to back it up and all he can do is wait and watch. According to the Witch, Huggins is certain of Mervyn's guilt also, but knows he can't sheet it home. Mervyn is cunning. I am getting very frightened of Mervyn. I must be careful.

The Witch claims she is a fortune-teller and has proved Toebeck Senior's murder with cards and a crystal ball. This is all bull, I guess, but she sure has weird eyes. She calls herself Madame Zombroni. Madame Baloney would be more like it. Here real name is Rita Zombroni and the way I get it she is an old whore. She was certainly Stanley Toebeck's mistress. She hates Mervyn. She said that her and Mervyn's father had been sweethearts for forty years. The thought makes me sick. But she doesn't seem to be Mervyn's mother, who must be dead. Customer would be a better word than sweetheart, I reckon.

She has some weird plan in her nut to haunt Mervyn and make him confess. She speaks clearly some of the time and then she just mumbles to herself. For all I know it may have been her watching on the tower, but against this is the fact that she claims she has been trying to find out where Mervyn was staying, without success. It certainly wasn't her who walked through the house by night. These things still baffle me. And so does the buried money.

Now for the immediate danger. I said I would play along with the Witch. She took me over to her house in Burton Street but I didn't go inside. What a dump! I have done what she asked me to. I don't know how I had the nerve to do it but I did it. I think I did it because the Witch could be right about scaring Mervyn. I can't see him cracking up and confessing but he might clear out and no one wants to see the back of him more than me.

God knows what will happen when Mervyn comes home and goes into the sleeping-porch. I don't mind admitting I'm scared. I've got to act the part; boy, I've got to act! This is the real test. I am frightened for myself and I am frightened for Granny. When I think of Mervyn I get a creepy feeling. He must be terribly evil and I can sense it. He may be mad. But not as mad as the Witch, that's for certain.

Cedric locked the document in the drawer.

55

IT WAS a beautiful evening but the crescent moon and the planet Venus were no longer in view. They had been visible earlier in the evening before tea and Cedric had taken his father and grandmother out onto the front lawn to see the spectacle for themselves.

"It's weird and wonderful," Granny had marvelled. "I've never seen anything like it before. The star and the moon look like jewels in a blue velvet box."

"Really looks great right over the tower like that," Martin Williamson said. "Damn good mind to go right up to the top of the tower and have a look at it. I think I will. Right up to the very top."

"You be careful, Martin," Granny said, "I wish you would fix that loose step you're always going to get around to fixing. And come down soon for tea."

"If people in this town had a grain of sense between them they'd be here in their hundreds begging to get shown up and over on a night like this." Having fired this bitter shaft, Martin shambled off across the lawn.

"You watch that loose step," Granny called after him.

56

GRANNY AND Cedric had Ovaltine and biscuits for supper on a railed side porch looking over the shrubbery. Martin had taken his supper into his bedroom. His light streamed through the branches and leaves. Soon after nine o'clock his light went out. Cedric and Granny sat in silence for a while and then Cedric told her all about how he was going to be a famous writer.

"Oh I'm glad," Granny said. "You're such a clever boy, Cedric. It's just the right thing for you."

After Granny had gone to bed, Cedric sat at the library table with a book open before him but not reading. He was too keyed up to read a word. He had left the library door ajar. He wanted to get the interview with Mervyn over tonight. It was no use deluding himself; Mervyn would smell a rat as big as an opossum. Close by, handy on the table, Cedric had placed what appeared to be an innocent article but was, in actuality, a sword stick which his grandfather the General had acquired at some stage of his travels.

The tiny but ornate clock on the marble mantelpiece ticked on. Cedric was sitting with his back to the half-open door into the hall, but he could see it clearly in the oval mirror which hung between bookshelves on the opposite wall. The after-theatre traffic hummed past and then the night grew very quiet save for a cricket chirping in the shrubbery, and the ticking of the little clock.

57

IT WAS nearly midnight when Cedric heard the kitchen door open quietly. His eyes flew to the sword stick. He swallowed. He lowered his head over the book but kept one eye on the mirror. The kitchen door closed again. Had Mervyn gone out again or was he standing motionless in the kitchen? The minutes passed. At last there came a light tap at the library door. For a big fellow Mervyn must be able to move very quietly, Cedric thought. He got himself under control.

"Who is it?"

"It's me, Mervyn."

Cedric turned around sideways in his chair. "Come on in, Merv."

The door opened slowly and Mervyn entered very quietly.

He was dangerously quiet. His fat face was pale. His eyes were little black holes.

"You're up late, Merv," said Cedric chattily.

Mervyn said nothing. He stared down at Cedric and then he looked around the library. He hadn't shaved that day and the stubble accentuated his double chin. He began to walk around the room drumming his fingers against the front of his check shirt.

"What's wrong, Merv?" said Cedric. "Nothing gone wrong, has it?"

Mervyn still didn't answer. He crossed to the tall windows, moved an edge of one of the velvet drapes and looked out. Then he turned and regarded Cedric steadily.

"You look as if you've seen a ghost or something," Cedric said. Mervyn looked up at the ceiling. His fingers still rested against his chest but had ceased their nervous drumming.

"I have."

"You what?"

"I have. I have seen a ghost." Mervyn's voice seemed even more highly pitched than ever, a positive squeak. "Or smelt one."

"What do you mean?"

Mervyn crossed to the library table.

Cedric indicated the chair at the head of the table. "Take a pew."

"I don't think I'll sit down."

Cedric began to turn cold. What was coming? Had he been wrong in thinking he had escaped unobserved that afternoon? He tried to smile.

"Aren't you going to bed? What's all this about a ghost?"

"Look, old son ..." Mervyn began. Cedric let his breath out slowly. Mervyn, after a long pause, continued. "Something very queer is going on around here. Have you seen anyone hanging around?"

"No," said Cedric. "Only Detective Huggins. I told you about that."

"Yes, so you did. You haven't seem him again, by the way?"

"No, I haven't. I've been thinking about that. I think you were right. It was nothing. He was just looking at the house. I guess. Or the tower."

"Were you around the house all afternoon, Cedric?"

"I went for a bike ride. 'Smatter of fact I nearly went into the billiard room looking for you."

"Why didn't you?" said Mervyn absently. "Damn it all. This doesn't make sense."

"What doesn't?"

"This," said Mervyn. From his pocket he produced a black curved-stem pipe. He put it on the table and stared at it with great distaste.

"What is it?" said Cedric. "You going to start smoking opium?"

"I found that in my room. Someone was sitting in there smoking that pipe. The room stinks of tobacco. A tobacco I know only too well."

"Well, it wasn't me." Cedric's tongue flicked quickly at the back of his teeth.

"No, I didn't imagine it was. You see, there's something funny about that pipe. Something that doesn't add up. Something I don't like particularly."

"Well. I don't know," said Cedric, scratching his thick switchback. "Who the hell would visit your sleeping-porch? Not me, not Granny, nor Dad, that's for sure. I haven't seen Dad with a pipe for years. Why would he go into your room anyway?"

"It wasn't your father," said Mervyn. "Who could it have been?"

"My father. You see, that's his pipe."

Cedric gaped at him. "But ... but he's dead."

"That's what kinda upsets me," said Mervyn.

58

WHEN CEDRIC awoke at 8 a.m. approximately, he was instantly aware of two things: the fateful nature of the day and a knot of apprehension in his stomach. Encouraged by the fatefulness, the importance of the day and, sickened by the familiar apprehension, he became angry. He sat on the side of the bed and churned his anger until it frothed. It was directed at Mervyn Toebeck and, to a lesser degree, the Spook. Who the hell were they to gatecrash his life, frequent his home, torment him? Why the blazes should he, Cedric Williamson, wake up worried and miserable? On account of them! He muttered a coloured three-word sentence he had learned in Snip's pool room and felt better straightaway. It was a sentence exhorting some Power or Being, unnamed but patently omnipotent, to have sexual intercourse (and by implication, violent, sudden and unwelcome to the recipients) with the said recipients, the number, age and sex of whom was not delineated but who were plainly despised and had the common denominator of illegitimate birth.

Cedric repeated the pithy sentence on the way to the bathroom. It was as well Granny was not within earshot.

In the kitchen Mervyn's fat face was cold and set. His nod to Cedric was almost surly. Cedric took a deep breath and resolved to keep his anger simmering, ready to boil into rage if need be. It gave him strength.

But, after breakfast, Mervyn's voice was its old unctuous high-pitched normal tone when he suggested to Cedric that they go and sit for a while in the shrubbery.

Cedric agreed. He said, "I'll just go and slip a shirt on first."

In his bedroom he wondered for the umpteenth time how he had screwed up the nerve, what had possessed him, to smoke that pipe in the sleeping porch? It occurred to him that maybe the old Witch had partially hynotized him. This did not seem a very convincing explanation. No, he thought, I was a bit above myself, a bit carried away, after that adventure with the bootleggers. I just didn't want the excitement to die out. And, true, the move had been in keeping with his policy of attack being the best defence: in keeping with his theory that by continuing to throw spanners in the works the machinery would finally jam and the truth would out. Also anything he could possibly do to get Mervyn rattled was a step towards getting rid of him. Impetuously as he had carried out the Witch's plans, they must have been in concord with a subconscious consideration.

Deep in thought, Cedric mechanically buttoned up his shirt and tucked it into his trousers. Mervyn was nobody's fool. He must be giving that pipe business a lot of thought. It seemed logical he would track down the possession of the pipe to the Witch. Would he approach her? Would she give the show away if he did? Only time would tell. Cedric decided to keep his bad temper handy. He'd throw a tantrum, he'd deny everything. He'd tell Mervyn to hit the track and keep going – the very idea – he, Cedric! ...

There was a garden seat in the shrubbery and Mervyn was sitting on it and staring intently at a huge stone frog, painted green and haunch-deep in mouldering leaves. If Cedric had not been so disturbed he would have sniggered at the unmistakable similarity in both Mervyn's and his graven companion's faces and expressions. As it was, the droll similitude seemed to underline a sinister aspect to this conclave in the shadowed shrubbery.

Cedric sat down on the other end of the garden seat.

"I know." Mervyn said immediately.

"You know what?" said Cedric grimly.

"I know who put that pipe in my room."

Cedric got control of himself. "Yeah. Well, it's got me beat. Who?"

"Huggins-ss-s," Mervyn hissed, "Snowy fuckin' Huggins-ss-s."

"But – Huggins. *Detective* Huggins? How the dickens – it doesn't make sense."

"It adds up to me." Mervyn broke the tip of a twig he was playing with and flicked it at the frog. "You saw Huggins hanging around. He's probably been lurking around lots of times when you haven't seen him. He knows Granny's just an old lady he could easily bluff if she saw him. He'd twig straightaway the sleeping-porch would be my room. He must be in his second childhood to dream up a stunt like smoking that pipe in my room. He ought to be pensioned off. He ought to be down at the seaside playing with a little bucket and spade. Putting on a screwball act like that only shows me how safe I am."

Cedric's eyes hooded briefly. "I still don't get it."

"It's like this," Mervyn explained. "As I've said before, I don't want to speak ill of the dead and all that crap but my old man was a no-good bum. He wasn't only a drunk but he was a pimp for an old whore called Madame Zombroni who reckons she can tell fortunes, but tells 'em on her back and the only crystal balls she ever had were jammed up against her poxy old arse."

There was a brief interlude here while Cedric's tension exploded in hysterics. Even Mervyn started to chortle. He threw something else at the frog.

He continued: "Well, this prize decrepit old slut is convinced in what's left of her brain that I finished up her precious Stanley-Wanley – that's my patah, ole boy – so who's going to help her drink methylated spirits out of silver goblets in her rose-scented boudoir now? Of course" – Mervyn looked steadily at Cedric – "I feel deeply for her. After all, old boy, when you've spewed in the same jerry as someone for forty years their sudden demise leaves a gap in your life. Not only that but it's bad for business. I mean to say who's going to fish around for blokes who want their fortunes told? Bring your own crystal balls."

Cedric stared hard at the frog and fought off another attack of hysterics.

"Well, this dear old soul has gone around the bend so far what with bad booze and diseased pricks that she has seen fit to sell Snowy Huggins the tale that I finished up her Stanley. I know this is right, Cedric. I keep my eyes open and my ear to the ground and I've got the grapevine working for me so I know this doddery old harlot-cum-fortune-teller with the accent on cum has recently been closeted with the brilliant Snowy Huggins, the criminals' avenging shadow, on many occasions. That's who he got the pipe from, you can put a ring around it. All I say is he's as mad as she is. One thing I know now is the only way the cops in this town could catch a man is if he posted them a signed confession and didn't use too many long words in it. Yuh, yuh, yuh!"

"Tonight," said Mervyn, and there was a lower, more malevolent undertone in his voice now, "we ring Ernie Fox. Tonight! While Snowy Sherlock Huggins and Madame two-bob-a-poke Zombroni are happily rocking their ouija board and writing notes to each other in invisible ink, we, you and I, Cedric old son, will be picking up our first fifty quids' worth of hush money. And not only that, my boy, but tonight we'll carry the Sashalite with us and we'll strike again. Tonight. My bloody oath we will! From now on we're in business. We'll pick up the money and then we'll have a quick think and find another guilty couple. The more the merrier from now on."

Mervyn rose up, stuck his hands deep in his trouser pockets and slouched restlessly around the frog. "A lot hinges on you, Cedric, old son. The way this crackpot Huggins is going on he's liable to pull me in and put me through the hoop anytime. He probably fondly imagines that I think my old man has come back from the grave to haunt me and I'm a nervous wreck by now."

Mervyn sneered at the frog.

"Anyhow I'm going to vanish for the rest of the day just to be on the safe side. I'll keep an eye on the Spook. When I leave for the phone kiosk at about half past eight, I'll send the Spook off to the school to that spot we worked out by the dental clinic where he can watch the sundial. You leave here about 8.15 and pin that note we've concocted in the telephone directory. Between the last two pages. That's right isn't it?"

"Yes," said Cedric. "The last two pages. Yellow pages. Just advertisements."

"Right. As soon as you've done that you slope for the school round the back way and meet the Spook over by the clinic. As soon as I've rung Fox I'll head for there too but I'll come across the sports-grounds and up through the tennis courts. It's just about as far from the west end as it is from Grant's Fields so I should be there in plenty of time. He's got to detour to that phone kiosk by the library. I don't think there's a chance of him making better time than me but, just in case, don't wait for me. Grab that loot and beat it. You'll be going the way I'll be coming so we can't miss each other. Everything straight?"

"It's the way we worked it out," Cedric said flatly.

"Right," said Mervyn. "Well, I'm going to fade. Coming?"

"No, I'll sit here for a little while."

Mervyn walked away out of the shrubbery. He stopped and looked back. "Cedric."

"Yeah?"

"Bring that Sashalite. That's something you simply mustn't forget. We're in business. man."

When Cedric was quite sure Mervyn had gone he winked at the frog.

59

THE NOTE that Cedric, Mervyn and the Spook had worked out and then printed in block letters read:

WHEN YOU LEAVE THIS PHONE BOX GO BACK ALONG THE MAIN STREET AND WALK STRAIGHT DOWN FENTON STREET TO THE PRIMARY SCHOOL. PLACE THE PACKET ON THE SUNDIAL IN THE GARDEN JUST INSIDE THE MAIN GATES. THEN WALK AWAY DOWN FENTON STREET AND KEEP OUT IN THE MIDDLE OF THE ROAD. NO TRICKS OR YOU WILL BE A SORRY MAN.

At 8.30 Cedric pinned this note between the last two pages of the telephone directory which hung in the phone booth opposite the public library. He had pretended to be speaking into the mouthpiece while he ascertained there was no one passing by.

He set off for the primary school, taking a back road. The Sashalite was bulky in his blue blazer pocket. He was playing by ear. All day he had tried to figure out some plan of action but his mind had kept stalling. He had opened up an exercise book and headed a page: 'Chapter One'; he had mowed a lawn and helped Granny fold some freshly ironed linen.

Cedric climbed over a stile, crossed a paddock, went across the cracked asphalt of a quadrangle behind the school, cut through the bicycle sheds, looked into the girls' toilet (something he had always wanted to do), moved around the big dark central block of classrooms and approached the dental clinic, a small detached building in front but to the side of the school. There was plenty of cover. Behind the clinic was a plantation of pine trees and through them a track led down to the tennis courts. Cedric had no intention of letting the Spook pull off one of his little tricks: when he was six or seven yards from the clinic he stopped and called loudly and firmly, "Spook, it's me. Where are you?"

But the Spook won the toss. When he spoke it was from behind Cedric. "Right here."

"Are you trying to give me a heart attack?" Cedric complained when he had recovered from his fright. "Come on, let's get organized. Let's get under cover. Where'd you spring from anyway?"

"I bin right behind you from the sheilas' dunny," the Spook explained cheerfully. "I bin reading all the limericks and pictures of cocks and things on the wall. You ought to smoke. You didn't have any matches to see by. Some of these sheilas can draw real good."

Cedric knew when he was beaten.

The dental clinic had a small porch with walls of trellis work and in here the Spook and Cedric ensconced themselves on a stone step. They had a good view of the circular garden laid out just inside the big wrought-iron main gates. In this garden was the sundial.

"Well, if you think I oughta smoke, give us a cigarette," said Cedric. He had just survived a weak moment when he had almost wished he had not warned Ernie Fox and so spoiled the true excitement of this perfect plot.

The Spook obliged, even to lighting the cigarette he handed over from the butt of his own.

As Cedric let the smoke of his first cigarette drift fragrantly out of his mouth and into his nostrils (smoke blue and forever like the first anything), the Spook chatted simply and amiably about the drawings and inspired writing on the walls of the girls' lavatories, and Cedric heard the chuckling voice of Maybelle Zimmerman. He fought hard to shut out the evil thoughts he had held at bay for some time now. He evoked a mental image of the solemn challenge in the grave childish features of cousin Jasmine vanished into the mist of Cape Town (alas for the creaking of a swing in an orchard: alas for a bygone, violet dusk). A lorry rumbled between him and a girl waving from a train, uh-who-ee-duh-who-ee, and Cedric put his forehead against the totara lattice work and he could see through a little triangular aperture the dark garden where the sundial was and he could see the lights of Fenton Street.

60

WHEN MERVYN came he was savage. With his back to the street lights he was faceless and transformed again into the evil fat slug of Cedric's nightmares.

"I got the raspberry," he said in a gruff choking voice. "And it wasn't Ernie Fox. It wasn't Huggins anyway. Whoever it was said it was the police but I think it was bluff. I think Fox has roped in a friend. He said the police would have me in a day or two. He said he knew who I was. It's just bluff, bluff, but it's still the raspberry. And what can we do? Nothing! Thanks to the brainless kid's idea of no camera. By God, if we had the photos it'd be a different story."

"Aw shit!" said the Spook. "I need the dough. My sister's given me the bum's rush again. I thought we were in the money and I could start paying my way. She's shoved one of the kids in my room already. Fancy a man's own sister calling him a jailbird! What'm I gonna do now?"

But Mervyn was walking away towards the gates. Cedric ran after him. He called, "Merv."

Mervyn kept walking and Cedric called again. Mervyn stopped. So did Cedric. He didn't get too close. "What did you say on the phone, Merv? Did you mention the note or the school here. Use your block."

"Don't you tell me to use my block, Little Lord Fauntleroy," Mervyn said in a dirty savage voice. "You and your bright no-camera ideas. Do you think I'm such a big mug that I'd be hanging around here if I'd mentioned the note or the school? They were too dumb to even trap me into saying anything. They just said – oh bugger it, let's get up the town, Spook."

Cedric hadn't realized the Spook was right beside him. He thought with some exultancy: It's over, they're going.

Mervyn said, "Sorry, old son. This has been a big knockback for me. Come on, Ceddy. Let the three of us go up to the village and sit down and have a quiet think over things."

Cedric thought: You cunning fat bastard! You know what side your bread's buttered on, don't you? But I'll be shot of you before this night's out. But watch your step, Cedric. Wait your chance.

They walked in silence up Fenton Street. When they hit the main street people spilled out of the Royal Theatre, lighting cigarettes and heading for the milk bar and soda-fountain next door.

"Interval," the Spook observed. "Crikey, I'm hungry. Fancy a man's own sister calling him a jailbird."

There were people all around them now. Some smoking and others licking ice creams.

"Nothing like a crowd to make you inconspicuous," said Cedric.

"I'm hungry," said the Spook. "I'm so gosh-darned hungry I could sit in the gutter and howl my guts out. If I could just get a feed and the price of some fags I'd jump a freight and take off to the Smoke."

"And be a big shot," said Mervyn and Cedric together.

Mervyn looked at Cedric and grinned. Cedric grinned back weakly. He deeply regretted this inadvertent eirenicon.

"We can't see a man go hungry," said Mervyn. Cedric could see the next step was to suggest going to his place, so he thought fast. He put his hand in his pocket and pulled out a handful of the silver from Mervyn's buried hoard.

Cedric said to the Spook, "Go get three pies. Get some Green River or something. Get yourself some fags. Keep the change. Merv and I'll go over to the parking area and sit over there and wait for you."

Mervyn and Cedric walked across the road, leaving the Spook looking for some small coin he had dropped. Crossing the road just ahead of them was a pair of trim plump buttocks moving provocatively beneath a tight short skirt. She was a young woman, petite, her legs strong and shapely and tipped up on high heels in shimmering sheer silk. The overall effect sucked a wolf whistle from Mervyn.

The arched eyebrows of Margot Bramwell and her pert elfin prettiness reprimanded Mervyn over her shoulder. The eyes, sexiness itself beneath the veneer of aloofness, took in both Mervyn and Cedric.

"Hoity, toity," said Mervyn, loud, coarse, flirtatious. Cedric banged him with his elbow. He had recognized her.

Margot's high heels tapped away down the right-of-way to the civic parking area.

"Whassamatter?" growled Mervyn. "What a grouse looking brush. She's asking for it. I'd like to slam a length into that."

"So would I," said Cedric, surprising himself with his own frankness. "That's old Vern Bramwell's second wife."

"So what?" said Mervyn. "All the better. He gives her the dough-ray-me and the boys give her bumps-a-daisy. I'll bet you a quid that's her outlook."

"Maybe so," said Cedric.

"Oh, to hell with it." said Mervyn. They mooched down the alley-way.

61

THE PARKING lot was a big, nearly square area of asphalt, all carefully marked out with parallel white lines as if in readiness for some outdoor game with kingsize chequers. The dozen or so lights on iron posts at intervals around the perimeter accentuated the resemblance to a stadium.

There were only about fifteen cars parked on the area.

Cedric picked out Margot Bramwell's silver grey two-seater Alvis with its hood up. She tapped her way past the Alvis and then Cedric lost sight of her. By this time he and Mervyn had sat down on a narrow seat which was built in a square around an old elm tree.

The Spook joined them with three hot pies in gravy-stained brown paper bags. He had three pint bottles of Green River with the tops off.

"A picnic," said Mervyn sadly.

The Spook rolled up his bag and threw it away while Cedric was still letting his teeth get used to the hot pastry.

"Starving," the Spook explained. "I feel almost human now."

"Pity you don't look it," said Mervyn and Cedric in unison. Cedric cursed this rapport which seemed to be determined to flourish.

"Now where," Cedric mused out aloud when he was nearly finished with his pie, "did that sheila go? She hasn't gone back to the flicks."

He had assumed Margot Bramwell had availed herself of the intermission to get something from the Alvis but the two-seater was still there and Margot had not returned.

"Who?" said Mervyn dropping his empty pint bottle behind the seat, "Green River! What would my father say? My son, my son. Can this be true? Do my eyes deceive me? Never, never! I see it all – you have put green ink in your meths to pull the wool over the eyes of the accursed Snowy Huggins. Bravo, my son! Long may your guts rot."

"Mrs Bramwell," said Cedric. "Wanna fag. Cedric?" said the Spook.

"No," said Cedric, "Thanks all the same." He dropped his rolled-up paper bag behind the seat. He tilted his head back to drink Green River.

Right opposite, across the parking area, was a two-storeyed building known as the Waverley Apartments. On a balcony, the centre one of the three, the bright tip of a cigarette glowed briefly. Someone was leaning over the balcony rail. A tiny shower of sparks bounced off the asphalt below the balcony. The smoker had tossed away his cigarette. French doors leading from the balcony opened and a man passed through them into the lighted room beyond. He turned to close the French doors. The click as they shut was enough to tell the long-jealous Cedric who it was. He nearly choked on his mouthful of Green River.

The balcony smoker was Blair Bramwell – slick, supercilious Blair Bramwell dressed in slacks and, incredibly, a sleeveless singlet. Surely Blair Bramwell lived in his father's big new home? Cedric knew full well he did. And he knew people like the Bramwells did not go visiting dressed in singlets.

And then Cedric just *knew*.

Like a fool he started to laugh and then he told Mervyn and the Spook why he was laughing.

"What a laugh! Serve old Bramwell right. I suppose he thinks she's at the flicks. And all the time his own son is doing the job. What a beaut! The more I think about ..."

Mervyn was squeezing Cedric's arm.

"What?"

"Give the Spook the Sashalite," said Mervyn, squeezing just a little harder. "We're back in business. This time it isn't for peanuts."

62

CEDRIC WANTED to shout out, "Count me out. I don't want to have anything to do with this."

He hated the Bramwells and this was his chance to really hit back as he had long planned to do. He was poor and maybe Mervyn was right – maybe this time there really was some big money in the air. But Paphnutious stood again at his elbow passing his hand over his features and feeling his own hideousness. What Cedric really wanted to do was to go home to his books and Granny and Gus, and – yes, even Martin with his tower. But the action and the excitement acted like a drug that left him speechless.

The Spook had the Sashalite in his pocket. He balanced himself on Mervyn's shoulders. Cedric steadied the Spook as Mervyn rose from his crouching position. The Spook grabbed the bottom rung of the short fire-escape beside the balcony and a thrill filtered through Cedric's confusion as the emaciated black shadow swiftly scrambled up, straddled the balcony rail and disappeared.

"I think the best place is back by the tree," whispered Mervyn. They began to walk towards the elm. "All hell'll break loose when the Spook clicks that button on the Sashalite. No one can pin anything on us sitting over by the tree, and we'll be able to see just what's happened. He should be down that ladder and gone through the other exit under the Memorial Arch before they're outa bed. We'll just stay put. We know nothing. We can saunter off right down the main drag whenever we like. We might even stop at Snip's and get a bottle of his Green River to celebrate. Cedric, you old son of a gun, there could be a thousand quid in this. What a spot these two are going to be in when that flash goes off! It does my heart good to think of two fellow pilgrims in a predicament like they are going to be in any moment now."

They had not been seated under the elm tree for many minutes before the light in the room behind the French doors went out.

63

THE SPOOK had never heard language like this on a woman's lips before. He had heard foul language uttered by the female of the species, but usually in rage – never before in low, throaty, cooing tones. In the darkness, Margot beseeched her lover to plumb every depth of sexual abandonment.

After the light had gone out the Spook had carefully and quietly pushed open one of the French doors some six inches. The lovers were not far from him. They were sprawled on the top of the bed. He had the Sashalite at the ready. The passion which pounded in him made him shake all over. His eyes had grown used to the dark and he could see the outline of Margot's naked legs wrapped around her swain. He could see her bare thighs thrusting, withdrawing, thrusting, hear her groaning with delight, urging him on with every filthy word she could think of.

The Spook got his thumb on the button, rehearsed under his breath the exhortation 'Say cheese', which had earned him Mervyn's and Cedric's congratulations ('brilliant') pushed wide the French doors and stepped through.

There was a step down he had not imagined existed. He pitched headlong into the room.

64

MERVYN GRABBED Cedric's arm. "The light's on again. I didn't see a flash, did you? We'd have seen the flash that old Sashalite gives off from here."

"I didn't see anything," said Cedric.

"Well, the light didn't go off 'til we were back here under this tree. Even a nut like the Spook would have waited 'til the light went out. We didn't see any flash. Hell, now the whole place is lit up."

The light had come on in the adjoining room also.

"There might be another room yet," suggested Cedric.

"That's it. I'll bet that's it. A bedroom. Well, that means we don't know what's going on. The Spook might be still waiting his chance. I hope those French doors weren't locked."

"It's too dark to see if he got through or not," said Cedric. "But I'm prepared to guarantee he's not still on that balcony. My eyes are getting used to the dark and if there's anyone on that balcony I'll eat my hat."

"I'll eat mine too," said Mervyn. "And, God damn it, they wouldn't lock doors that only open on to a balcony."

"They've got a lot to lose," said Cedric.

"They're going to lose it too. We'll just have to sit it out. If it goes on too long one of us will have to scorch back to your place on the off-chance the Spook has slipped out some back way. I'm prepared to swear he hasn't come back out this side. Could he get out the other side?"

"I can't see it," said Cedric. "I'm not absolutely certain but I think those Waverley Apartments back on to another block of buildings. There could be another door. I'm not saying there isn't, but frankly I don't think so. I think the Spook would either have to come back the way he went or cut through one of these entrances under the balconies."

"By God, if he's been nabbed we could be in the cart," said Mervyn.

Cedric shivered. He felt sick.

65

THE SPOOK made a mad leap in the direction of the balcony, collided with the edge of the French door he had opened, and went staggering back across the bedroom. The Sashalite was dropped, gone. He saw that the man had sprung from the bed. The Spook groped along a wall. He was trapped.

The light went on. He was standing right in front of a door. He wrenched it open and plunged into another dark room. He tripped over a small table and went sprawling forward.

Blair Bramwell in singlet and socks and nothing else, appeared in the lighted doorway. He switched on the light. He walked slowly into the room. The Spook, still on the floor, wriggled away from him. Bramwell moved around the Spook. He reached out and took from the wall the bejewelled scimitar that he and Margot had admired earlier over their drinks.

"Don't move," said Blair Bramwell. He swished the scimitar through the air above the terrified Spook.

Margot appeared in the doorway pulling her dress down. "Don't you touch me," the Spook babbled. "If you hurt me I'll tell everybody about you and Mrs Bramwell."

"You will, will you?" The scimitar swished again. Blair's voice was cracked. From the doorway Margot emitted a bubbling moan. Her hands were cupped over her mouth.

The Spook decided to make a bolt for it. He decided to charge towards the door and push the woman aside.

He never reached the door.

66

THE CINEMA was out and people were returning to their automobiles in the parking area. The main street was noisy with traffic. Cedric and Mervyn watched in silence. They had exhausted every line of speculation and there was nothing to talk about.

Soon the only car left was the Alvis.

67

MARGOT'S FACE was grey. She sprawled limply back on the settee, her mouth hanging open. Her head lolled despairingly. Her eyes were turned away and riveted blankly on a wall adorned with guns, horns, boomerangs, blow-pipes, tapestries, tiger skins.

Blair Bramwell was sponging blood off the carpet. He had found a newspaper and was tearing pages from it. He kept pouring cold water from a glass on to the carpet. He screwed up and threw each exhausted piece of paper into the fireplace.

"Thank God it's a dark carpet," he said. "I'll have a look at it by daylight tomorrow. I'll probably have to buy some cleaning shampoo. The thing I can't make out is that flashlight. It hasn't even got a camera to go with it. If he were a professional at this sort of thing or if the old man had hired a private detective or something, he'd have had the whole works. It's got me beat. He must be just some prowler."

The bejewelled scimitar, pride and joy of Gerard Hemingway's globe-trotting heart, was back in its place on the wall among the other curios.

"I tell you no one will ever know, Margot," Blair said.

"All we've got to do is keep our heads."

"Oh my God! Keep our heads! My God!"

"Oh, for Christ's sake, shut up," snarled Blair. "Can't you see our cake's dough if we make one slip. What's worrying me is who he is. Or was. How did he know your name when you reckon you've never seen him in your life?"

"I tell you I don't know him from a bar of soap," moaned Margot, her eyes screwed shut. "Get rid of it, will you, get *rid* of it. For God's sake did you have to cut his head off! ... Oh, oh ..."

"I'll get rid of it, damn you! Just try to keep calm. Hemingway'll be gone for a year at least. I'll dump the body and everything away to hell and gone somewhere. I'll have to use the Auburn. You'll have to run me around to the Auburn and then head for home."

"Don't say *head*," screeched Margot.

"*Shut up!* You want Monty Harrop to come nosing around?

Look, Margot, he had to die. Can't you see that? What difference does it make how it was done? I didn't mean to do what I did, God knows. I just swiped and it was done. That thing's like a razor. Margot, if he'd talked we were washed up."

"You didn't only swipe, you hacked. Again and again."

"What did you expect?" snarled Blair. "Sew it back on?"

"I can see it in the paper now. Guilty pair sentenced to death ..."

"Oh, stop talking through your neck, will you?"

"There you go again," cried Margot. "Don't keep saying things like that!"

She leapt up, took a look at the awful thing that Blair had dragged over to the fireplace so that it was off the carpet, and spun around covering her eyes. "We'll swing. We'll both swing. What a fool I was to listen to your schemes!"

"Swing nothing," rasped Blair. "I tell you it's a piece of cake. You're my biggest worry. If father smells a rat we're gone a million. You've got to get yourself home fast." He looked at his watch. "But fast. I'll have to park down the street and slip around to the gardener's shed for a spade."

He set fire to the paper in the grate. "I'll clean up some more some afternoon. The big thing now is to get this body out to the sticks somewhere. That rug the – er – other part's wrapped in is a problem, I may have to burn it. I'll have to replace it somehow. It's going to be a damned hard rug to replace. Just the sort of fancy thing a nut like Hemingway would have. Let's have a brandy and get round to the Auburn. All you've got to do now is keep a still tongue in your head."

"Oh shit," groaned Margot. "There you go again."

68

MARGOT BRAMWELL came out of one of the private entrances to the Waverley Apartments and headed for the Alvis. She wasn't mincing along in her normal manner. Her gait was more of a totter.

The parking lights of the silver-grey two-seater glowed and then the automobile, its perfectly tuned motor almost inaudible, circled around and parked outside the entrance. A tall slim man appeared, a door was shut firmly. The man climbed into the car and the Alvis was moving before he could have been properly seated. The Alvis purred down the right-of-way to the main street.

"Come on," said Mervyn.

They stood beneath the balcony and they both called in turn, several times.

"Spook!"

"Fred!"

There was no reply.

"What're we going to do?" said Cedric.

"I'm damned if I know," said Mervyn. "There must be a back way out. All we can do is head for home."

My home, thought Cedric, not *your* home or *our* home, damn you.

"This has really got me bamboozled," said Mervyn. He tried the doors of the various entrances but they were all shut tight.

"We've simply got to get our brains into gear," said Mervyn. "The Spook went up that fire-escape with the Sashalite. He never came out on this parking area again to date. You agree with me there?"

"Unless he's turned invisible," said Cedric.

"Presumably he crouched down on that balcony until the light went out. He's not up there on the balcony now. So he must have gone in. If he shinned back down while we were walking back to the seat under the tree he'd have seen us and come over."

"Maybe he didn't. Maybe he got cold feet, slipped down, took the Sashalite and he's headed for the Smoke to be a big shot."

"Hmn," mused Mervyn. "It doesn't sound right. The only other explanation is that he found another way out and he's waiting for us by your old man's tower as planned."

"But it's hours and hours," objected Cedric.

"There's one other explanation," said Mervyn grimly, "and it's one I don't like one little bit. He got nabbed."

It was an explanation Cedric didn't even want to think about. But it had to be faced. He asked, "Would he talk? Would he spill the beans?"

"I don't really think so. But here is a point. Bramwell wouldn't get the cops even if he thought the old Spook was a burglar. He couldn't. How can he explain being up there with his father's second wife? The whole set-up is fishy. The Spook isn't such a dunce that he wouldn't know he had the drop on Bramwell. They'd just have to kick his backside and turn him loose."

"Or do him in," said Cedric.

Cedric and Mervyn looked hard at each other in the wan moonlight.

"Christ!" said Mervyn.

They started to run just then – really run fast – and they just found cover in a doorway as the lights of a car lit up the parking area.

It was the maroon Auburn sports car with the top down. It skidded up to the private entrance Margot had used. Blair Bramwell got out, left the motor ticking over, lifted the lid of the rumble seat and then entered the building.

In two or three minutes he was back with a limp body clutched to his chest. He dumped the body in the rumble seat.

"Murder!" said Mervyn. "Holy God! Murder!"

Cedric was close to crying. He was terribly frightened. Blair came back down the stairs and jammed a smaller bundle into the rumble seat. Then in and up he went again.

"He's not getting away with this," said Mervyn. "And, by Jesus, I'm a different proposition from the Spook. He won't do *me* in!"

Bending low, he left the doorway and sped behind the Auburn. Cedric saw him hook something out of the rumble seat, have a quick look down, and come running back. He was blowing hard.

They heard a door close. Blair Bramwell banged down the lid of the rumble seat. The big sleek car moved off. It took the other exit, out under the Memorial Arch.

"It's murder all right," said Mervyn. "We're donkey deep this trip. The poor old Spook was jammed down with just his feet sticking up. They must have bashed him over the head. What's the bet I haven't got the murder weapon, a club or something, wrapped up right here in this rug or whatever it is?"

"We'll have to go to the police," whispered Cedric.

"The police! Are you nuts? We'd be in the dock ourselves, you dumb-cluck. I tell you we've got our thousand quid and maybe twice that right here in my arms and this time it's just a two-way split. Money won't help the Spook where he's gone. Let's head for your place down every back street in town."

They went under the Memorial Arch, a stoop-shouldered youth and a fat fellow with a splay-footed gait who clutched a bundle in his arms. There wasn't another person to be seen on the streets anywhere.

69

IN THE sleeping-porch, while Mervyn was fumbling for the light, Cedric bumped against the bundle Mervyn was carrying. When the room lit up it revealed that this brief contact had put Cedric in a worse mess than Mervyn. Mervyn's dirty old check shirt was dark and stained, but on the lapel of Cedric's blue blazer and down the front of his light grey shirt the stain was unmistakably blood.

"Look at my blazer," said Cedric. "Look at my shirt." "Look at my bloody hands," said Mervyn. For once he could have been using the epithet literally. Cedric felt ill.

"Spread that newspaper out on the floor," Mervyn ordered.

He dumped the bundle on the newspaper. Cedric looked down at it and gulped.

"It's a pretty fancy sort of a rug," said Mervyn. "Chinese or something. I tell you, man, we've got the murder weapon here. It's a club or something."

"I feel as if I'm going mad," said Cedric. "Look, I've got to wash this blazer and shirt. What if Granny comes out?"

"We'll get to a tap in a minute," said Mervyn. "Let's have a squiz at what's wrapped in this rug."

That was one 'squiz' neither of them was ever to forget! Cedric didn't remember groping his way out of the sleeping porch. Under the lilac tree he heaved up the pie and the Green River. While he was mopping his face with a handkerchief he heard Mervyn saying urgently, "For God's sake don't make such a row. Is there any kerosene or benzine or something?"

"In the woodshed," croaked Cedric. "In a gallon tin."

He leaned against a veranda post. His knees were weak. Soon he could see a flickering glare from the backyard.

Mervyn came back. "I've set fire to that rug in the incinerator, good and proper. I soaked it in kerosene and there won't be a strand left."

"That – that – that other thing won't burn," said Cedric thickly. "God, I'm scared. What are you trying to do, Mervyn? You must've gone mad. We're covering up a *murder*. We're just as liable to get blamed for this as Blair Bramwell. More. He's got money. You know he always gets away scot-free. It's us that's going to be in the cart. People have seen us around with the poor old Spook."

"You've got to listen to me," said Mervyn tensely. "I don't think anyone's even going to know there's been a murder.

Bramwell will bury the body somewhere. He'll go right out into the bush somewhere in that car of his. What a fright he's going to get when he can't find that bundle. Well, we've burnt the rug. We'll have to bury the – er – other part. The Spook's sister has kicked him out. She'll think he's left town again like he did before and so will everyone else if they think about him at all."

"You can't bury that on this property," said Cedric. "I'd never sleep again."

"We'll bury it miles away," said Mervyn soothingly. "Now, look, I've kicked some paper over it. Can you get a box or a sack or something? Anything so we can handle the damn thing."

Cedric felt so dazed and worried he began to walk around in circles. Mervyn grabbed his arm. "Haven't you got a box or an old biscuit tin or something?"

All Cedric could think of was one of the cartons he had a collection of in his den. He tiptoed through the kitchen and along the passage to his den. When he came back Mervyn grabbed the carton. "Attaboy! Just the thing."

"You'll have to do it," said Cedric. "I couldn't bring myself to step inside that room while that's in there."

Mervyn entered the sleeping-porch and came out with the carton held in front of him. His fat face was grey. He said, "Get a spade and let's get moving. This is the worst chore a man ever got landed with."

The kitchen door opened and Granny stepped out. She was in her dressing-gown. Cedric's and Mervyn's nerves were stretched so taut that they both cried out and the carton seemed to jump out of Mervyn's hands of its own accord and land right at Granny's feet.

Cedric never knew how he did it but he stooped and picked up the carton and walked behind Granny into the kitchen.

"Cedric," said Granny. "Do you know what the time is? What're you doing? What's in that box?"

"Some books," cried Cedric. "Yes, books."

He bolted right through the kitchen. He went up the stairs two and three at a time. He reached the dark closet connecting the two upstairs bedrooms. In the distance from below somewhere he heard Granny call his name. Up the step-ladder he went. He thought he heard an awful sniggering sound from the carton but somehow he forced himself on and up and pushed up the trapdoor into the ceiling.

70

WHEN GRANNY tracked Cedric down he was in the big ornate upstairs bathroom, his face and hands lathered with soap, his shirt and blazer still wet from frantic sponging.

"What's the idea?" said Granny, who could be stern when she was worried and thought something was going on behind her back. "Why wash up here? What've you been up to? Has that Mervyn got you into some mischief?"

"Look, Granny," said Cedric towelling his face. "If you must know, I'm late because we ate a pie up town and it made me sick. I've been awful sick, Granny, but I'm O.K. now."

"Sick!" cried Granny. "Poisoned! A pie. I'll get Dr Buick." "Please, please," said Cedric. "I tell you I'm all right now. I brought it all up. I didn't want to worry you and that's why I washed up here. I was a bit sick on my sleeve and shirt."

"There's something funny about this," announced Granny.

"If I thought for a moment that that Mervyn ..."

"Look, Granny," said Cedric firmly, wondering if he could stand the strain much longer. "I tell you it's nothing to do with Mervyn. The pie was my idea. I'm as good as gold now. All I want is a cuppa tea. You go down and put the kettle on and I'll be right down."

Cedric was cunning enough to know that Granny regarded tea as some sort of a panacea. "The quicker I get a hot cup of tea into me the better," he said.

In the kitchen Cedric saw Mervyn beckon him from the veranda.

"You sit down, Cedric," said Granny. "I won't be a second," he replied.

Mervyn led Cedric down the steps on to the side path.

He said, "My nerves are shot. I'm heading up to Snip's to get a bracer. I'm going to pour a whole bottle of rot-gut over my tonsils tonight. Look, Cedric, if I cleared out, do you think you can handle it from here?"

"What d'you mean?"

"I mean, can you get rid of that box? Where is it, anyhow?"

"It's safe," muttered Cedric. "Until tomorrow."

"Well look, Cedric, I've wiped any idea of trying to put the black on Bramwell. This is just too hot to handle. I've got Huggins on my hammer and God knows what. If I can slip quietly out of town I'm sure I'm doing

164

the right thing. You explain to Gran I've been offered a job out of town. Tell her tomorrow. Then all you've got to do is get rid of that carton, say after dark tomorrow night. Be careful."

"All right," said Cedric. It was a development he had prayed for – though not in these circumstances – but he had a deep-seated, uneasy presentiment of breakers ahead: big, huge, bad breakers. "You think everything's going to be O.K.? I mean if anyone talks …"

"Who is there to talk?" pointed out Mervyn. "The Spook's made his last speech. I'm not going to talk. Neither are you. If they catch Bramwell – well, he knows nothing about us. Sure we were pals with the Spook but, as for where he went tonight, we know nothing."

"That Sashalite," muttered Cedric. "What became of it?" "Bramwell will get rid of that too. Even if it turns up, what can it suggest to anyone? Nothing. I tell you, Cedric, old son, get rid of that carton and forget the whole business."

"Forget it?" Cedric gave a hollow laugh.

"Cedric," called Granny from the kitchen doorway. "Coming," said Cedric. Mervyn stood back in the shadow as Cedric went inside. As soon as the kitchen door closed, Mervyn tiptoed to the woodshed and found the spade. He crossed to the meadow, and, watched by an unsmiling Gus, dug up the buried sack. He put the spade back in the shed. In the sleeping-porch he grabbed one or two personal belongings and stuffed them into his pockets. At the gate he had a good look up and down the street. He headed for town with the sack dangling in his right hand and bumping against his knee as he walked.

71

CEDRIC SAT at the kitchen table and sipped hot tea. He tried to assess the situation from every angle. Mervyn was probably right. All he had to do was sit until after dark tomorrow night and steel himself to get the carton out of the loft – he shuddered.

Granny said sharply, "Cedric, you *are* ill. You're poisoned. Your hands are shaking. I'll get Dr Buick. It's late, but Mrs Lloyd won't mind me using her phone. And Dr Buick is kindness itself. I've had him here to attend to your father later than this and he never minds one little bit."

"I'll have another cup of tea, Gran, and I'll be as right as rain. Then all I have to do is have a sleep and I'll be a new man in the morning."

"Are you sure it was just a nasty old pie?" said Granny.

"I'm beginning to think the quicker we see the back of that Mervyn the better. And as for that thin man ..."

"Please," squawked Cedric.

"Cedric, what is up with you?"

"Look, Granny, I'm all right. I'll tell you something too, Granny, I think we've seen the last of both Mervyn and the his friend. Mervyn's been offered a job out of town and if he takes it I think they'll both go. Then I'll settle back into my swot and I'll write a novel too. You just watch me."

"Well, I'm glad to hear there's a chance he's going. I began to think he was a bit like the horse in the tent."

"What d'you mean?" Cedric asked disinterestedly between sips of hot tea.

"Well, I mean he's the sort you let get one foot in the door and in the end it's you that has to get out. These people were in a tent and it was raining and they felt sorry for their horse and they let the horse put his head inside ..."

Cedric blew out a mouthful of tea.

Granny said, "Did you choke, Cedric? You're not feeling sick again?"

"I never felt better in my life," Cedric lied monstrously.

He stood up and went over to Granny and kissed her. "I'm going to have a good sleep now. I feel fine."

"Yes, you have a good sleep," said Granny. "Nothing like getting your head down ..."

72

MERVYN TOEBECK walked purposefully towards the business and shopping area. His mind was very busy. He slowed down as he neared the phone booth opposite the public library. When he was fifteen yards or so distant he stopped to put the sack down. He had been so engrossed in his calculations that he had not given the sack a single thought. It had been just where he had buried it, it felt about the right weight and that was that. However, there was something about its soundless collapse when he lowered it to the footpath that prompted him to give it a suspicious prod with his shoe. Disbelievingly, Mervyn tipped the sack up and let earth and pine-needles trickle into the gutter.

He stood perfectly still for some moments. Then he put his hand on his forehead and shook his head violently. Nothing about this seemed to make sense at all. The only solution he could come up with was that his arch-enemy Huggins had been concealed somewhere and watched him burying the sack. This was another of Huggins' little pranks – like the pipe. Mervyn was convinced now that Huggins had gone quietly mad. But, he had to admit, it was uncanny and frightening. Angrily he pitched the sack over a tin fence. He looked nervously up and down the street. Right then the town clock on the post office just around the corner chimed the full hour and emitted one resounding boom.

Mervyn felt so unnerved that he very nearly did keep on going and get clear of the town. He scowled blackly. Now he had no money at all. He had imagined that the last of his worries would have been small change. He went through his pockets and found exactly one penny. It seemed like an omen. He knew he would never have a chance like this again to get his hands on some big money. It was late. The streets were deserted. He went boldly towards the phone box. Then his nerve failed him. He thought about his plan. He paced up and down. He looked to left and to right examining every shadow. At last he stepped into the phone box.

He looked up Vernon Bramwell's number and dialled it.

When he heard the receiver being picked up and a voice saying, "Yes, who's speaking?" he dropped his penny into the slot.

"Who is it?" the voice repeated.

"I want to speak to Mr Blair Bramwell urgently."

"This is Blair Bramwell speaking. Who is that?"

"My name doesn't matter. Did you lose anything tonight?"

"Who's speaking, please?"

"I have no time to answer questions," said Mervyn. "You killed a man tonight and I have a rug and a nasty little something to prove it."

"For God's sake!" Blair Bramwell sounded frantic. "This is an extension phone."

"O.K." said Mervyn. "Now listen, you'll get away with this all right but it'll cost you a thousand quid. In small bills. Got it? Nothing bigger than a fiver."

"I haven't got that sort of money. A thousand. You're nuts."

"Then you'll swing. I think a thousand is cheap. You can raise it. It's just after one o'clock. At this time tomorrow night I'll ring again and give you directions. It'll be your last chance."

"Listen here ..."

"Listen nothing. You listen. Surely you've got enough brains to see you're trapped. You're lucky you're dealing with me. Don't you try to fool with me. I know everything and one trick from you tomorrow and the police will have you. For murder!"

"Shut up, you fool."

"Right," began Mervyn, but just then the town clock began to chime the quarter-hour and he waited. Then he said, "I'll ring after midnight tomorrow. You be handy to that phone and have the money parcelled up neatly. I'll tell you what to do."

"You bastard ..."

But Mervyn had hung up. Just before he left the booth he had an inspiration. He looked to the back of the directory and there, sure enough, between the last two yellow pages of classified advertisements was the printed note they had concocted for the eyes of Ernie Fox. Mervyn read it through carefully. Thoughtfully he closed the directory, leaving the note where it was. He punched his right fist into his left palm jubilantly. It was perfect. There would be one thousand pounds on that sundial instead of fifty. And no three-way split. Mervyn, positively drooling, left the phone box and crossed the road.

He made his way to Snip's Pool Parlour and went down the steps. There was a door, closed and padlocked, across the passage leading to the big room where the tables were. He began cautiously to step down the dark narrow stairway on his left. When he was a few steps down, a telephone began ringing. He stood still.

The telephone kept up its clamour. Then a light showed beneath a door at the foot of the stairs and someone picked up the receiver. Mervyn waited until he heard the ting of the receiver being cradled, went on down the stairs, knocked on the door and then opened it.

The winking man was sitting on the side of a stretcher made up as a bed with grey blankets and a grimy pillow. He looked up, startled. He was dressed in combinations – singlet and long underpants – of that indeterminate shade which is difficult to accuse of being downright dirty.

Mervyn beat him to the first wink. "Hi, Winker. I heard the phone. Business as usual?"

"Always business as usual," said Winker, winking. "On call, day and night. A man gets less sleep in this game than he would on his honeymoon."

"I can just see you on a honeymoon," grinned Mervyn. "Is that your Italian singlet you're wearing?"

"Eh?" The winking man was wearily pulling on a sock. "The one with the spaghetti on it," elucidated Mervyn. The winking man grunted. He was going to pull on the other sock when he desisted and looked up at Mervyn. "I suppose you're on the bludge as usual? Why don't you earn it this time? The bridge builders and riggers out on the Aranaga Viaduct are having one helluva pay-night pissup. I took six dozen of the brown out before and now they want three dozen of the red. Jesus, there'll be some fat heads out there tomorrow. I wouldn't go out on that viaduct for love nor money let alone with a hangover. Just as well the stuff's pure." He winked.

"Yeah," said Mervyn. "Pure poison."

"You take it out, eh? Three dozen of the brown and ditto the red. Won't take you five minutes to load it into the Nash. It's only three miles out there. They threw me a quid for mileage last trip so just charge 'em for the grog on this trip. Six doz, that's nine quid. You do the job and a quid's yours. I'm stuffed. I want to grab some shut-eye."

"I've got no licence to drive," said Mervyn.

"We've got no licence to run booze either, son. And I know you can handle the car all right. It's late. There's no risk tonight. Snowy'll have sucked up his Ovaltine and be tucked up in bed long ago. You might get yourself a crow out there, Merv. Some of the crows out there might want to come back with you by this time of night. They'll all be shickered. They'll be pushovers."

"You must think I like my bread well buttered," sneered Mervyn. "They'll be pretty second-hand by now."

"What difference does it make? Here's the keys of the Nash and the big one's the key to the padlock into the room. Take the padlock in with you and run the bolt."

"I know what to do," said Mervyn testily. "O.K. I'll do it, but not for a mouldy quid. I'll do it for the driving practice. I might get myself a car pretty soon."

"They tell me these Rolls Royces are quite a good buy," the winking man derided Mervyn.

"You might be surprised," said Mervyn. "Now, when I come back I'll help myself to a bottle and sleep in the room. I'll open up for you early."

"Don't you pile up that Nash."

"Don't you worry about me."

"I'm worryin' about Mr Rolls and Mr Royce. Hate to see them lose a sale."

Mervyn shut the door on the winking man's cackling.

73

THE NASH was a disc-wheeled touring car, ten years old but still a good car mechanically. Its body work was starting to go because it stood in the open most of the time against a wall of the Borough Council sheds.

Mervyn got in behind the wheel, puffing and perspiring after two trips carrying three crates, each containing two dozen bottles of the brew, up from the underground storeroom and stacking them on to the back seat. The motor fired first kick.

While the motor warmed up Mervyn took a big suck at an extra bottle he had brought along. It made him cough and splutter, but, when he had recovered, he grinned an almost tigerish grin. A thousand quid, he thought. He drank again. He could feel the fumes already mounting to his brain.

The Nash slowed down as it emerged from Burton Street. It turned towards the railway station and picked up speed.

The official police car, an early model Ford V8 Sedan, was driven lightless from an alley-way between a warehouse and a joinery factory. Detective Huggins was at the wheel. His eyes never left the red tail-light of the Nash some two hundred yards ahead.

"We'll get Sanderson this time," he said to the young constable who sat beside him. "It'll be interesting to see how good he is at winking out through bars. Snip Hughes won't bail him out. He'll drop him like a hot spud."

"Do you think Sanderson will squeal?" asked the young constable.

"Frankly, I don't think so. He's a real old lag and he'll just say nothing. Snip'll probably put up the money for a mouthpiece, but if we can only catch Sanderson unloading that poison red-handed, we'll get a conviction for certain. Barrow's just waiting for us to put someone in the dock. He'll throw the book at him. It's a wonder some people haven't gone blind around these parts drinking that stuff."

The Nash had turned left towards the Adgeworth road.

At Westend it turned right. About a mile further on Mervyn pitched his empty bottle over the hood. He was drunk now.

"A thousand quid," he mumbled. "All for little me. Boy, I'll never look back after this! This dump'll never see me again. There's no way Bramwell can wriggle out of this. He'll raise that money as sure as hell. His car must be worth more than that."

Mervyn settled down to drive faster.

74

"THAT THING can move," muttered the young constable uneasily. Driving without lights out here in the dark countryside with just the red glow ahead for a guide was tense and tricky work.

Huggins seemed unperturbed. "I know. Snip Hughes reckoned he made the city in four hours in that car and that means averaging sixty all the way."

"Can't we involve Hughes if he's the owner of the car?" asked the constable, sitting forwards and pulling in his navel.

"No, it's in Sanderson's name. Has been for the last year ever since we started to put the heat on. He's a crafty lad our Snip. He plays life like he plays billiards. If he can't make a hundred break, which he can most of the time, he leaves the balls safe."

"We must be hiking," said the constable. "Man, he's moving."

"It's not like Winker to drive like that," said Huggins, puzzled. "I hope he hasn't woken up we're on his tail. Thirty is his limit usually. We're hitting seventy. Aha, he's turning off."

The Nash crossed the railway line and wound down a narrow dirt road.

"Good," said Huggins. "Now we can take it easy. My guess was right. Pay day out at the viaduct and the boys are throwing a party. We'll fall back so we can use our lights on the bad corners and we should time it nicely. We should arrive just at the psychological moment."

75

THE GORGE carved out by the Aranaga River was deep, and by daylight the spot where the gorge was straddled by the old viaduct and the partially constructed new one afforded a tremendously impressive view. By night, however, it was an eerie place hemmed in by densely bushed razor-backs. All that could be seen of the bridgework were the red signal lights along the old viaduct. The silhouette of a huge crane loomed skywards. There were lights in the cluster of old railway carriages which housed the small army of engineers, riggers and labourers. A fire was burning in an open oil drum and men were clustered around it. A guitar was being strummed and the voices of men mingled in sporadic outbreaks of song. In the heart of this scene Mervyn parked the Nash.

He left the parking lights on and the motor idling. He climbed out and willing hands helped him unload the crates. Most of the men were already staggering, their voices thick.

"The mileage is on the house," Mervyn told a tall thin man who appeared to be the spokesman of the shadowy figures. "Nine quid is the price of the plonk."

"And cheap at half the price," said Detective Huggins, coming around the back of the car. "All right, Sanderson, your number's up this trip."

Mervyn was drunk, but he quickly realized Huggins had mistakenly taken for granted that the Nash was being driven by the Winker. There were men between him and the two advancing policemen. The only real light was the flickering glare of the bonfire in the oil-drum. He fled.

He dared not run too fast. He knew this place was built on the very edge of a ravine. All the lights were behind him. He stumbled towards the railway line. Just as he reached it the young constable collared him low. They both hit the ground rising up to the tracks.

"Get up," snapped the constable, standing over Mervyn.

Mervyn groaned. The constable stooped low and grabbed him by the collar and a sleeve. Mervyn let himself get hauled to his feet, sagging limply as if all the fight had been knocked out of him. The constable grabbed him by the shirt front with both hands. Even with their faces six inches apart neither could make out the other's features. Mervyn brought his knee up viciously: the constable gave an agonized yell and buckled up. Mervyn drove his fist into his jaw with all his weight behind it.

Huggins, who had followed up carefully, keeping the beam of his torch just above ground level, skirted around the grappling figures. With carefully calculated force he rabbit-punched the shorter and unhelmeted shadow on the back of the neck twice. The young constable who had gone staggering backwards and Mervyn who dropped like a stone reached the ground about the same time.

Huggins shone a torch down on his victim.

"Toebeck," he murmured. He felt Mervyn's pulse. Mervyn groaned and tried to move. Huggins undid his coat and produced handcuffs.

76

MERVYN'S NECK was so stiff and sore after stopping Detective Huggins' two side hand chops that he couldn't move his head an inch either left or right or up or down without suffering pain. The bottle of 'the red' he had tossed off in such high spirits had turned dog on him. He was on the verge of nausea and kept swallowing saliva. He didn't know whether it was the wood alcohol or the blows or a combination of both which had left him seeing double, but the fact remained that, across the desk in the watch-room of the police station, he could see the chest, shoulders, face and silvery mane of two Detective Hugginses, neither image very distinct and the one with the most hazy delineation partially superimposed on the other.

He was still handcuffed, and right behind the chair on which he slumped, the young constable towered menacingly, his lower lip split and thickening. One hand deep in a pocket of his police trousers supported a very painfully bruised part of his anatomy.

"I'm going to sue you for this," Mervyn said malevolently. "This is wrongful arrest. The pair of you assaulted me. Winker said I could use his car anytime. I was invited out to that party. I didn't know there was grog in the car. Take these handcuffs off."

"You'll have to do better than that, Toebeck," the two-torsoed, two-headed incubus that was Huggins intoned. "Constable Dawson and myself both distinctly heard you charging nine pounds for that rot-gut you delivered. Which version do you think Justice Barrow will believe? Several men out at the camp have admitted ordering the muck by ringing up Ned Sanderson. They've admitted that Sanderson delivered a supply earlier in the evening. The best thing you can do is make an honest statement. We can make things hot for you over this, Toebeck, very, very hot. You're on probation for theft now. You have no driver's licence, you resisted arrest and assaulted a police officer by kneeing him in the groin, you were delivering six dozen bottles of bootleg liquor in a no-licence area. It'll surprise me if an analyst's report doesn't prove that a liberal consumption of this muck could cause death or blindness. Let's see now, what else can we think of? Ah, you exceeded the speed limit, you were drunk in charge of an automobile ..."

"I was not drunk."

"You're stupid with drink right now, Toebeck. You're only a young fellow and I know you've had a bad start in life so I'd like to help you."

"Yeah," sneered Mervyn. "I bet you would."

"I'm rapidly losing patience. You must have enough sense to see that you can't dodge jail this time. It's just a question of how long you're going to get. I'll remind you that when you're on the inside every extra month will seem like a lifetime. Make no mistake, Toebeck, you're going to have plenty of time on your hands to remember your mistakes. It carries a lot of weight if I can stand up in court and say you were contrite and co-operated with us."

"We'll see," mumbled Mervyn. "I'm not making any statements tonight. I've been assaulted and I want to lie down. I just might die, the way I feel."

"If you die it'll be that wood alcohol you filled yourself up with."

"Do you think ...?" Mervyn began and then angrily checked himself from displaying weakness. He had nearly asked his mistily distorted inquisitor if there really was a chance of the drink he had consumed causing blindness.

Huggins' two heads looked up at a spot behind Mervyn.

Mervyn heard the door shut.

"Aha," said Huggins. "*Mister* Sanderson. How good of you to arise at this hour of the morning to oblige us."

Mervyn heard another voice – that of a third policeman say, "I wouldn't actually say he did it with very good grace, Sir."

"Dear me," said Huggins, falsely benign. "Well, none of us like losing our beauty sleep."

"I don't know what all this is about," said Winker querulously. "A fine thing when an old man can't even grab himself a bit of shut-eye. Always reading about things like this going on in Russia and Germany and all the time it's just as bad, if not worse, on a man's own doorstep."

"Sit down, Sanderson," Huggins snapped. "We've got you and Toebeck absolutely sewn up. We've got positive proof and plenty of witnesses that you were rung up to deliver bootleg liquor and that for a sum of money you obliged. It was bulk dealing and absolutely flagrantly commercial. Toebeck's assaulted a police officer and he is in serious trouble. I've got men searching under the building behind the billiard room and at any minute now they'll be reporting in to say what they've found. So what do you think they'll find, Sanderson?"

"Now, how would I know?" The winking man spread out his hands helplessly.

"You wouldn't have a clue, would you?" said Huggins.

"Too bad. Well, Justice Barrow is just going to take one look at you two bright sparks and he'll listen to what we have to say and my guess he'll start thinking in terms of two to five years."

"Bullshit," said Winker.

"You hear me out, Sanderson. You've dragged a minor into this dirty racket now. That's going to prove this moonshine is practically poison. I've explained to Toebeck that your only chance, both of you, to get leniency is to come clean. Why should you and Toebeck be the fall guys for Snip Hughes? Come clean and I'll promise you a light sentence."

"Did you say a life sentence?" asked the winking man.

"I said a *light* sentence."

"I'm sorry, I'm not as young as I used to be. I've had a hard life and my ears don't work too good. Funny thing but my memory's going too: Getting yanked outa the stretcher like this when a man's trying to grab a little shut-eye is a cruel blow to the memory. I feel all confused. I'm beginning to wonder if I even know my own name. This is a frightening experience for a man of my age. Where am I? Who am I?"

"Toebeck is young enough to remember," said Huggins grimly, but obviously impressed and amused in spite of himself by the histrionic ability of the winking man. "He's too young a rat not to leave a sinking ship."

"Toebeck," said Winker, his eyes wandering vacantly around the room. "Who's Toebeck? Is the ship sinking?" He sprang up. He had slippers on, showing along with the cuffs of crumpled trousers under a ragged brown overcoat. "Man the lifeboats! Man the lifeboats! We're going down with all hands and the cook. Down to Davy Jones' locker. Don't you just stand there, skipper. Do something."

"We'll do something all right," said Huggins. "All right, boys. See what they've got in their pockets and tip them into the cell for the night. They won't cook up a yarn that's going to get them out of this mess."

77

THE WINKING man had a handkerchief. Mervyn had a safety razor, a shaving brush, the three handkerchiefs Granny Williamson had given him for Christmas, a toothbrush, a comb that needed dentures and a packet of contraceptives. "You can keep them," Mervyn said apropos the latter, showing his teeth to the young constable he had kneed and punched and who was now making a written inventory of his belongings. "You can use 'em if you meet up with a sheila with a white walking-stick."

"They look to me like you've been carrying them around for a long time," the constable said nastily over his sausage-like lower lip.

"You like another kick in the balls?" said Mervyn. There was a stump of a pencil lying on the desk. Mervyn flipped it into the palm of his hand with his finger-tips and cupped his hand to hold it in place. It stopped there even when Detective Huggins unlocked his handcuffs.

Two policemen – Constable Dawson and an older officer – conducted Mervyn to a cell: the only one the station had. It was furnished with three beds and a small table. The winking man was already stretched out on one of the beds. There were tins under the beds.

"How cosy," said Mervyn. "What do you do if you arrest a woman?"

"There's a room put aside for females," said the older of the policemen stiffly.

"If those tins are what I think they are," said Mervyn, "what do you wipe your arse on?"

The older policeman slapped Mervyn hard across the face.

It came as a nasty shock to Mervyn. He had estimated him to be reasonably good humoured.

"'Just try to act and talk like a human being, Toebeck," said the older policeman.

"I want to go to the little boy's room," gritted Mervyn, tears in his eyes more from the pain in his neck caused by his head being jerked than the actual slap. "I wanna go biggies, Poppa."

They took him down a passage and showed him a door. "And don't be long," said the tough cop. "Or I'll come in there and bang your head on the concrete wall. That acts better than a dose of salts, Fatty."

In the little dark room Mervyn groped for the light switch, found it and pressed it down. There was no bolt on the door. Slowly and silently, perforation to perforation, he tore a piece of paper off the roll. He pressed his shoulder hard against the door to resist sudden invasion, held the paper firmly against the wall and, with the stub of pencil, began to print in block letters:

I PUT THE BLACK ON B.B. FOR 1000 QUID. GOT PICKED UP BY THE COPS BEFORE I COULD TELL YOU. PICKED UP FOR BEING DRUNK. DON'T WORRY. RING B.B. AT HIS FATHER'S HOME AT 1 O'CLOCK TOMORROW MORNING. TELL HIM JUST WHAT I WAS GOING TO TELL FOX. THE NOTE IS STILL THERE. I SWEAR I WILL COME BACK AND KILL YOU IF YOU DON'T. PLEASE DON'T FAIL. THINK £1000! IT IS A CERTAINTY. THERE IS NO RISK.

Mervyn read the note over as well as he could with his blurred vision. It was just readable and that was all, but he felt reasonably certain Cedric would understand it. He folded it carefully and tucked it into one of his socks. He urinated and pulled the chain.

A minute later the cell door was slammed on the two prisoners. A key turned the lock.

78

TEN THIRTY, Thursday morning

In the upstairs sitting-room Cedric sat and watched the glow-worms quitting the black cave of the fireplace: that was all that remained of his document on Mervyn Toebeck.

On an oval claw-legged table beside Cedric stood his pen and pencil set, a Hall and Stevens Algebra textbook, a pad and the exercise book with 'Chapter One' printed at the top of the first page.

Cedric's eyes strayed up the wall above the mantelpiece and picked out, in the ceiling moulding, the tiny tell-tale darkness of the spy hole through which he had peered down into this room and watched the skinny, black-trousered leg of the Spook swinging to and fro from the knee. Cedric swallowed hard, remembering how he had crawled through the loft between ceiling and roof. He shivered as his thoughts swung, magnetized, to the carton up in the loft, complete with its dreadful contents.

"Tell me it isn't true," he prayed. "It must be just a nightmare."

Somehow, Cedric realized, he had to live out the day. If Mervyn's summing up of the situation was right there would be no mention of the slaying in the newspaper. Cedric had been over and over every aspect of the previous night and he was inclined to feel hopeful that Mervyn would be proved correct. Blair Bramwell and his father's young wife would most assuredly keep silent. Blair had a big fast car and it was a certainty that the remains of the Spook would by now be far away in a safe place. "A safe place," thought Cedric desperately. "Is there any such thing when a murder is involved?"

The more Cedric pondered about where to hide the carton the more worried he became. He wanted it to be gone from the ken of man forever. Down a well? Some day, someone would clean the well. Bury it deep in some wood somewhere?

Some day, for some reason, workmen would fell the trees and shift the earth as they were doing right now in the gully. He could hear the grunting and snorting of the great, clumsy grading machines. Cedric had read a lot of detective fiction and he knew how much science had come to the aid of the law in reconstructing crimes. He wanted to *know* it was safely hidden, gone for good so he could sleep easy. Not just tonight but all his life. Where? A skull!

"Jeepers creepers," muttered Cedric. He paced around the room, so steeped in thought he didn't see Detective Huggins coming through the front gate.

Yes, Bramwell would have hidden the Spook's body away out in the country and hidden it well. Cedric wished he owned a car. That would certainly simplify the disposal of the carton and its gruesome secret. If the Spook's bones were ever turned up they would be those of a headless skeleton and *that*, Cedric figured, would give any Sherlock Holmes a headache. A headless skeleton. Whose? Would the Spook have carried anything in his pockets to assist identification? Would Bramwell have thought of that angle? These were lines of mental inquiry leading nowhere, Cedric realized. Mervyn had reckoned that nobody, not even the Spook's sister, would ever wonder what had become of him. This could well be so. And if she did? Well, Mervyn was a well known associate of the Spook. Cedric was glad that he himself had hardly ever been glimpsed in public with the Spook. Mervyn had gone. But, of course, if the worst happened, the police would find him. Mervyn would say nothing – that, Cedric felt, was for sure.

He had to hide that carton and then erase the entire awful episode from his mind. Once that carton was gone Cedric could start forgetting. He would know nothing, nothing.

79

CEDRIC, CROUCHED in the private sitting-room, heard footsteps coming up the stairs. He heard his Granny's voice, then the deeper voice of a man. He experienced a hot feeling in the pit of his stomach. He felt weak, giddy.

The door opened and Granny entered followed by Detective Huggins. Cedric fought off an impulse to steady himself by grabbing the edge of the table. He took a sideways step to keep himself moving, to ward off a feeling of faintness. The smile he conjured up was a ghastly failure.

"That Mervyn," Granny began wrathfully. "That …"

"Mrs Williamson," said Detective Huggins soothingly, but with insistence, "I would like to tell Cedric about it myself and see if he can help me."

"Cedric's not in any trouble?" Granny asked imploringly. "None at all, Mrs Williamson. I just want him to tell me a few things about Toebeck that might help me. You just let me have a little private talk with him, Mrs Williamson. I assure you that you have nothing to worry about."

After subjecting Cedric and the benign Detective Huggins to a hard suspicious look, Granny reluctantly left them alone.

Cedric tried to let himself go limp, relax. He sank into a chair and then hastily folded his arms to hide his shaking hands. He knew his face was drained of all colour but, about this, he could do nothing.

"What's Mervyn done?" he croaked.

Detective Huggins pulled up a hard chair close to Cedric – so close, Cedric felt he must be able to see his trembling hands and knees.

"Your friend Toebeck is in jail."

Cedric's Adam's apple felt as big as a pumpkin. It did a sort of hand-spring, then it started practising push-ups.

"Whaffor?" Cedric managed to get out.

"He's in serious trouble, I'm afraid. Did you have any idea he was on probation?"

Cedric shook his head. The skin on his face felt taut. "My reason in coming to see you, Cedric, is this: we have Toebeck on some serious charges now, running bootleg liquor, assaulting a police officer, all sorts of offences, but I suspect him of something even worse. Much worse."

"Golly," said Cedric.

"Whereas we have positive proof of these other misdemeanours," Detective Huggins went on, "this big one is very, very hard to sheet home. In fact, unless Toebeck confesses – and short of torture I can't imagine him doing that I'm afraid he is going to get away scot-free with a dreadful crime. Probably not committed in cold blood or premeditated but nevertheless a dreadful crime."

"Such as?" asked Cedric, digging his fingers into his armpits.

Detective Huggins looked long and hard at Cedric. He timed it nicely. "Murder."

It wasn't difficult for Cedric to look shocked. In fact it was a relief to have an excuse to sit upright and let his horror show.

"Cedric, I want your assurance that you tell nobody of this conversation."

"N-no, I won't of course," stammered Cedric.

"Toebeck has been living in your home for some weeks now. He met you, in fact, the day his father died. That was the day you first chummed up."

Cedric's brain was racing. "Well, Sir, we didn't really chum up. It's just that I felt sorta sorry for him and then we sorta couldn't get rid of him."

"Yes. I suspected something of that nature. Now, Cedric, what I am really interested in is whether, at any part of your association, in any of your conversations, Toebeck let drop anything that may have made you suspect that he had anything to do with his father's death?"

Cedric felt his heart slowing down, the pressure easing.

He looked blankly at the detective. "He committed suicide, didn't he? That's what I thought."

"Yes," said Detective Huggins slowly, thoughtfully. "I suppose that is where the matter will have to rest."

"But ..." began Cedric. He left the word hanging, an unformed question.

"We'll forget about it," said Detective Huggins. "Now I understand he left here last evening. He had his razor in his pocket when we arrested him. Your grandmother said he told you something about getting a job away from here."

"To tell you the truth," Cedric said earnestly, "I ate a pie last night and it made me sick. Mervyn said something about leaving and I was so pleased to know he was going out and what with feeling crook with the pie I just didn't ask any questions. Having him hanging around was an awful nuisance. I wanted to get on with my swot" Cedric nodded at the algebra textbook on the oval table.

"Good boy," said Detective Huggins, nodding his silvery head of hair in approval. "I've been rather concerned at knowing he was staying here. I had an idea you were unaware that he was on probation."

"What was he on probation for?" asked Cedric. "Shoplifting: petty theft generally," Detective Huggins said. "A very light-fingered type. And common. I was far from happy at seeing him trying to foist himself on a very respectable home and into the company of an honest well bred boy like yourself."

Cedric had quite thawed out now. His relief and the flattery were his undoing: anxious to impress the detective with just how respectable and law-abiding a citizen he was, he blurted, "I nearly came to see you once, sir. Mervyn buried money in our meadow and I dug it up." His voice tailed away. A blunder! His Adam's apple got back into its hand-spring push-up routine.

"Did he now?" said Detective Huggins, pouncing softly, catlike. "Where is this money, Cedric?"

The room lurched.

"I – I – I," said Cedric. His brain had stalled. "How much money?"

"I couldn't understand it," Cedric heard himself saying.

"It was all in small change. Pennies, sixpences."

"He buried it and you dug it up?"

Cedric nodded. "I was going to bring it to you but I really didn't know what to do. You see, I was fixing a leak in the roof and I saw him digging a hole."

Huggins stood up. "Come on, Cedric. Show me this money."

"I'll go and get it," Cedric mumbled. He started for the door on unsteady legs. Huggins was right behind him.

Cedric stopped out in the passage. "I'll get it. I didn't tell Granny. I didn't want to worry old Gran."

Huggins smiled tightly. "Lead on, Macduff. We shan't tell Granny."

Cedric knew when he was beaten. He wished he were dead. The Spook was better off than he was. It was all over and done with as far as the Spook was concerned.

When Cedric entered the long dark closet where the step-ladder still stood he was close to fainting. It seemed to Cedric that the place smelled of death. The ladder, as Cedric mounted it, betrayed his agitation. It creaked and shook. Detective Huggins, keenly interested, steadied it. They had not closed the door opening from the sunlit bedroom and there was enough light for the detective to watch closely. Cedric pushed up the trapdoor and his groping fingers touched first one carton and then the other. They were side by side, each with an end tipped up on a joist. Cedric whimpered.

"What did you say?"

Cedric didn't answer. "You idiot!" his brain screamed at him. "Try for God's sake to remember which is which!" Beads of cold sweat appeared on his forehead. Surely the one on his left was the first of the cartons to be hidden? He dragged it over the joist towards him, praying he would hear the clink of coin against coin.

80

AFTER LUNCH, Cedric sprawled out in the shade of a pine in the meadow. Nearby Gus champed diligently at the grass. The meadow was an enchanted place this shadowdappled afternoon, the air aromatic with blue gum and pine. Sitting over here while Granny took him through his Latin vocabulary seemed a memory from a prior existence. He raised his eyes to the big Williamson house. Beneath that roof ...

Cedric clenched a fist and pressed it against his lower lip. Now the awful contents of the carton would have to be tipped into some other container. He was going to hide the – what he had to hide – where he hoped it would never, ever be found, but Huggins had seen the twin carton and Cedric intended to run no risks. A sack would do the job, he had decided. He had already located a suitable sack and put it in the box ottoman upstairs.

What became of the Sashalite? Cedric wondered. Had Bramwell disposed of it?

"Look here," Cedric muttered to the nameless and unreasoning dread which kept welling up within him every time he managed to think himself into a comfortable state of mind. "What've I got to worry about? I've done absolutely nothing. How would you like to be in Bramwell's shoes? Boy, Bramwell is sure paying for his sins! Poor old Spook. Oh well, he was doomed to be a no-hoper anyway."

It irritated Cedric to realize that to a large extent his own security depended on Bramwell getting away with it. In a week or so Blair Bramwell would be his old urbane handsome self – and with a successful murder to his credit also.

"Damn him," Cedric growled. Gus subjected him to a questioning look and then lowered his huge head groundwards again. Cedric now grinned faintly. It had just occurred to him that by picking up the phone some day in the future and whispering some cryptic remark to Bramwell he could easily destroy that gentleman's equanimity. He shook his head. If everything worked out all right the best plan was to forget it. Or try to forget it. There was just that one horrible job ahead of him: from then on he would know nothing, absolutely nothing. If he was ever accused of anything connected with this grim affair or questioned on any point, he would just shake his head and plead ignorance and innocence. Another thing that irritated Cedric was that here was a beautiful plot for his novel fallen like a ripe plum into his lap and, confound it, it was one he could never dare put on paper.

My God, he thought, closing his eyes, I wouldn't be lying here in the shade of an old pine like this if I'd chosen the wrong carton this morning. Phew! Then the fat would have been in the fire and that would be the understatement of all time.

For Detective Huggins, Cedric felt an affection approaching hero worship. Once Cedric had assured him he did not have the faintest idea how the money had been obtained the detective had been kindness itself.

The strain had proved too much for Cedric and he had begun to cry. This was when they both returned to the upstairs sitting-room with the carton full of small change. "I didn't want to worry Gran," Cedric had sniffled. "And I'm frightened of Mervyn. If he knows I found that money and gave it to you he might find me after he gets out of jail and hurt me."

"I don't think there is any sense in ever mentioning this money. I should have guessed about Toebeck myself. This pilfering money from milk bottles was an old dodge of his father's when he was desperate for drink money. Whole streets were cleaned up around Christmas and New Year and I never thought of Master Mervyn. I must be slipping a bit. Anyway, we've got enough on him to put him away for quite a while without trying to pin this on him too. I'll give this money to the milk contractor or whoever got cheated most. Your name won't be mentioned, Cedric. I certainly wouldn't like to be responsible for him doing you a mischief. He's very unpredictable. Actually, I think he'll come to a sticky finish. At any rate he'll be behind bars for some time and the odds are you'll never see him again."

Huggins had been so kind to Cedric, he almost seemed like a fellow conspirator. When they heard Granny coming up the stairs he had stowed away handfuls of loose money into his pockets and actually winked at him.

81

LATER, CEDRIC had burned the carton. He had no special reason for doing this: just some impulse to destroy anything associated with his predicament. He thought of the other carton with its grisly passenger and felt genuinely sorry for it. A lonely boy, he had early acquired the habit of investing the inanimate with a personality. What a way for his good old cartons to finish up, he thought.

He arose, brushed pine-needles off his clothes, and mooched back to the house. Somehow he would have to kill the hours until nightfall.

Martin Williamson was standing on the path where it curved behind the house and beneath the kitchen window.

Martin was saying, "Are you sure it's only the ninth of the month today? Doesn't seem right. Seems to me it ought to be later than the ninth."

"It's the ninth," Granny answered him through the window over the sink bench. "I'll have no money until the fifteenth. And the mill is shut until Monday, anyway."

"Shut," exclaimed Martin. "The mill shut!" He wandered away disconsolately in the direction of the tower.

Cedric went into the kitchen and, to his deep dismay, saw that Granny was crying. Hastily she turned away, flipping a corner of her apron up to her eyes.

"Oh Granny," cried Cedric. "What's wrong? Dear Granny, don't cry."

"It's nothing," sobbed Granny.

"Tell Ceddy," said Cedric. "Don't cry."

"Poor Martin." She tried hard to regain her composure but Cedric had surprised her and now she couldn't stop her tears. "Poor little boy. That's all he is, Cedric. He's your father, but since that fall he's just been a little boy. A dear, kind little boy and everyone laughs at him and his tower. He's not hurting anybody. He always liked to build things. It's him that's been hurt, hurt by that fall and by the world. We were robbed by Vernon Bramwell and now poor Martin …"

Cedric kissed and hugged her. He prevailed on her to sit down at the table.

"I'll put the kettle on."

"I'm all right now," said Granny. "I'm sorry."

After they had drunk a cup of tea, Cedric went around to the front lawn and there, sure enough, was Martin, his hands clasped behind his back and his gaze fixed at a point high up on the tower. Cedric also looked up at the top of the tower and, because a big white cloud was drifting with majestic swiftness across the blue sky, the whole great crazy edifice seemed to be falling towards him. Cedric moved on into the shrubbery where the big graven green frog crouched in all its ugliness and inscrutability.

Not only the frog awaited Cedric. Standing furtively behind it and cringing somewhat was Winker.

82

DETECTIVE HUGGINS had cut out smoking back in the nineteen twenties by the simple device of putting his amber-coloured cigarette holder in his mouth every time he felt the craving but without a cigarette in the end. Even after all these years he still carried the holder and stuck it into his mouth, particularly when he was alone and planning something.

Huggins was a widower and usually postponed having a hot meal until after nightfall, sometimes well after. For lunch, this Thursday, he ate a ham sandwich and drank milk. Then he stuck the amber holder in his mouth and stroked his silver hair.

At eleven-thirty, back from his interesting conversation with Cedric, he had attended the local court-house where two justices of the peace had remanded Mervyn and the winking man for trial. As Huggins had expected, a barrister had appeared on their behalf. Edward Sanderson had been granted bail, but Mervyn Toebeck was back in the cell.

Over one hundred crates, each containing two dozen bottles, of 'the brown' or 'the red' had been found in a cunningly walled-around compartment beneath the building behind Snip's Pool Parlour. Samples were already in the care of an analyst.

A constable had been sent to interview the milk delivery contractor and had been instructed to take notes painstakingly as to exactly who had been robbed of how much. Huggins knew that the contractor had supplied quite a few households, although their bottles were devoid of money, but after that had dug in his heels. The drawer of the desk in the detective's office was filled with piles of carefully sorted small change.

His teeth clamped on the amber holder, Huggins decided that he would keep his promise to Cedric about not pursuing the matter of the stolen money. He liked Granny Williamson and he liked Cedric. That Cedric had succumbed and taken a few shillings for himself, Huggins had quickly deduced by the poor boy's extreme and ill-concealed agitation. Huggins had lived in this town a long time and, clever and professionally inquisitive man that he was, he knew the score. He was very sorry for the Williamsons. He carried no brief for a poufter like Vernon Bramwell who he knew had swindled the General's widow.

The puzzle of Toebeck Senior would also have to be, if not forgotten, at least shelved, he decided. Huggins, as a C.I.B. man, was the boss. Such decisions were up to him.

Constable Dawson of the thick lip and still slightly self-conscious gait put his head around the door. "A Mr Fanthorpe," he announced. "Anxious to talk to you about something, Sir. Won't tell what."

"Show him in." Huggins put his cigarette holder in the inside pocket of his suit jacket.

83

"I'VE GOT to think," Cedric, sitting on the side of his bed, said to himself. He hammered his knee. "Think. Think. Think."

Sick at heart, he glanced at his bedside table where lay the crumpled and only just decipherable note handed to him by Winker. There was no need to read it again.

But Cedric found he couldn't think logically. He put his head in his hands despairingly. He thought of Granny crying in the kitchen. Poor Granny and his poor father, robbed by the Bramwells. Half a thousand pounds was five hundred pounds. That was a lot of money. He thought of Detective Huggins. He thought of the carton in the loft. He thought of the line in the note: 'I SWEAR I WILL COME BACK AND KILL YOU IF YOU DON'T'.

He whimpered. He felt so beaten he could have just slumped forward in a heap on the floor. He got control of himself and stood up. He put the note in his pocket and went to his den.

84

CONSTABLE DAWSON ushered Mr Fanthorpe into Detective Huggins' office. He was a man of medium height, in his middle fifties, of wiry build, red-haired, his thin face remarkable only for the intenseness of his blue eyes and the smallness of his nose. His nose wasn't much bigger than a new born babe's, but it was freckled and each nostril featured a small tuft of gingery hair. Huggins who was hair-conscious, being so well-endowed himself, observed that Fanthorpe was concealing a bald pate by growing very long what still remained of his red hair and combing it across. In a side wind, Huggins thought, you'd blow along the street like a Chinese junk.

Mr Fanthorpe had a rather large black book under his arm and for a second Huggins placed him as a solicitor, but he then revised his impression. The way Fanthorpe was dressed was wrong for the legal profession. His shirt was open at the neck and the sleeves were rolled up the thin freckled arms. Furthermore, he wore shorts right down to his knees and socks right up to them in that ridiculously pukka sahib tradition that leaves only the narrowest circle of knee cap exposed to the caresses of nature.

Huggins indicated a chair on the other side of the desk:

"Take a seat, Mr Fanthorpe."

When Mr Fanthorpe sat down, Detective Huggins observed to his dismay that gold lettering on the back of the black bound book pronounced it as the Holy Bible.

"I trust this is a police matter, Mr Fanthorpe," he got across quickly. "I've a very busy day before me."

"Undoubtedly a police matter," said Fanthorpe, fixing Huggins with his pale, intensely blue eyes. He had obviously noticed Huggins' startled recognition of the Bible. "But Captain, are not all matters, matters that concern God? Not a sparrow falls etcetera, etcetera. Are we not every man of us in our respective walks of life servants of an all-merciful and benign Father?"

Huggins had missed out on a lot of sleep and was irritable.

He put his hand in his pocket and fumbled around, fingered a ten shilling note and a small coin. Then, on an impulse, he opened the desk drawer and lifted out two shilling pieces from the milk money.

"Whatever cause you are collecting for, Mr Fanthorpe," he said, "I'm sure it's a good one. Owing to the work I have to do and will have to do all by myself without supernatural aid or alleviation, I am afraid I am disinclined to discuss it further. Please accept this small token of my appreciation of your good deeds, past, present and intending."

While Huggins was speaking, Fanthorpe had placed the Bible on the desk. The detective reached across and placed the money on the book. He started to stand up but Fanthorpe raised his right hand. "Captain," he said, his blue eyes glittering.

Huggins was perched on the extreme edge of his chair. He said irascibly, "My rank is Detective-Sergeant, Mr Fanthorpe."

"Forgive my ignorance," said Fanthorpe. "Then Detective-Sergeant shalt thou be. I, Sir, am a tiller of the good earth. My life has been spent in extracting God's bounty from the soil and doing His work. I read neither newspaper nor fiction, Sir, only the eternal truths set down for us in the Scriptures. My days are spent in being at peace with my God, my beloved wife and my family. I wage war only on evil, on the demon rum, on lust and fornication."

"You specialize in those particular manifestations of evil, eh?" queried Huggins keenly.

"They are rampant, Captain – that is Sergeant," snapped Fanthorpe. "And it is owing to my ceaseless vigilance in stamping out such evils where it is in my power to do so that I sit at this desk in this room now."

"Come to the point, Mr Fanthorpe, if you would be so kind."

Fanthorpe picked up the two shilling pieces off the Bible and put them in his pocket.

"Although the last thought in my mind was a contribution to God's work I will not spurn those few pence. Rest assured, Sergeant, this gesture on your part, quite uncalled for as it was, will make its humble contribution to the hungry and suffering of this earth."

"Buy them milk," Huggins suggested. "Or perhaps even you yourself need a drink, Mr Fanthorpe. Now please … "Fanthorpe again raised his right hand imperiously. Huggins breathed deeply and contained himself.

"Last night," said Fanthorpe, "my good wife, God bless her, and myself were deep in prayer. It was an hour, Sergeant, when most fellow mortals were asleep. My wife and I pray frequently throughout the night so that the deep love we hold for each other shall be approved by the Almighty. Only prayer can distinguish love from lust, Sir."

"Before or after?" said Huggins.

"Both," cried Fanthorpe. "Do you mock me, Sir?" His tiny nostrils quivered.

"No, no," said Huggins soothingly. "I was just wondering, that was all."

"When two mortals of the opposite sex are so moved by their devotion to the Lord, Sergeant, that they are brought to their knees, firstly in supplication and then in thanksgiving for His bounty, can not then all carnal desire be sublimated?"

"On your knees, huh?" said Huggins. "Well, well, well."

He nearly added, "at your age," but refrained.

Fanthorpe went on fiercely, "Imagine our disgust when we heard, in the stilly night, an automobile using one of the bush tracks which wind through the valley behind our home. They lead nowhere, Sir. What else could I possibly suspect but fornication?"

"Quite," said Huggins. "With possibly the demon rum thrown in for good measure."

"Exactly."

"Well, we appear to be getting somewhere. What happened?"

"I arose," said Fanthorpe, his blue eyes now glazed and fixed at some point beyond Huggins. "And then ..."

"Put on your pyjamas," prompted Huggins, in a mumble. "Left the homestead carrying a horsewhip. I took the path down through the native bush behind our home and, guided by the stars, sought out the trespassers."

"This is your land, is it?" asked Huggins.

"All of it, every acre of it, tilled by my own hands and the hands of my sons. Not the bush, of course, which is on steep hillsides. We have been plagued by trespassers over the years in this fair valley. The place has been despoiled by drunkards and fornicators. The trees grow close to the road and it has been impossible to fence it adequately. Notices have proved useless. The land on the other side is unfortunately open country and these evil-doers are as liable to trespass on my land as anywhere. My home is hidden from the road. There are several lanes between the trees and they are like a magnet to these people seeking privacy to indulge their evil passions. If you could only realize the conversations I have heard and the sights I have witnessed on many occasions ..."

"Before you could use your horsewhip," said Huggins, wearily sarcastic.

Fanthorpe decided to ignore this. "Last night," he said, his voice now gruff, "I saw something I shall never forget. I should have come earlier to acquaint you as an officer of the law, but my wife and myself prayed so deeply on my return to the home that we both slept deeply and late."

"For Christ's sake," yelped Huggins. "What did you see?"

"A ... big ... sports ... car," Huggins repeated in an enfeebled voice.

Fanthorpe's chest heaved. He said quickly, "I knew the car. A very expensive American car. It belongs to the son of my lawyer, Mr Vernon Bramwell." He lowered his eyes to the Bible, placed his hands on it, one on top of the other, and closed his eyes. His lips moved.

"Mr Fanthorpe," said Huggins leaning across the desk.

"Please continue. What else did you see?"

Fanthorpe's pale blue eyes opened. "I saw a man digging a grave," he said and relapsed into prayer.

85

SITTING AT the desk in his den, Cedric read over what he had written:

(1) There can be no question that Mervyn intended to doublecross me and keep the £1000 from Bramwell for himself. Then he was arrested and has had to appeal for my help.

(2) Blackmail is a dirty filthy racket. But I do feel that to blackmail a skunk like Blair Bramwell is nowhere near as bad as tormenting a poor stupid bastard like Ernie Fox. Let's face it. I've often had evil thoughts about Maybelle myself. Ernie Fox is only human and, like me, poor. I think I can be proud of myself for putting him out of his misery. But Blair Bramwell is wealth. His family robbed my family. Blair crippled a little girl on a bicycle. One of the maids at the Bramwell house died having an abortion because of him. That's equal to murder. And he killed poor old Spook. Bramwell should definitely pay for his crimes. Who knows what harm he may do next? But it is too dangerous for me to go to the police. An anonymous note is still too dangerous. God knows what might come out. Bramwell has money and influence. He has the knack of getting away with things. I might even end up in serious trouble myself. That would kill old Granny. Granny cried today because of Dad, but in the first place the Bramwells caused everything. Perhaps Granny cries much more than I know. If I have five hundred pounds I could invent some story about getting a half prize in the Art Union or something and give it to her. And forking up £1000 would really hurt Bramwell. In a way it's justice. On top of these things there is just that chance that Mervyn would kill me or burn the house down or something if I fail him. Detective Huggins said he was dangerous. I don't think there's any doubt Mervyn killed his father. If I gave him £500 as his half I'm sure he would go away and at least I could sleep easy. It looks like the logical thing to do is to go through with it although I don't feel very proud of myself. But I am trapped. Let's analyse it for risk, and so on.

(3) The Spook is dead. His body, headless, is undoubtedly buried where it will never be found – well, not for a long time anyway. If and when it is found it will be unidentifiable. His sister is bound to think he has left town as he did before. She ordered him out. It could be ten years before anyone asks any questions. Mervyn will never talk. I will never talk. Blair Bramwell and his stepmother (the dirty rats) will never talk. If the Sashalite is found somewhere, what significance has it? None. Right. The note we wrote is still in the yellow pages of the telephone directory. I had better ring from that box because it's closer and I can get to the school in time and hide by the dental clinic. I don't think anyone could catch me in those school grounds. I know every hole and corner. I will be able to see that Bramwell is alone. I must remind him on the phone to leave his car at the telephone box and walk. Anyway the note makes

that clear. I'll read the note quickly over again. Will it be risky using that phone at one o'clock in the morning? Well, I won't be in there long. I'll just have to have a good look up the street first. Anyway, who knows what's going on? A friend of Bramwell's might go past. So what? Bramwell won't be telling a living soul about this. All I'll say is, "That you Bramwell? Go to the phone box opposite the library. There's a note between the last two yellow pages of the directory. Read it and do what it says. Don't forget to walk. Leave your car in town." Then I'll hang up and make tracks for the school.

Cedric, having read through the document, picked up his pencil to add something further, but his hand was shaking too badly. He had broken out in a clammy sweat.

86

DETECTIVE HUGGINS and Constable Dawson walked back through the trees to the clearing where the Ford was parked. Two other constables had been left to guard the shallow grave and the naked decapitated corpse it had given up.

"You don't look so hot, Dawson," Huggins said as they climbed into the car. (Actually he looked a bit white around the gills himself.) "Positively seedy. You're beginning to think you should've been an insurance agent or something and not a policeman, I suppose? Kick in the pills last night and a headless corpse today. Never a dull moment."

The Fanthorpe estate was about seven miles in the back country where there were still stands of bush and deep wooded gullies despite the intensive felling of timber over the years by the Grants of Grant's Mill who had, in the very early days, wangled some sort of monopoly.

They drove for the most part in silence, Huggins at the wheel, his amber holder clenched between his teeth. Nearing town, he said, "I don't anticipate any trouble clearing this up. I don't think we'll even need those photographs and I won't bother yet to get casts of the tyre treads of the Auburn. The boys will see that the hospital wallahs don't muck them up anyway. It'll be nice and tidy if Bramwell just comes clean and signs a statement. I'm only praying this crackpot Fanthorpe identified the car accurately. There's always the remote chance that a similar vehicle could have come from miles away. If Bramwell plays it cool or has jacked up an alibi it could be tricky. There's big dough in the Bramwell outfit. We'll just have to pounce and scare a confession out of him. He can't have the faintest idea we're on to him. That is, if we're not barking up the wrong tree."

A few hundred yards from the main street they drove past a big garage and Constable Dawson tapped Huggins on the shoulder. "The Auburn," he said. "Bramwell's car. In the garage. In the showroom. Either that or it's a twin."

Huggins U-turned and pulled in at the kerb by the garage. "You better stay in the car. We don't want anyone stampeding."

There were three men, one in overalls, standing looking at the Auburn. As Huggins entered the showroom window a big bald man, who Huggins knew was the manager, opened the driver's door of the maroon roadster and closed it again. It made the soft click of perfect coachwork.

"Afternoon," said Huggins pleasantly. "That's young Bramwell's car, isn't it?"

"Was," said the manager. "Ours now."

"Oh. I say, do you think you could spare me a moment?
Just something I'd like to find out. You may be able to help."

"Sure."

They went into the manager's office which was walled nearly right around with glass and looked right across the showroom.

"There's no need to repeat this," said Huggins. "But that Auburn. How much? It's impertinent, I know, but between you and me it could be an official question."

"I wrote him a cheque for nine-fifty. Offered him eight but he stuck out for a grand. We settled on nine-fifty. It's steep, but it's a car I wouldn't mind myself, actually."

"Why would Bramwell get rid of that car?" Huggins said. "Did he make any inquiries about a new car or anything?"

"He said he'd been thinking about getting something else and I mentioned that grey Jag over there but he didn't listen too hard. I'll tell you something. He went straight over to the bank with our cheque. I sat here at this desk and watched him cross the road and walk up the steps."

Huggins went across to the bank. Ten minutes later he climbed in behind the steering wheel of the Ford.

He said to Constable Dawson, "Bramwell sold the car. Then he went to the bank. My first idea was he was getting all the money together he could and then skip. But the bank tells me he didn't want anything bigger than a fiver. Nine hundred and fifty in fivers! The bank had to send a girl around to collect a few to make up the amount. But Bramwell said that's what he wanted and it was none of their damn business why. He walked out with – let's see – one hundred and ninety fivers. It's ridiculous. But it tells me a story. Now, Vance, you've taken this game on. What do small bills in big chunks mean to you, Sherlock?"

Dawson thought hard. He looked worried. "A lot to carry around?" he ventured.

Huggins closed his eyes. "Try again."

Dawson pondered. Then he said brightly, "He's going to play the horses."

Huggins got out of the car. "You take the car back to the station, Vance. I'll be along in a few minutes."

Dawson slid over behind the wheel. His brow was still furrowed.

Through the window Huggins said, "When you've been a detective as long as I have you'll know what insisting on small bills means."

"What, sir?"

"He's frightened of being taken short," Huggins told him. Huggins went back to the garage. Dawson scratched his temple and then drove off. Five minutes later the Auburn stole out of the garage with Huggins at the wheel. He headed for the police station.

He parked the Auburn on the lawn behind the station. He had a quick look in the rumble seat and got the impression it had recently been sluiced out with water, probably hosed. He was pretty sure he had this business sewn up, but he decided to run no risks. In his office, after ringing the hospital and giving the location of the Fanthorpe property, he put through a toll call to C.I.B. headquarters in the city. He wanted some laboratory men, experts, he told the city branch. City promised them within six hours.

87

A SHEEPISH Constable Dawson entered Huggins' office. "Sir," he began.

"Yes?"

"I was just thinking," said Dawson.

"I thought I could smell something burning. Do you know I haven't had a cigarette for sixteen years? Sixteen miserable, wasted, stupid, frustrated, holder-chewing years. Dawson, give me a cigarette."

"Certainly, Sir." Dawson plunged out of Huggins' office and went back to the watchroom. He came back with a packet of Players. He tapped the bottom of the packet and offered it, with one cigarette end protruding, to the detective.

"Give me the whole packet," roared Huggins. He yanked open the drawer where the milk money was and fired a handful of sixpences across the desk.

"But, sir!" protested Dawson. "Pick 'em up. Keep 'em,"

When Dawson looked up from gathering the sixpences, Huggins was smelling the open packet of cigarettes. His eyes were closed.

"Tobacco," Huggins murmured. "What fragrance! What flower could compete? What rose would be even in the hunt? Tobacco! Magnolias in the moonlight, daphne after the rain, verbena leaves burning softly in the dusk – PAH! Tobacco."

With a magnificent flourish Huggins put a cigarette between his lips.

"Matches," he roared. The cigarette flew out of his mouth but he caught it neatly.

Dawson fumbled for matches. He lit one and extended it. Huggins had his eyes closed but one eyelid flickered open just wide enough for him to guide the tip of his cigarette to the match. He inhaled. "Ash-tray," he murmured.

Huggins put the cigarette down on the ash-tray. "Yes, Vance?" he said. "You were saying?"

"Blackmail," said Dawson. "It just sorta occurred to me."

"My boy," said Huggins, picking up the cigarette and waving it under his nose, "you will go far in this world. Your brain is like the mills of God. They grind slow but they grind exceeding small. That might be all wrong, but Fanthorpe would know. Must ask Fanthorpe. Check everything."

Huggins inhaled. "Yes, Vance Sherlock Dawson, blackmail is the answer. And with the complication of a headless cadaver and one moreover that has had a spade slashed through the fingertips and is naked, and the further complication of a wealthy suspect, educated and cagey, blackmail is the angle we must concentrate on. Fanthorpe's evidence could not stand up unsupported in the face of a ruthless King's Counsel's cross-examination. Night-time in the bush. Shaky ground, Dawson."

Huggins laid his half-smoked cigarette in the groove provided in the rim of the ash-tray. "Sixteen wasted years," he mused.

"Yes, sir," said Dawson.

Huggins sat and leaned forward on his elbows. "Somebody is putting the acid on Bramwell. It's too much of a coincidence to even consider that it has nothing to do with the buried body. And the sale of the car. This very day. No, Bramwell is our man without doubt. But unless we can establish the identity of the deceased, motive may be hard to prove. Bramwell may well deny everything. Where are we then? Well, we have his car. The rumble seat of that roadster is going to be subjected to a microscopic inspection by experts. Bramwell could say his car was left somewhere where anyone could have used it. What jury would convict? Young Bramwell is clever. We've got to outsmart him. I think we'll play this blackmail angle. We've got to *catch* this blackmailer, Dawson."

"Yes, sir."

"Now, Dawson, what do we know about this blackmailer?" Dawson thought. "He knows Bramwell buried that guy we dug up."

"Brilliant. Let's say he knows about the murder anyway, or he knows why. And, more important, he knows who the victim was. That's something we simply must know. We can't hang a man for cutting the head off a spook. The old judge is going to look up so many books he'll go cross-eyed. We've got to hand him this case on a plate."

"Well, Mr Fanthorpe wouldn't have blackmailed him," said Dawson. "Or else he wouldn't have come to us."

"That seems to make sense, Vance. But only just. Fanthorpe and his missus were so deep in prayer before and after and, for all I know, during, they probably didn't think of it. Otherwise he might have tried it on just to raise the wind to send Bibles to the Persian Gulf or somewhere. No, Dawson, the man we're after knows more than Fanthorpe. Come on. Let's attack. I have a plan, Watson."

88

HUGGINS AND Dawson took the Ford and went to the three-storeyed building which had always been known as Bramwell and Thornes.

"We would like to speak to Mr Bramwell – Junior," Huggins said at the inquiry office.

Blair Bramwell rose from his desk at their entry. He looked handsome and suave. He wore a dark suit, white shirt and knitted tie. He shook hands with both Huggins and Dawson and sat down again. He indicated chairs.

"And to what do I owe this pleasure?" he said.

Huggins stared at the ash-tray on the desk. It was heaped high with butts.

"It's hardly a pleasure," Huggins said. "I'm afraid you've gone a million. The Auburn car is around at the station with laboratory men coming to light with more positive evidence all the time. We've already dug up your hapless and headless victim. Just as a matter of interest, where is the head?"

Blair Bramwell said nothing. The blood had drained from his cheeks. He groped for a cigarette and lit it. His hands shook.

"Useless to fight, Mr Bramwell," said Huggins. "If ever there was a cut and dried case this is it. But there is one very puzzling aspect. Why did the person who blackmailed you tip us off before you paid him?"

"The sod!" Bramwell struggled to say. "The crazy sod! I raised the thousand."

"I know," said Huggins sympathetically. "I've been to the bank. A hundred and ninety fivers. Quite a pocketful."

Bramwell stared at Huggins. "You've really got me over a barrel, haven't you?"

"Well, we've got a job to do. Come clean on the whole affair and you probably won't swing. It's the best offer I can make."

Bramwell went over to the window and stared down the street. The office was on the second floor.

"I wanted to have a look at this man Hemingway's flat. Monty Harrop had the keys. I heard this Hemingway had a marvellous collection of curios and I wanted to see them. Monty lent me the keys. I was having a look around the flat at all the things this guy's picked up in Africa and the Amazon and places when I heard a window being forced open. I immediately thought of a burglar. I took down a sort of curved sword off the wall and turned off the light. A man entered the room. It was a burglar; I could tell by the way he moved around. I clicked on the light and there was this skinny guy all dressed in black. As soon as he saw me he pulled something out of his pocket. I thought it was a gun and I swiped at him with this sword. I swear it was just a natural reaction in self-defence. He sprang at me just as I slashed and – Oh Jesus!"

Blair stumbled back to his chair at the desk and collapsed into it.

"Proceed," said Huggins.

"I'd cut his bloody head off," said Blair. "Clean off. Christ Almighty! I can never tell anyone how awful it was. Just one swipe. The sword was like a razor. I didn't know. I thought he had a gun in his hand."

"Was it?"

"No, it was some sort of flashlight. I threw it over a bridge somewhere. But the way he pulled it out of his pocket fast I was sure it was a revolver."

"You'd never seen this man before?"

"Never."

"What did you do with his clothes?"

"I burned them. Every stitch. Siphoned some gas out of the car and soaked them and set fire to them."

"Anything in his pockets?"

"Nothing. Some matches and a few loose cigarettes. And about two bob in shrapnel."

"What happened to his head?"

"You tell me and we'll both know. I wrapped it in a rug and put it in the rumble seat with the rest of him. But when I buried the body it wasn't there. I tell you I nearly had a heart attack."

"When did the blackmailer contact you?"

"At quarter past one. I heard the chime over the phone."

"In the morning?"

"Yes."

"When does he ring again?"

"One o'clock this morning."

"It was the town clock you heard chiming?"

"Yes. It was loud."

"Hear a penny in the slot or anything?"

Bramwell was lighting a cigarette. "I've told you everything I can. I acted in self-defence and then, like a fool, I panicked. I should've come straight to the police but, God, man, when you've just cut off someone's head you can't think straight! He was only some scum anyway and I thought of my father and his reputation. My own too. It was ruination. Because of some small-time cat burglar. So, all right then, I tried to save my own skin. But the fact remains I acted in self-defence. Then I think I went temporarily insane. It's like a bad dream."

"It may not be so bad, Mr Bramwell," said Huggins. "But I'm afraid I'll have to ask you to come with us. Just a brief statement. This will all make for leniency you know. I can see how easily this tragedy occurred."

"Well, let's get out before my father comes crashing in," said Blair. "I'll walk down first. You know this town. If anybody sees a man with a cop they think he's committed a murder."

89

TWENTY MINUTES later, his statement typed out and signed, Blair Bramwell was sharing the cell with an unshaven, bleary-eyed stiff-necked Mervyn Toebeck.

In the watch-room, awaiting the arrival of a fire-breathing Vernon Bramwell, phoned by his son, Huggins said to Higgett, the oldest constable of the local force, "Round up Dougherty. Tell Ted Watson the night watchman. Go and hook old Fleming out of retirement. At one o'clock tomorrow morning I want every phone box in this town under close surveillance particularly the one opposite the library. We'll nab this blackmailing rooster and then we can tie this case up."

90

GENERAL ARNOLD Williamson had never been a drinking man, but, on the other hand, had never been known to publicly condemn the stuff. He had placidly gone along with his wife Beatrice (Granny) when she had become a prohibitionist, mildly at first, and then, influenced by Martin's wife, rabidly so. However, the General was expected to entertain Governor-Generals and Field-Marshals and even take the King in his stride if he had honoured him with a visit, so there stood on the great sideboard a crystal decanter full of vintage cognac.

At eight thirty on the night of the ninth of January 1936 the stopper of the crystal decanter was pulled for the first time in perhaps fifteen years, by the shaking hand of Cedric. The neck of the decanter chattered against a goblet. Cedric took a deep breath and lowered two fingers of the venerable fluid into his quivering interior.

The dining-room was lit only by a hall light streaming through the open doorway. Cedric knew that Granny was busy in the kitchen. In the nigrescence, Cedric gently put down the goblet on a silver tray.

Not until Cedric had seated himself at the dining-room table did the smooth old liquor assert itself. A golden glow began in his stomach and sent out exploring emissaries to every outpost of his system. Another trip to the sideboard to drain the goblet and Cedric was rock steady.

He went purposefully to his den. The tying up of loose ends, the obliteration of all evidence, was becoming a mania. He took Mervyn's crumpled soiled note and read it through yet again, carefully. From the drawer in his desk he took the notes he had made that afternoon. He perused these thoughtfully, nodding now and then in agreement with his earlier reasoning. But again the ghosts of fear and vacillation stood behind him and he returned to the sideboard.

Cedric went up the stairs aware of a pleasant floating sensation. In the private sitting-room he burned the papers he carried in the fireplace wherein still lay the charred ashes of his earlier analysis of the situation and the carton which had contained the milk money.

Cedric had been more thorough in his destruction of the horror carton. After its contents had been tipped into a sack, that bloodstained container had been soaked with kerosene and set alight in the incinerator. Cedric had done all this just after nightfall. His activities had not aroused Granny's suspicions and it is just as well that she had not chosen to investigate as one glimpse of Cedric, white faced, shaking, jumping and twitching violently at every sound or movement, real or imagined, would have condemned him.

After the papers had crumpled into a black red-rimmed nothingness in the fireplace, Cedric went to the closet. He took the step-ladder and heaved it out of an upstairs bedroom window. He listened to the soft crash and swish of branches as the big clump of bushes below cushioned the ladder's fall. Downstairs he padded. In a few minutes the step-ladder was back in its corner of the woodshed. Now the sideboard called to Cedric again as the rude imperious surge to an old sea-dog.

Seated at the dining-room table again in the purblind light, Cedric reflected that he was handling things well.

91

THAT AFTERNOON, wandering around in a worried and jittery state, with every new solution as to where to conceal the Spook's head beset immediately with objections, Cedric had watched with increasing interest the metalling and tarring of a new road through the gully which had once been Williamson property.

At five o'clock, the road workers had packed up. An old Thornycroft truck dripping tar and the huge smoke belching steam-roller had lumbered off back to the Borough sheds. A hundred yards or so of levelled dirt remained to be metalled and sealed on the morrow.

Just after eight o'clock at night, Cedric had darted through the shrubbery bearing a sack and a spade. In a cold sweat and ready to head for the ditch at the side of the road at the first glimpse of either car or pedestrian, Cedric had dug, in the dead centre of the as yet unmetalled stretch of road, a hole some eighteen inches square and two-feet-six deep. In had gone the sack with its grim burden. Cedric had made as good a job as he could of patting down the returned earth to level.

Even recalling the strain and heart pounding excitement of this manoeuvre sent Cedric to the decanter again, but common sense prevailed – he must keep a clear head for the tough task ahead. Also he had to kiss Granny goodnight. He went and cleaned his teeth and rinsed out his mouth. But the brandy stilt glowed like a beacon in his belly.

In his bedroom he stretched out on his bed in the dark.

There was virtually no moonlight. He had brought a small clock with a luminous dial from the library. Turning his head on the pillow and squinting, Cedric saw that it was now just 9.30. "Well," he thought, "it's got to be done. I've thought it over from every angle and there isn't any risk. There's more risk in not doing it. I don't want Mervyn gunning for me. Besides, five hundred quid isn't to be sneezed at. If I do it, it's for Granny's sake. It's only a pittance compared to what the Bramwells have robbed her of. And that smug smarty Blair Bramwell should have to pay in some way for his sins. It's unthinkable that he should slip away unscathed again."

Cedric rehearsed what lay ahead. Take a penny, take two pennies, take a small piece of paper and a pencil, in case, when he checked, the note had gone. First, the time. Say, leave the house at 12.45. Better have a nip of brandy. Go quietly by the side door. Head for town on foot. Into the phone box and check the note. Ring Bramwell. Say my piece smartly. Head for the school. Lie good and low. Swoop home down the back roads. Hide the thousand quid (in the dark, Cedric's brandy-flushed face relapsed into a triumphant leer) under the frog in the shrubbery. Just scoop out the dead leaves and poke in the money …

Cedric, his face still sagging in a vacuous smile, slumbered.

92

CEDRIC WAS still sleeping soundly when various cars drew away from the police station. Several policemen, ex-policemen, the night-watchman, the son of one of the policemen and a local warden had been dispatched to keep all public phone boxes under close surveillance.

The booth opposite the library was at the top of the list: one of the laboratory men from the city had volunteered his services. An examination of the Auburn's rumble seat was to begin early in the morning. The older of the experts who had arrived had retired in Huggins' guest room. Huggins stayed behind in charge of the station.

In the cell, both Mervyn and Blair Bramwell lay awake.

Bramwell, despite his father's fury and influence, was still under lock and key pending a preliminary court hearing. He had been aloof to Mervyn, scarcely deigning to exchange pleasantries, but now, when Mervyn grumbled about the noise of the cars drawing away so late at night, he felt constrained to say to the darkness, "Why should a bastard blackmail someone and, before he picks up the money, tell the police? It's just cutting his own throat. It doesn't add up. The more I chew this over the more I think two separate parties are involved in getting me in this mess."

"What's this about blackmail?" asked Mervyn, propping himself up in bed.

"That's what that expedition you just heard leaving is hunting," replied Blair. "My blackmailer. He rang from the public box near the town clock. I heard the clock chime and I heard a penny in the slot. If he rings me at one he's gone a million. If he does ring he can't be the person who told the police. But if he doesn't ring, then we'll never know. Never. It's got me beat. I thought I'd done everything slickly but it looks as if the world and his wife knew every move I made."

"Tell me more," urged Mervyn.

"Go to sleep," said Blair. "For Christ's sake!"

Mervyn slumped down in bed again. He rubbed his whiskers. He felt sick.

93

IT WAS the frightening so-real dream again, the dream of some zombie-like creature of the night pacing past his room, which awoke Cedric.

He lay still in the dark for some moments, his mind befuddled with sleep and the dying fumes of the cognac.

The hand of the luminous dial of the little clock said 12.55.

Cedric rolled out of bed.

"Oh God," he mumbled. "I can't go through with it. Damn and blast Mervyn and the Bramwells and everyone. I wanna go to sleep and forget it."

But Cedric knew he had to force himself along. He was fully dressed right to his shoes. The pennies, the notepaper and the pencil were on the bedside table. Like an automaton, he shoved them into one of his trouser pockets.

Cedric was cold and frightened. He wondered if the cognac would, one more, dismiss his terror and give him strength. His mouth felt dry and furry and water appealed to him most.

"Well," he thought, "water first and then we'll see if the decanter still has the magic touch." He opened his bedroom door cautiously and was appalled to see a light streaming through his Granny's bedroom. Her door was ajar. Cedric drew back into his room and closed the door. "Curse the woman," he gritted, and then felt deeply ashamed. Poor Granny!

Quickly, Cedric dropped out of his bedroom window. The mission would have to be accomplished without the good offices of alcohol. "I'll be back home in no time," Cedric told himself. "Safe. Rich. Just move fast and keep my eyes open."

The first thing his vigilant darting eyes picked out was the shadow on top of the tower. Cedric crouched low. No doubt about it, just for a fleeting second he had seen the unmistakable silhouette of a watcher on the tower. Instead of fear, rage flooded him. He would put an end to this persecution. He must know. Who was it? What damned pest dared to ascend the tower and spy on his every move? This scotched any trip to town. He would be followed. Was it Huggins? Was it the Witch?

Cedric skirted the big front lawn, flitting from shrub to shrub. He entered the tower. He knew just what he was going to do: he knew every inch of his father's tower. Right at the top of the second flight of steps he pulled hard on one of the steps until it sprang free from its dovetail on one side. Cedric knew it was the step that Martin was forever promising Granny to make secure. Cedric twisted the step until, instead of presenting its side to a descending foot, it presented its edge. He listened. Yes, someone was slowly descending. Or was it the sound of his own heart?

Cedric squatted down about twenty feet from the tower and awaited the outcome of his trap. His ruthless move had given his rage a vent to escape and now he wondered if he had, perhaps, done something wicked. Who would it be? Not some kid, that was for certain, at this hour. Could it be Huggins? Why watch this house? Damn Huggins.

He thought: all I can do is crouch here and wait. What shall I do if this midnight prowler falls? Make a dart for town or back to my room and play innocent? First I must see who it is and make a decision then. It can't be much after one o'clock. In the jam Bramwell is in he will wait by the phone.

There was a muffled cry from the tower and then a clattering sound followed by two loud thumps. After a second, or a split second, the prowler came pitching down the next flight, the lowest one, and a limp form thudded into the floor of the tower just inside the doorway.

Cedric bounded forward and peered at the limp figure. He recognized his father, more by the voluminous white pyjamas than any familiar outline, just as a tiny distraught figure came stumbling across the lawn.

Cedric was never to forget his Granny's awful screaming.

94

MISERABLY CEDRIC stared out of a side window at the dawn light groping its way into a courtyard hemmed in on three sides by the brick walls of the hospital.

Granny came along. He didn't hear her approach. She touched his shoulder. "Come on along, Cedric. Dr Buick is going to take us home."

Cedric felt sure his father was dead. In the back seat of Dr Buick's car he queried tremulously, "Is Daddy dying?"

Granny took his hand. "No, no, Cedric, Dr Buick thinks everything will be quite all right. He will have to rest for a long time but there is a chance of a silver lining."

Cedric didn't understand. He thought they were breaking it to him gently. Dr Buick, his broad but rounded shoulders slumped low, drove in silence. Cedric saw that he was still wearing his pyjama jacket under his top coat. Cedric had left his moaning Granny cradling the unconscious Martin's head in her arms and fled to use Mrs Lloyd's phone. The doctor had arrived only a few minutes before the ambulance. Cedric had been frozen. He wanted to die.

Now, as the tower hove into sight against the dawn sky, Cedric began to cry.

Dr Buick told Granny he wouldn't come inside. From his case he took a small bottle and counted out four white tablets.

"Take two, Mrs Williamson, and Cedric can have either one or two. Then rest. I'll be around after lunch."

Cedric and Granny drank tea in the kitchen, but neither of them took the tablets.

"You see, Cedric," Granny said. "He is badly concussed but he seems to have gone right back to the time he fell from the scaffolding. He was quite lucid for a while and Dr Buick thinks that all these years in between that first fall and this one have been wiped from his memory."

Cedric, not quite understanding, drank his tea. He could see no point in confessing his guilt. The damage was done. He had been a fool, but how, he appealed to his conscience, in God's name, could he have guessed that the tower so preyed on Martin's mind that he walked in his sleep and ascended it? Granny should have told him the night he had been so terrified by the footsteps. Confused and distraught, she believed that something similar had happened this time: that Cedric, awakened by the footsteps and curious, had watched from close by.

"He's not going to die is he, Granny?"

"Definitely not, Cedric. Dr Buick assured me he will be all right."

"Promise? You're not just saying that?"

Granny, on her way back to the table with her cup refilled, kissed Cedric. "I promise. True, he's going to get well again. Perhaps better than we think."

He suddenly realized what Granny was hoping for. "You don't mean – will Daddy be sorta, y'know, you mean he may …?"

"Yes," said Granny, nodding. "There is just a chance he may be quite normal, Cedric. There is one big catch though."

"What is it?"

"Cedric, would you mind leaving our old home here? Dr Buick has made me a wonderful offer for the house. A wonderful offer. That's something at least we didn't have stolen from us. We can start again in a new town. Dr Buick thinks that if your father remembers the tower at all it will only be as a dream. He thinks the tower should come down and, if we can, we should move away. He's frightened that if Martin sees the tower when he leaves hospital it may shock him into a relapse. He wants these years and the tower to be just a dream to him."

"Why, yes," said Cedric slowly. He wouldn't be 'Pisa' Williamson any more. They would live in a new town, somewhere over the rainbow. Maybe the town the little girl on the train had been going to.

"Why, yes," he said again. "Sure, Gran. Anything to get Daddy well."

"You're such a good boy, Cedric. You're sure it's not too great a sacrifice? I know you love this old home. Our new one won't be very big, Cedric."

"I don't care," said Cedric. "As long as Daddy gets well.

Y'know Gran, maybe everyone has a tower in their life that just becomes a dream."

He didn't quite know where the thought had come from but he was quite proud of the remark.

Granny reached across the table and took his hand. He said after a moment or two. "Granny?"

"Yes?"

"Granny, can we take Gus?"

"We'll go one better than that," Granny said, quasi-brave through her tears. "Gus can take us."